Quest

Cover image: Abi Perkins

Design: Abi Perkins

This book is dedicated to my Mum and Dad for introducing me to books and encouraging my creativity when I was young.

Quest

Book synopsis

Survival in a post-apocalyptic world is not for the faint hearted. It requires difficult decisions and the deployment of extreme violence to hold onto what you have and take what you need.

A motley clan of survivors is making its way across the country to fulfil a mysterious mission accompanying an enigmatic character.

Beset by challenges, they are held together by a combination of their own will to live and their ability to share the individual skills they possess, as they continue their quest.

There are others though.

From another desperate place where they are also fighting for their very survival. They too are on a quest.

The futures of both groups are inextricably linked.

This is their story.

Opening Chapter

2031 - Roasted Sheep Camp

Lost in their own thoughts, faces lit up by the flickering flames from the fire slowly roasting the sheep, the clan was eagerly anticipating their one cooked meal of this day. It had been a lucky discovery so close to what had been a town. They had got used to tracking deep into the countryside to find such fine fare.

Once cooked, they would eat what they could and then wrap what they could cut from the carcass when it was cold, for their onward trek. For now, fat dripped down from the butchered and skinned sheep as it cooked. The smell of good food had them salivating. Then Radar spoke and the spell was broken.

"Visitors!" he announced. Just one word. It was enough. It captured their complete attention. No-one with good intent arrived in the hours of darkness. They all knew that.

Steel was the first to jump up. He always seemed to be ready, sometimes even when he looked like he was asleep, he could rouse and stand with an ease of speed that shocked the unwary. He scanned all around but could not see anything out of order and so waited for Radar to continue.

The carcass continued spitting fat out from its roasting, but nobody else moved. They were waiting for Radar to speak.

"Carrying hardware and coming in one skirmish line from that direction" as he pointed away from him and slowly swept his arm in a narrow arc. "Five or six, could be a couple more. They are in a tight group. Some are hidden behind others."

Steel nodded to the two newcomers, a pair of children in their early teens, to follow him and strode off purposefully into the darkness, sideways and to the left of where he knew the intruders were approaching from.

The rest picked up their weapons and moved into a well-rehearsed semi-circle. Those that needed to, smeared soil from the ground onto their faces and moved slowly away from the fire towards the arc that Radar had defined.

Radar remained where he was. His silhouette would continue at the fireside, partly because he knew he would be no good in a fight. Not anymore. However, he recognised that his main role at this point was to act as bait for the intruders. To demonstrate that someone was at the fire, barbecuing the supper.

The smell of the cooking would waft towards the outsiders and draw them in even more. Food was hard to come by right now.

The clan did not run away. They had lost valuable resources when they had run away in the past and they had also lost irreplaceable clan members in retreat.

They had worked out it was better to defend with malice than run away. Their core baggage was hard to come by and it was what the attackers wanted. Tarpaulins, cooking kit, spare weapons and food. Survival depended on resources.

Besides, they would scavenge the dead of the attackers and hopefully add to their own clan's armament and ordnance in the process. They had a well drilled routine.

They went to ground in an arc away from her on either side, curling back towards Radar, cradling their preferred means of fighting, taking the opportunity to smear more soil and dirt into their faces and cut down their reflection and make sure their weapon was free and ready to use.

Most of them had guns, handguns in the main but also a pair of shotguns, which would be useful in the forthcoming close quarter combat. Others had hunting crossbows the strings already drawn. Each also held unsheathed machetes. Home-made from aircraft engine rotors, the short heavy blades could hack an arm off in one swing or cripple a leg.

Best of all they were silent. Burnt black, they were also impossible to see in the dark of a night.

Dark haired clan leader Raven realised that it would be a few more moments before their night vision kicked in, so she faced down and closed her eyes. Normally, without that preparation they would have been at a distinct disadvantage but with Radar's warning, they would probably have enough time.

Raven knew that Steel would provide the edge, coming from his flanking move and she understood that her role was to hold the centre ground firmly and face up to the enemy coming straight at them. Have their attackers facing the defensive line between themselves and the fire.

Raven lay there waiting and trying to remain calm, her heart was thumping away in her chest as she knew that combat could leave their numbers dwindled by dead. Worse still, having to manage the wounded and those who could not walk or work.

They all knew that they had to remain useful for the clan or there was no place for them in it. Med, the redhead, had her combat capabilities. It was her job to patch them up, try and keep them in the fight but even she had limitations and it wasn't possible to save everyone. Alive and functional, they were useful to the clan. Wounded or dying were not.

That was not Raven's concern right now.

Raven briefly thanked the special skills that Radar possessed to have given them the opportunity to protect what was theirs. She had no idea how or why he should be able to do what he did. It defied all logic.

Despite all rational and logical thought, Raven simply could not comprehend how the old man had lost his sight but not only had his other senses become more acute, he also had something akin to a machine-like ability to "see" things that others could not.

Radar had also given them the idea for the machetes after they stumbled onto a crashed fighter aircraft in the early days after the main wars had ended. The jet had broken apart and the engine blades were easily retrieved from the wreckage.

The finely engineered parts had been partly reshaped and honed to form fine edged fighting blades that each member of the clan carried. They also had spares bundled in rags in the barrow. Useful replacements, or to arm new clan members.

Controlling her breathing, she looked up and could now make out the shapes from the shadows in front of her. The clan knew to stay low and look up at the intruders who would be marked out against the slightly lighter shades of the night sky above them.

Lying prone made them a smaller target but also left them in a weaker combat position, as they would need to rise to press home an attack.

They had practised endlessly and whilst not as fast as Steel, they could rise from their prone positions on the ground and into combat swiftly. Steel had taught them all well.

It was then that they heard the first sound from the group of intruders approaching. Radar was incredibly good, but he could not always make out the exact numbers when people were packed together. Though he could often see arms and armaments. She realised that they were going into this fight with insufficient information, so any reduction in those numbers would therefore be good.

It was a cry of pain that was immediately followed by a mad rush of leaves and branches. Then a gurgling sob of some description. It seemed that someone had stumbled into one of Steel's perimeter traps.

A former gamekeeper turned poacher, Steel laid snares in what seemed to be a random fashion, sometimes they snared game before their morning trek outwards and onwards. To Steel's trained eye however, they were not a haphazard selection.

The places he chose were on natural paths between the obstacles of trees and bushes for both animals and people. Easy for him to visualise the routes they would take, after that it was just a matter of setting the different types of snare.

Head-height loops were held in place on a trigger of wood in the cleft of a bent sapling. Once snagged, it could take a head clean off as the natural weight of the human and gravity, caused a pull against the sapling springing away from its release.

Sometimes it would just cut through a throat and dig into the spine causing the human or large mammal to dangle and choke to death on their own blood. They had once snared a deer that way and lived off venison for quite some time.

The low loops were for the rabbits, dogs, cats, anything ground hugging and small. Often caught by a leg and sometimes by the throat. The low snares could also trip up a human.

The traps were an effective tool to create a defensive perimeter when the clan stopped to make camp and gave them a bonus of food for the pot or the roast later that day when they had made distance.

Steel had moved swiftly in the dark away from the campfire, with the two teenagers sticking closely to him. It pleased him that they had picked up some of the stealth that he insisted on and to be fair, they had survived all this time together before they were allowed into the clan and he also knew that they had both proved themselves fearless.

He held his hand up to pause. Pointed to his face and wafted his hand. The two newcomers dropped to the floor and quickly scooped up dirt to rub into their faces and leave only their eyes showing any reflection.

Steel had no need. His dusky brown skin gave him some natural advantages in the dark. Then he raised his hand. They indicated they were ready with a nod of their heads and moved off with him on the hand signal. Both carrying their machetes held out and ready for use.

No gun for steel. He held a crossbow, with a small clip of bolts attached to the stock and pockets full of the little flighted steel killers, plus a catapult and handfuls of steel ball bearings.

Steel also carried a machete in a scabbard and knives on his belt. He could revert to any of them quite easily when the combat degenerated into hand-to-hand fighting, as it invariably would that night.

Right now, though, he had to make sure that his flanking move was carried out swiftly and silently. No words, he urged the newcomers with pulls, pushes and jerks of his hand to hold, to move forward or to the side as he required.

They were making good progress when they too heard the strangled gurgling sound and as he brought them to an immediate halt with one raised hand, Steel smiled to himself. He knew that his snares were deadly.

There was a thrashing sound and then a return to silence. He slung the crossbow over his shoulder and silently unsheathed his machete. Then Steel patted his hand forward gently and the trio advanced more slowly now and in the direction of where the distress had sounded but poised and ready to attack.

They just needed a signal and that would come from Raven.

It had not always been like this of course.

Chapter Two

2030 – The Collapse

Raven was alone back then. Hiding in the forest. Sat on a log under a camouflaged tarpaulin as the rain fell steadily, with larger drops falling from the branches above, tip tapping louder in between the constant drumming sound of the drizzle.

At least it was keeping her dry. She had decided that there would be no more walking today. It meant she had time to think for a change. An opportunity to stop looking over her shoulder or reconnoitring a trail path ahead along with being constantly wary.

She thought back to how it had come to this and in doing so recounted the sequence of events that had begun with the Pandemic the year before in 2030.

"It was nothing like anything that had been experienced before. Ever."

"The world must have thought it was prepared. That it had learned from the Spanish Flu which killed over 50 million people worldwide at the turn of the twentieth century and then successfully managed Bird Flu, SARS and COVID."

Raven recalled the endless documentaries on the television which showed that the world had advanced medical knowledge, expertly trained key workforces and vast reserves of personal protective equipment for medical and care staff. *"Politicians and newsreaders were telling us all that we had it covered."* She thought, *"How could so many people be so wrong?"*

She had watched the Politicians and leading scientists on the news showing off what seemed to be endless banks of antidotes, vaccines and well-rehearsed methods of isolation, protection, and treatments. *"There to reassure us that everything would be alright"* she thought. *"Keep us in our little boxes."*

Sat in the isolation of a wooded ravine. Raven had all the time she needed to work through how it had come to this. She opted not to start a fire. It was still daylight and the smoke could be seen. She wasn't that cold anyway.

Despite the positive messaging and all the reassurances. It was clear to Raven that the world had not been prepared for the latest pandemic. Akin to a combination of Ebola and Tuberculosis. It was both deadly and swiftly transmitted and she shuddered at the memory of images being shown worldwide.

The World Health Organisation come onto the television back then and accorded the virus with a scientific title P-ebola-TB-1, or Petub1 for short, if she remembered it properly. It had been the first of its type ever identified and hence why it had a number 1 in the categorisation.

However, the media and world population quickly called it "The Plague" and it wasn't long before everyone forgot about the technical name.

"There really was no other word to describe it" she thought. It happened so quickly and was so deadly that the pandemic identification never assumed its specified name in the eyes of journalists and world commentators.

Raven remembered how the news channels had showed fancy graphics depicting how quickly it was spreading. Interspersed with horrific scenes being filmed by roving camera crews in different countries. At first it seemed to be happening *"Over there"* or *"Somewhere else"* she thought. *"Then it came here…."*

"The Plague swept through countries with a ravaging speed that governments could not comprehend. Multiple waves over the course of a year. Each one reducing the size of the population and its ability to look after itself."

"The elderly, weak and infirm went first but they were followed very quickly by others who did not fall into the description of being vulnerable or had any underlying medical issues."

The horror of it all came back to Raven then and she quietly began to sob into the sleeve of her camouflage jacket as she sat alone.

She knew that the plague attacked young people, fit people, healthy people. The medical and care professions were decimated. They were on the front line, they tried to help, to care, and to show kindness to those affected. They tried to stop them from dying. Then those carers were dying themselves and there were fewer and fewer people to help, to care, to save anyone, anymore.

The news reported that heads of government died, as did their teams and then the politicians who replaced them. Senior civil service officials stepped in but then died themselves. National leaderships worldwide began to falter.

Raven had watched as society began to crumble, as law and order failed to support the communities.

People stopped going to work. Money no longer held any value. The only worthwhile effort was to try and survive and stay alive.

News bulletins were then being controlled by the government, or what was left of it. The messages were different then, remembered Raven. Hourly at first and then degenerating to just once a day at noon. Messages telling people to remain at home but there was no-one left to maintain that sort of order.

Raven's job had been in construction back then, but no-one was building anything anymore.

The water stopped being pumped through plumbing, electricity was not being produced. Utilities maintenance and repairs stopped almost overnight. Food stopped being delivered to supermarkets and corner stores. Those stores that remained were ransacked.

Some of the independent radio stations that remained active reported on various military factions around the world, who tried to step in and create their own order but they in turn fell to the Plague and to greed, as many tried to seize opportunities in their own countries or took to the countries of others, perceived to be better, to be safer. With food or energy resources, whatever the excuse was.

It was the invasions and the Wars that had started on an international scale that impacted them the most. This was when it started to get bad for Raven and her husband. They tried to survive together after getting back with each other.

Then the national fighting degenerated into civil wars, followed by regional actions as the capability to fight further from home became more and more difficult.

She could remember the radio reporting on Enormous Electrical Magnetic Pulse (EMP) bombs that had been detonated to permanently dismantle the digital and technological weaponry.

Those attacks had wiped out any military advantages of the developed countries overnight. Then the only radio channels still working were the old analogue ones.

They reported that the EMP's were a game changer and levelled the playing field in terms of national or even regional capability to wage war and dominate the battlefield.

Thankfully, in Ravens eyes, the use of thermonuclear devices had been avoided in accordance with the 2025 world nuclear non-aggression pact, which had already led to large scale de-armament of such risky total annihilation weapons.

However, some tactical nuclear weapons, such as neutron bombs were used in both offensive and defensive manners during the Struggles, as those who wanted power and control held their moment in time. Such detonations could eliminate large scale military formations and heavily armoured fortifications, whilst also impacting on nearby towns and cities.

She remembered watching all the posh ceremonies on television, as treaties were signed by eminent politicians back in the day. Raven and her friends had all thought that it signalled a move to world peace and she shook her head and gave a sorrowful sigh, as she wiped away the tears with the sleeve of her jacket.

It was because those nations who could, had invested time and effort to create new generations of non-nuclear bombs that could cause just as much devastation. Those bombs had been used to dramatic effect. She could remember the big explosions, seeing shock waves in the distance and feeling the ground tremble so many miles from their epicentre.

By then, only a handful of radio stations had continued to report that worldwide and nationally, civil war was rife. It caused the collapse of society everywhere. Cities fared the worst as the epicentres of the pandemic or the target of small tactical nuclear missile attacks or the more modern massive EMP bombs.

Raven had already moved out of the city to avoid the bombing and thankfully missed the worst of the looting.

Supermarkets and other food stores were overwhelmed, as if by locusts. Nothing was left. When the food ran out in the shops, the mobs raided houses, took up residence in tower blocks and other substantive structures, which they fortified and where they ruled with the power of the gun and the knife.

People flooded out into the countryside in search of safety from the pandemic. In search of food and to get away from the looting mobs in the dense urban environments. They in turn fell onto the smaller rural communities in their desperate battle for survival.

Raven managed to travel back to her home in the countryside. Avoiding the larger groups of people and sticking to the trails that she used to run along for her triathlon training.

She needed to leave the city, as with no-one to work at the utility plants, there was little to no electricity, unless a generator was possessed and only then if it could be fuelled. Gas mains were on fire until the supplies were exhausted and there was no running water to extinguish the flames. The city was ablaze when she left.

She saw that some communities had tried to set up hand pumps at water hydrants but had witnessed them give up that precious commodity to the mob. Violence ruled the day.

There was only a single government radio station still on-air, operating analogue channels. It reported that the armies and militia continued to fight in different parts of the world. They continued in the Struggles that followed the wars, for the control of fuel for their armoured vehicles, ships, and aircraft but fewer and fewer as clans realigned and fought each other to a standstill.

Fought for what they had and what they could take from others. Many that survived the war and the struggles, fell to the last ravages of the Plague.

On the ground here, the mob mentality had gone to the extreme. Those who developed a fever, or a cough were ostracised and often killed without question. Anyone who had anything that someone else wanted, was killed and their belongings taken. Families and clans of like-minded people began to isolate from one another, as the Struggles continued to play out into 2031 and beyond.

It took just over a year for the Plague, the Wars, and the Struggles to decimate all the societies on planet earth and those few hardy people who remained, did what they could to survive. Less than ten percent of the population made it into 2031.

Raven was one of them.

Those who survived, had their own tragic story of how they have stayed alive. They got used to fighting. Being able to inflict and respond to extreme and sustained violence. They got used to being part of a dystopian world.

Raven knew she wanted to be a survivor. She wasn't about to give up.

Chapter Three

2031 - The Clan

They were a diverse clan. They had banded together out of necessity not a matter of choice or planning. Their numbers had grown and shrunk because of encounters with other people. Rarely neutral, they had become used to fighting to hold what they had or take what they needed.

Running and hiding were their primary tactics but when they had to fight, they could do so with a ferocity that frequently shocked their adversaries.

Each of the clan had their own story, their own losses, and their own emotional survival experience. Staying alive had been their immediate priority then but more recently they had begun to think longer term. That there might be a future, though at times it was hard to imagine.

Raven led the clan. Tall, lithe and a rugged looking Hispanic. She was a former triathlete with strength and stamina in depths. She could run all day, swim swiftly and had excellent aerobic abilities to recover quickly from hard effort. She had been trained in unarmed combat by her husband, who had not long since left the Army where he had been a paratrooper when the Plague started.

His name was Roberto, and she was called Maria. They loved each other with a passion. Roberto had served in the Army for over ten years. A handsome guy, he had fallen in love with Maria the first time he bumped into her in a bar where Maria had been working. Their love making was legendary, in Roberto's opinion, and he often referred to it as "jungle fucking" as it could be that intense. Almost animal like. Two physically strong and able human beings enjoying each other's bodies.

Roberto had originally made the decision to leave the Army so that they could start a family and be together more often. Maria was thankful now that they had not had any success in that department, as she had seen so many young children and babies succumb to illness or perish in violent attacks.

However, Roberto had been caught up in the first big wars, then his unit had become isolated and fought through the struggles which had been his signal to leave and return to his home. He wanted to be with his Maria. He left his former comrades in a silent night-time exit from their camp.

It was Roberto who first identified the change in behaviours across society, as law and order began to crumble during the early days of the Plague, the Wars, and finally the Struggles. From their isolated place in the countryside, he began to teach Maria all he knew about field craft. How to hide. How to survive off the land. Lay traps and use a crossbow to silently hunt for food.

However, his greatest gift had been to teach her how to fight. Grappling, wrestling, choke holds, twists, and turns. They had added it to their daily aerobic programme as they saw the deterioration across the community commence.

They would both run for hours and then finish off the session with a grapple. Sometimes the grappling became something else, and they could be lost in a passionate embrace that Roberto would use to try and turn to his advantage.

It added some edge to their sex play as it got rougher and turned into jungle fucking. Wrapped in tight embraces and demonstrating their fierce love for one another.

Roberto never hurt Maria though, as he worshipped the very ground she walked on. He just wanted her to be able to defend herself in any situation if he could not be there to help.

They had escaped the worst ravages of the pandemic out in the countryside. Roberto was back from war by then, but the Struggles continued. They witnessed explosions on the horizon as the remaining armies battered each other to a standstill.

Roberto and Maria were planning to move out of the house and into the wilderness once the fuel for their generator ran out and they had created sufficient ration packs to take with them. Some had already been created and held dispersed from their house as grab packs, something Roberto had learned out in the field.

However, their plans were overtaken when an armed gang surprised them when they broke into their home one night. Whether it was for provisions, drawn by the dimmed lighting they had, or for their last remaining fuel or to rape and kill. It was hard to say, it could have been any combination of those things.

As the attackers burst through both the front and back doors, one entered the kitchen where they were eating their evening meal. Roberto stepped across and blocked the approach of a large male brandishing a sawn-off shotgun and Maria snatched up Roberto's bayonet from the table.

Roberto attempted to tackle the intruder head on, but the man fired the shotgun and Roberto took both barrels in his chest and face. He seemed to disintegrate in front of Maria, and she felt her heart burst in the pain of seeing her man die.

She responded by slashing out with the large bayonet, as the intruder struggled to pull out a handgun. She killed the attacker outright with a cut to the throat. As he bled out in a spectacular spray of blood, he fell backwards, gurgling horribly.

Maria glanced down at the dead form of Roberto and her heart continued to stab with hurt and tears welled up in her eyes. Maria knew that she could not remain there. So, she jumped sideways, turning slightly, and smashed out of a window backwards. Scrambled away from the property in the darkness of night and went to ground outside.

Looking round, she could see other forms at both the front and rear of her property exit and look around. Silhouetted against the house lights. Probably alerted to the sound of breaking glass and so Maria set off at right angles from the house into the nearby woods where she began to deploy the evasion techniques that had been drilled into her, repeatedly by Roberto.

She lay out in the darkness and heard the gang tearing the house apart. Maria calmed herself down as much as she could before searching out and collecting the emergency packs that Roberto had hidden. Then she made off into the night. It would not be good to stay around. Roberto was dead and there were too many intruders to tackle by herself.

That first day after Roberto was murdered had been exceedingly difficult as the immense grief of losing Roberto washed through her. The anguish that Maria felt was gradually replaced by a burning hatred of those who had harmed him. Along with the injustice and unfairness of life in general. It made her heart harden.

As she foraged for food using all the skills Roberto had taught her, it made her more determined to survive and gain some vengeance. She would live as a memory to her lover. How she would gain revenge was not completely apparent to her at that time, just a seething resentment that slowly built up inside her.

A few days after Roberto had died, Maria came across a mixed group of white adults and children, living rough in the woods.

She watched them over a period of two days, not sure what to do. She watched them trying to look after each other, steal, or hunt for food for two small children in their midst first and then themselves.

Maria wasn't sure whether to show herself and join them for protection but could not make up her mind.

It was during a period of observation that she had noticed two intruders sneaking up and preparing to launch an attack on the families. They were ahead of her and nearer to the family group.

At that moment, Maria had a choice. Do nothing and move away or stay and prevent another murder. She chose, in that moment, to do something, use it to avenge Roberto. Anger welled up in her as she saw the family group being herded together by the guns that both the attackers wielded.

Maria was still some twenty yards away when both assailants without any challenge or warning, began shooting. Too late to unsling her crossbow, she had to launch her attack with what she had in her hand. Roberto's bayonet.

Maria screamed at the top of her voice as she sprinted forwards and plunged the bayonet into the back of one of the shooters as he tried to turn round. Realising at the last minute that it was a woman, not a man, they fell to the ground, caused by Maria's momentum. They collapsed into a heap.

The second attacker had already emptied both barrels of his sawn-off shotgun, as two of the remaining adults in the small group hurled themselves into him. As they tumbled and scrambled, they gradually took control and wrestled the remaining gunman to the ground with one of them grabbing him in a choke hold, and the other holding onto his arms. They continued to grip tightly until the life was choked out of him.

Maria pulled the bayonet out of the dead woman and stood facing the remaining two adults, all three of them panting heavily. Their fixed gaze was broken by the horrible sounds coming from a woman on the floor behind them.

Maria could see that both of the children were dead. The young boy had been shot in the chest and the other, almost headless figure of the girl both lay still.

The remaining woman was rolling around holding onto her stomach with blood jetting out of several wounds and screaming at the top of her voice.

Not knowing if there were any more attackers, one of the two defenders, a huge man, had gently put his hand over the mouth of the screaming woman to stop the noise.

The other, a red-headed woman tried to tend to the wounds and despite showing some skills and encouraging the man and Maria to assist, it was all to no avail.

The woman bled out silently staring with shocked eyes at the sobbing man holding her down, with a hand over her mouth, until she no longer moved. He moved his hand up and placed it over her glazed eyes and shut them with a gentle movement of his fingers.

After a long period of silence, Maria carried out a perimeter check and could see no further attackers. When she returned, she could see the big guy and his companion, digging graves with a combination of a steel plate and their knives. Sadly, they would not be deep graves and probably susceptible to future incursion by wild animals, but it was the principle of the moment she guessed.

As they tired, Maria helped and the three of them got slowly fatigued, sweaty and dirty labouring over the chore. It was during this time that they shared their stories.

The group had originally been two families related by the marriage of two sisters and they had tried to escape the worst of the violence by tracking out into the wilderness but did not possess the skills to survive there.

One of the children, a young girl got sick and died within the first few weeks they had camped out, without ever understanding what had killed her. The red-headed, pixie-faced girl said her name was Sheila and was a trained paramedic. Not very tall, she packed a lot of strength in a small frame.

Sheila lamented the lack of equipment and medication to save the poorly girl or stop her sister from bleeding to death in her hands. The big guy just sat and sobbed.

Eventually the big guy introduced himself as Gordon, a restaurant chef and a giant of a man standing well over six feet six inches tall, with a mop of black hair partly covering his face. Gordon said he was a whiz with a knife in the kitchen when it came to meat preparation but until today, had never been in a fight. Never witnessed anyone die in such bloody circumstance. Maria had.

It was Gordon who explained that both guys had returned to the urban areas to scavenge for food, leaving their wives and children safely back in their makeshift camp. Or so they thought.

They had probably been followed back to their camp by the attackers. He broke down and cried again assuming it was all his fault. Sheila tried to console, and they sat in an embrace for some time before reasserting some degree of silent composure.

Maria told them about Roberto and how he had shown her how to survive in such circumstances and she would share that learning with them if it would help. By sticking together and pooling their skills and resources they may be able to survive. All agreed it seemed to be the most sensible thing to do.

Gordon said that it was his wife that he had smothered to keep quiet and broke down sobbing again. Maria knew that he would have to toughen up or he would soon be overcome by grief and despair. Making him way less than useful.

Maria made the decision to help them. Take them on as survival trainees, much as Roberto had done with her. More mouths to feed but mutual support to remain alive longer. Being able to rest whilst someone else stayed awake. That sort of thing. She tried hard to remember everything that Roberto had taught her about staying alive in the field. She would share what she could with them and try to survive together.

They stood there by the four graves of their family together and first Gordon and then Sheila said some tender words about their loved ones.

They elected not to bury the attackers but removed from them any item of value. More ammunition for the sawn-off shotgun and the handgun, a penknife, their hats, and coats. Then they left the bodies where they were, to the vagaries of the carnivores, rodents and other scavenging wildlife and headed off further into the wilderness away from the town.

Gordon silently imagined their bodies infested with maggots and thought *"It would be a fitting and grisly end to the bastards who had killed his family."*

Over the next few weeks, they picked up enough skills and a degree of fitness that they were able to scavenge in smarter ways, but it is doubtful they would have survived that long without the arrival of the poacher.

They discovered a pair of rabbits hung up by their legs in small clearing in the woods. Throats slit to drain blood from their bodies. It was whilst staring at the find that they realised they had been drawn into a trap when a voice rang out across the clearing.

"Do not move. Do not shout out. Drop all of your weapons and raise your hands in the air!"

After looking around and not being able to see anyone, the three of them complied. Lowering the handgun, shotgun, crossbow, bayonet, and knives to the floor. Then the disembodied voice showed himself, accompanied by a young male. They both approached covering the trio with a hunting crossbow, carried by the adult that had a speed clip attached to the stock for rapid re-arming. The youth had a small hunting bow, with a quiver full of arrows slung over his shoulder.

The slightly built, bearded, dark-skinned man and the smaller youth were both in camouflaged fatigues. The man said "Me and my son have been watching you over the last week or so. We could have killed you at any point during that time. However, I think that you have demonstrated the right sort of attitude to help form a survival group."

Which got their complete attention.

He further explained that It was unlikely that individuals alone would endure during these desperate times and recognised the need for companions. The right sort and hence this approach with the rabbits as a lure.

The man introduced himself as Andy Steel but told them to just call him by his surname as that is what he was used to. He had been a gamekeeper but now he had used those skills to turn into a poacher. His son was called Rufus, or Roof. The group bonded over a few days hunting and it was then that Steel was able to demonstrate his excellent field skills, which were undoubtedly his greatest asset.

Not the biggest of men, his wiry frame belied a strength of body and mind that could overcome harsh challenges. Steel's pockets were full of wire snares. It was an apt name in many ways. He earned Maria's immediate respect with his knowledge and abilities to read the terrain and thought that Roberto would have liked him too.

Roof was still learning his trade and supported his father on all his expeditions.

Any wire, any bits of metal that Steel could salvage, filled his backpack and he could make them up in minutes and sometimes deploy them even quicker. He also positioned a cheese wire garrot over his shoulders, with both pegs sat on each breast for rapid use. *"It all looks quite gruesome"* thought Sheila.

Steel by name and by nature. He had the ability to remain concealed, to move around undetected and to pounce with a level of ferocity unmatched by his three new companions or his son but they began to learn. Roof was clearly still in a learning phase as well, as he often displayed similar errors to those of the city-dwellers that Gordon and Sheila really were.

"Given names were a thing of our past.", had said Steel. "They were a memory of when society seemed to be civilised and it was a softer, warmer place to be. We cannot dwell on that and I suggest that we all assume names that mean something to us as individuals and more perhaps more importantly. Our function or contribution to the clan."

It was Steel who named Maria as Raven. Not just because of her jet-black hair and piercing eyes. It was because he could see that she was a natural scavenger and saw opportunities that most people missed.

Highly intelligent, she acquired new skills with consummate ease and was a born leader. Steel and Raven held each other in mutual respect, exchanged skills and brought the other three on with them. The two of them often sat for hours exchanging opinions and sharing the skills that they both possessed.

Gordon picked the hunting and hiding up quite well, but his greatest skill was clearly his cooking. A genial character generally, he wanted to assume the name Butcher because of his knife skills. However, it was Steel who named him Gastro after bringing the game they caught to life, with wild herbs and fruit when it could be found. His cookery skills in such circumstances were imaginative and enabled them all to eat well.

Gordon held onto the belief that it was only a matter of time before the rest of the group would call him Butcher, but it was after a hissy fit about not being called Butcher that Gastro stuck.

The rest, now knowing this, were just more determined to compliment him on his cooking. An unending trial of will, which Gastro was not winning.

It left the genial giant acting surly and sour sometimes but thankfully it did not affect his culinary capabilities, which only further secured his name.

The red-headed Sheila assumed the role of combat medic and after a while just went by the name Med. She possessed a decent combat medical kit, constantly strapped to her side whenever she was not in a resting mode. She also gained a broad range of methods for snuffing people out, which came surprisingly easy for someone who had at one time dedicated her life to saving people.

Rufus was a great climber. He could nip up a tree faster than a primate and often shot up to scan the horizon and simply shin back down again. He said it was like being on the roof of the world up there sometimes. So, his nickname and purpose were aligned. Roof.

Over time, the little group managed to acquire a small number of medical items, which found a place in Sheila's kit bag. Stolen in encounters with other groups and once from a raid on a well-stocked, well-guarded farm. May be not that well-guarded, as Steel was able to sneak in, grab a haul that included a pair of long-barrelled shotguns and sneak out, without ever being detected.

However, they had not anticipated being tracked down by the gun's owners. Something that would have fateful consequences.

Camped for the night, with Gastro sat by the fire awake and on guard, with the rest asleep. They had been shocked by the suddenness of an attack on their little camp. A shot rang out that got their immediate attention.

It had struck Gastro in the shoulder and threw him back over the log he was sat on.

Steel reacted the quickest, throwing dirt over the fire to extinguish the flames and reduce the imposition of being silhouetted against the light of the fire.

There was a swish and whoosh as a number of arrows were fired speculatively into where they had been lay around the fire, but none hit.

They could hear shouted instructions around them, and it was difficult to pinpoint where the attack was coming from.

It was Raven who broke the stalemate by hissing that they needed to withdraw from the fire and move away from where the shouts were coming from. She said," Move on my signal. I am going to fire the shotgun. Ready?"

Raven counted to five, brought the shotgun to her shoulder and fired one shot then the other, across a narrow arc in front of her then turned and ran, with the rest of the clan in tow.

It was difficult running in the dark. The first time they had needed to. They could hardly see as their night vision had been interrupted by the firelight. So, it was hard to avoid obstacles. Low hanging branches tugged at their clothing, hit them on the head and slashed across their faces as they ran. It was chaotic.

Running hard, they all ended up in a stream they had failed to notice, and it took a few long seconds to recover their wits, scramble up the bank and it was Steel who shouted at them to halt, take cover and face their attackers.

Everyone but Steel, held guns facing over the stream. It was then that Steel let out a low cry of despair. Roof, his son, was not with them. He started to rise from his position, and it was Raven who held him back and whispered "We need to wait. We need to know how many there are. Don't go back into that. Please?"

Steel though would not be held back, and he ripped her arm away and slipped back into the water and crossed to the bank on the other side. Then disappeared into the black of the night.

To be fair. He was probably the only one who could make his way back to their camp. He had the skills, the covertness and he desperately wanted to find his son.

Raven took stock of what had happened. They had all been able to carry their weapons and some of their backpacks and slings but their bedrolls, tarpaulin sheeting and basic cooking stuff had all been left behind in the headlong rush to get away.

They lay there in the dark, on the bank of the stream, weapons held ready for several hours before Steel made his way back. Med took the opportunity to tend to her brother-in-law's wound and after carefully helping him to remove his jacket, she inspected his injury. Clean entry and exit holes reassured her that there would be less risk of infection.

Med rinsed out the wound with fresh water from the stream. Then she squeezed some antiseptic cream directly into the bloody holes and patched a dressing on both sides, held tight by some duct tape.

She smiled wryly thinking what she could have done with a full trauma kit but that was just a dream now as she helped Gastro pull the smock jacket back on.

They sat in a defensive position ready to fight for hours before Steel returned.

He announced his arrival by saying who he was and calling out Raven by name, to hold fire as he crossed the stream and re-joined the clan.

It was a vastly different Steel who came back. Gone was his confident manner. He slumped down and lay against a tree. Tears welled out of his eyes and he wafted his hands around trying to explain but no words came out.

Raven put her hand out to him and touched his shoulder, which caused Steel to sob silently for a while. Raven moved closer and gave him a hug whilst he composed himself and explained what he had found.

Steel said "I approached the campsite carefully so as not be spotted but when I got there, I didn't see any of our attackers. Nor did I see any of our stuff. Everything had been taken."

Raven could see that is not what had upset him. She had already guessed what was coming next.

Steel continued speaking as he sobbed, "I found my son. The bastards had stripped him naked and left his body about a hundred yards or so from the campfire. He may have tripped up and possibly knocked himself senseless. There was a gash and lump above his eyes. However, it wasn't the gash that had killed him. Someone fucker had slit his throat, but not before they had taken what clothes of his they wanted." Then he broke down in sobs and could not continue for some time.

Raven hugged her friend. It was all she could do to help him in that terrible moment.

When he recovered, Steel explained that all their camp baggage had also been taken. He had no idea how many were in the group but felt he alone could not follow them. He also needed to do something decent for his son and so he had dug a shallow grave, with his bare hands and a knife. That is why he had been away so long.

All his story came out in sobs and showed a tender side to him that the clan had not been aware of before. Once he had settled down Raven said "You know we have to move, don't you? We cannot go back in case they return and ambush us again. We need to get away from here. Are you ready to lead us?"

Steel nodded and stood up. Having raided their farmhouse, he had some idea of the size of their force and that it completely outnumbered the clan many times over. He looked around at the rest of the clan and indicated they should follow him.

Moving in the opposite direction from whence they came, he led them all through the night and into the false dawn before he permitted them to rest. They camped without a fire for the day and picked up the hike again at dusk. Putting many miles between them and their attackers.

Steel and Raven talked at length about varying their pattern of direction, checking carefully that they travelled without leaving too much sign for anyone following them.

Steel believed that they must have had an expert tracker to find them but once they had lit a fire, it must have acted like a beacon. They really must take care that they are far away from possible danger before lighting fires in future.

Raven said that they needed to replenish their baggage and whilst it was dangerous, they need to approach towns and farmsteads to do so. However, in future they would have a smarter plan. It cannot always rest on Steel to be the pathfinder but at that moment in time the clan did not have any other alternatives.

It was on their second raid that their little group grew by one.

They had moved from the wilderness towards a town, to gain resources. Not a natural environment for Steel but he still took point on the raid and it was slow going. Their path was often blocked by collapsed buildings, burnt out vehicles and the remains of humans. Many of which had attracted the attention of vermin and carrion eating birds alike. Flies needed to be wafted away as they moved along.

There were some slim pickings. A canvas sheet from what had been an open backed haulage truck, a backpack full of rotting food was rinsed out in a pipe leaking water and would help carry stuff once the smell was washed away and some cutlery salvaged from a burnt-out diner.

As they entered the town, Steel thought it best that Raven, Gastro and Med remain holed up in a single storey building on the outskirts of the seemingly devastated and unoccupied settlement.

Other remains were being gnawed at by rats in numbers so vast, he was almost treading on them as he moved through the town. It also shocked him that they continued feeding warily as he walked past. It was almost as if humans no longer mattered.

The death and destruction that must have taken place there was horrifying and it made him even more cautious in how he searched.

Bodies had been stripped of any useful clothing or valuables. The shops looked like a plague of locusts had hit them. There was no food left anywhere. The carrion and rats were finishing off everything else that was edible. To them, that is.

Steel carefully searched around and was moving between buildings, when he was alerted to a solitary figure, picking his way along the road. Walking towards the place that Steel had concealed himself in. Steel froze.

Steel could see his irreparably damaged face. The man had no eyes in his sockets and horrendous scars around them. Steel was intrigued as to how the man was making his way along the road unaided and walking with purpose.

Easily avoiding the endless obstacles of damaged infrastructure, abandoned vehicles, the rotting carcases of what had previously been humans and other debris scattered aimlessly across the footpaths and what was left of the roads. He used neither a stick nor had any obvious support by person or by animal.

The badly scarred man had called out to Steel, even though the poacher thought he had concealed himself well. After a brief exchange, Steel made the decision to lead the blind stranger to where the rest of the group was hiding and share with them the man he had discovered, or who had discovered him. It quite simply defied words.

It was at the rendezvous point that Steel explained to the rest of the group that the man with the broken face and no eyes, had been able to spot him in the undergrowth adjacent to a road, which raised the eyebrows of those who could.

The stranger went on to explain that he had been working in the military but was a little coy on exactly what he did. Something about when their base came under attack during the Struggles, he had been deployed in an advance role. Their observation post had come under attack and he ended up like this. Clearly a story still to be told.

Not a young man and it was questionable why a man of his age should be on the front line at all, but Raven guessed it may have been needs must. His innate detection or sensory capability added a new dimension to the group and was welcomed and immediately and appropriately named on the spot as Radar.

Whilst he could feel his face, he had no idea how he really looked and had been persuaded by Med to wear a cosmetic bandage over the gaping holes just to prevent the others from continually staring at him. She explained that she had inspected the terrible wounds but as far as she could tell, they were all cauterised, not weeping or bleeding in any way. However, she suggested it may help prevent any further damage or any form of infection.

Persuaded on medical grounds, he wore the bandage like a blindfold, but only when he knew he could still "see" stuff, despite the covering. The others thought he was magical and held the man in some degree of awe. A Gandalf kind of wizard who would help them move forward from this no man's land kind of existence and help to keep them aware of others. An early warning system.

Radar carried a backpack with some military ration pack, with odds and ends in it, including a marked up large-scale regional map. Of no use to him anymore, it was handed over to Raven to manage. She noted a few markings on it and decided it would be helpful to record locations that could be of use in the future.

They had become a clan. They had a mixture of capabilities and felt confident that they could survive.

Truly little of value was recovered from that raid and so they decided to move on. It was Radar who suggested that they move west. When questioned as to why west, Radar would only say that there were solutions out there, by the coast. People to find. Answers to questions. That sort of thing.

In the absence of anything else, it provided the fledgling clan with some degree of purpose. More than just survival, a reason to go on living. So, after some discussion, they all agreed, and the clan began to move west and escort Radar on his quest.

They were camped in the ruins of a barn one evening when Radar said that they were being approached by a solitary figure. He was walking slowly, coming into their camp with both hands held high in the air but the clan took precautions anyway, and hastily arranged themselves in a defensive arc awaiting the figures arrival. Once Radar confirmed that he could not "see" anyone else, in any direction, they allowed him to approach unharmed.

Once Steel saw it was a solid looking man in a camouflaged military outfit, with a sub-machine gun strapped to him, he told him to lower the gun and any other weapons to the ground.

After a short pause, the man removed the machine gun, two handguns and variety of knives, bent down and laid them on the ground. Then he stood back upright, removed his forage cap to reveal a shaven head and dropped the cap on the weapons. Then without being asked stuck his hands up in the air again, whilst everyone else looked agog at his personal arsenal.

Steel and Raven then approached the man in a bracketed move, one to either side of him before Steel challenged the stranger on what an army man was doing here.

The guy shrugged and explained that he was the lone survivor of a unit that had been involved in the Struggles. He had become disillusioned with the strategy and the tactics of the group he had joined up with.

At first, he thought they were making a difference. Acting as saviours and being heroes but that charade soon fell away in a series of actions that saw them annihilate another militia group and then enslave those who remained alive.

Heavy punishment, torture and death for no reason was not for him, so he ran away.

He said he had found it difficult to do the right thing in the circumstances he found himself in. Encounters with others always ended violently and he had defended himself several times from small groups and pairs of other people who wanted what he had.

Managing to survive on the few rations he had taken with him and those he ripped from persons who attacked him, he had been roaming aimlessly. Wandering about, until he saw the motley clan from the distance of hills using his monocular. A tactical single field lens capable of viewing things from some way away and probably why Radar had not noticed him.

Steel commented that if they could be spotted that easily by an individual, it was likely they were at risk to larger and more predatory groups.

They had thought with the lack of technology, no drones, or aircraft of any description anymore that they were largely safe out in the wilderness. The candid observation by the new army guy put them all on edge and got them thinking.

Steel suggested that in future they would travel in first light and last light only, when it was harder to pick out people in the landscape, even with good lenses.

The army guy then continued that the clan looked like it had a purpose, and he needed the sanctity of good company before he was picked off by those whose intent was not good. He could not be sure from what he observed but this clan seemed to know what it was doing and had a plan. It attracted him.

He went to say that if they didn't want him, he would bid his farewell and continue on his way to find some other group. If such good people existed.

The clan conferred and the soldier was informed that he could join them at the small fire they had, cooking some rabbits and wildfowl on sticks. However, he would be on probation and the automatic weapon would have to be handed in until such time as the clan trusted him.

He remarked that as a gunner in the army, he was not supposed to hand his weapon over to anyone but understood the clan's fears. An automatic weapon could take them all out in one go under the right circumstances.

The gunner said his real name was Ged and explained that his role in their armoured combat unit was to man a swivel mounted heavy machine gun and provide covering fire. The sub-machine gun being his back up weapon. However, the Struggles had exhausted his unit's fuel and whilst the heavy ordnance had been removed and installed in fixed positions at their last encampment, it had rendered the combat vehicles obsolete.

Some of the armoured vehicles had been dragged and positioned to form a defensive perimeter ring but those that required electro-mechanical means to fire were useless. The remaining mechanical guns that did work were placed to create lethal enfilades that had stopped their enemies from incursion to their camp.

When he walked away, the gunner had taken his own personal weapon and several ammunition pouches, plus whatever food he could carry. He had been followed and it took all his fitness and skills to outrun his pursuers and continue his journey away from them. He said that he had wandered for a long time. Surviving on scraps and what he had recovered from those who did try to rob him.

The next few days were a little tense as the clan adjusted to having someone new within it that had yet to earn their trust, and all kept a wary eye on the athletic looking gunner. To be fair, he in turn was also not that sure about things and so for a while always kept his eye on the others in return and observed them closely.

It was not long after Gunner joined the clan that they came across a natural barrier. A river. More than a river really, it was a gorge and it seemed to stretch forever in each direction.

They were used to traversing man-made barriers of highways and byways, streets, and bridges in the more habitable areas of the region. Each demanded great care. Culverts that crossed underneath roads had often been laid with booby traps and bridges exposed those crossing to sniper fire.

Night-time manoeuvres were no guarantee of success and so the clan mounted separate plans each time they encountered such marvels of engineering. Often laying low for several days to monitor any activity and crossing such things in stages, whilst always trying to maximise the cover and whatever firing points they could discover. This raging gorge, however, was a different challenge completely.

The obvious route was to follow down river and find a place where the ferocity of the water was less intense, as it would naturally widen out at some point but also very risky. There were likely to be encampments close by, at or even on the water course itself, as it was a natural source of life.

The map didn't show any obvious crossing points in the vicinity of where they were.

The river was also a magnet for animals to take on water and the human hunters who wanted them for meat. All in all, as downriver posed a higher risk than going upriver. With every chance there were likely to be more people whom they could encounter. The clan decided to head upstream.

So, they made their way along the gorge, with the river on their left. It was hard going. They were trying to find a means to cross the river and found just what they were looking for. A big tree that had fallen and provided the perfect bridge across.

However, it was high up and there was a long drop down to the gushing water and rocks that protruded from the foaming river.

Steel was all for walking across one at a time, but he was the only one with the belief to do so. Radar said his balance was good but did not sound that hopeful. It was clear that Steel had confidence in his own ability to balance and the nerve to make it. So, they agreed that he would walk across and take the length of rope with him. Secured on each side, it would act as a handrail.

A little more jiggling about with belts and they could create as safe a method of crossing the gorge as they could. With each person's belt attached to the rope. If that person slipped, then at the very least they would be dangling from the rope. Though the clan had not considered how they would then retrieve the person dangling by their belt, as there was no more rope.

Perhaps by holding out a long branch that they could somehow pull themselves up with it but who would stand there and hold it? There seemed to be more questions than answers. All in all. It was a hasty plan, had a paltry safety device and had little in the way of alternatives other than to carry on walking upriver.

Steel was being a bit gung-ho and several of the clan told him so. It was Raven who decided that they would camp by the tree trunk bridge, whilst sending Steel ahead to reconnoitre the land to see if there was indeed anything better than this. For now they would try and work out how to retrieve someone who fell.

The clan spent two full days and a night at the tree bridge before a tired Steel returned just before it went dark. He was welcomed back with their usual banter and brief hugs and handshakes, given some food and his water flask was topped up with fresh water for him.

Their water bottles had been topped up by lowering them down into the river using the rope. Then they patiently waited for his debrief.

Steel reported that he clambered for about five miles upriver before returning. All he would say was that it was extremely hard going, and he found nothing any better than this tree trunk bridge, which he nodded at.

He said the sides of the gorge were sheer and there was no way of clambering down, wading across and climbing back up again. It all looked less safe than the tree crossing he had originally proposed.

The clan had used the camp time to cut down and strip a number of saplings that they could use to reach out in case someone slipped off the tree trunk.

They did not sleep that well and those required to stand guard did not take much to waken.

It was an end of summer misty dawn, which made the crossing just that little scarier than it already was. Mist shrouding the danger of the rocks and fast flowing river below.

Steel nimbly jumped up onto the felled tree trunk and after securing one end of their single length of rope, he cautiously made his way across the gorge, balancing carefully as he went. Then he secured the other end of the rope to a well rooted tree on the other side and stood beside it, after pulling furiously at it to test its hold.

Radar attached his belt to the rope and made his way across. He did not look nervous at all and in no time had landed on safe ground and stood next to Steel. He was followed by Raven, who didn't hang about either and stepped purposefully across the tree trunk maintaining a firm grip on the rope.

Med went next, holding onto the rope with one hand and carefully picking a route along the tree trunk. She was almost halfway across when her foot slipped on a mossy part of the trunk and they all gasped as her hands tried to grab a hold and she slowly slid off the tree and dropped about twenty feet down the gorge.

Steel immediately gripped the rope on the tree and shouted across for Gastro or Gunner to do the same on the other side as he saw her slip. Med jerked to a stop and swung gently from side to side.

Once they were all were satisfied that the rope was holding, as was Meds belt, the clan needed a way of recovering her. Raven asked Boy to grab one of the poles. The longest and push it out towards Med but it would not reach her, as she had sagged so low down into the gorge.

To be fair to Med, she did not panic at all at this turn of events and just hung listless and quiet. Perhaps she had worked out that wriggling may affect the security of her hanging position, but she if she thought that, she did not say it.

It was Gunner who reacted next and said he would stand on the tree trunk and take up the slack and asked Steel for his assistance. Leaving Radar and Gastro to hold the tied ends, Steel followed Gunners lead and stood on the tree trunk leaning back to take the strain.

It had some effect and lifted Med up about five feet. It was then the two guys realised they would have to step out onto the trunk and lessen the angle to raise her up but place themselves at risk by doing so.

The way both men leaned, had them moving sideways along the trunk towards each other, at an angle of about 45 degrees, with Med acting as a sort of counterweight. As they inched to the middle, Med slowly rose until she could reach up and take a hold of the tree.

This was a very delicate part of the operation as to lose her counterbalance body weight, could have had both Gunner and Steel falling backwards. It was an inch-by-inch action, as the three of them now acting as a team, helped Med up, without either guy falling off.

It took a lot of effort and some time before the three of them could each stand vertically. As tired as they were, the three of them inched over to the far side of the gorge. It was only then that they all realised that both Steel and Gunner had carried out the rescue, without any form of safety. Med hugged them both tightly in turn, gave each a peck on their cheek and said a very tired thank you to each of them.

Genial giant Gastro did not even try to walk. To be fair he was still taking care not to re-open the wound in his shoulder, but he hugged the tree trunk and very slowly leopard crawled along it gripping it tightly with his hands, arms, knees, and legs, which despite the seriousness of the situation had them all laughing uncontrollably when Gastro finally arrived on the other side.

More so when he gave his reason that he could not see how any of them could have generated sufficient weight to pull him up had he too fallen. A moment of levity at a difficult time for the clan. Gastro did go on to make the point that his method was probably the safest and wondered why no-one else had considered it. A fair point conceded some.

Steel hopped back to recover the rope, studiously avoiding the greener parts of the trunk, then they camped on the other side. They stopped to give all the clan time to recover from the crossing and it was a great source of humour and comradery during the evening until the point it came to stand guard or get some shut eye.

Before they got their heads down, Raven made a formal gesture to hand the machine gun back to Gunner, in full view of the rest of the clan. She thanked him for initiating the saving of Med, to which Med gave a thumbs up and blew Gunner a kiss. He grinned in return and inside was glad he had made the decision to join them. A good bunch of people.

It was a few days after the gorge crossing that they were joined by the final members of the clan. The newcomers. A teenage boy and girl, yet to be named, they were also on probation. They were scruffy urchins. Skinny, unkempt, and quite morose. They did not explain where they came from because they could not.

Mute by choice, accident, or birth, they communicated with each other in a rapid form of sign language. How they had managed to survive for as long as they had done, was testament to their strength of character and ability to conceal themselves.

For reasons known only to himself, Steel decided to take them under his wing and called them so. His wings. He was in the process of teaching them all he knew about covert activities and they in turn were sharing their sign language with him. They hung off his every word.

An extraordinarily strong bond was developing between the three of them as they continued learning. It may have been compensation for the loss of his son but if so, Steel never mentioned it. They in turn possibly saw a father figure that may nor may never have been in their own life story. No-one ever found out.

The newcomers already knew a lot about covert movements and had slid silently into their camp. It was only Radar who had spotted their approach and when he could see they were not carrying guns, were they allowed to advance into the camp. They did so under the cover of darkness and were apprehended trying to steal resources.

Gunner was all for slitting their throats and stripping them bare of what valuables they did possess. A paltry treasure trove of two penknives and a small bag of dried cooked meat but they did introduce a child's trail buggy that they used to carry their camping kit. It was Raven who stopped the execution and determined they could join the clan but only under probation.

At an undetermined point in time, they would either be named and join the clan, or she would let Gunner slit their throats and leave them behind. So far, they seemed to be a good addition to the team, with the skills that Steel was imparting.

They were known simply as Girl and Boy. So far so good. When they weren't on guard duty, the pair would be found curled up in each other's arms and everyone just got used to their intimacy. If they weren't curled up together, they were communicating in their own sign language about all sorts of things that no-one else could understand.

Right now, the clan were moving in the direction set by Radar.

They had left a main city behind, after a protracted and fruitless search for resources and were heading for the coast. To a location that Radar could not explain, only that it held some answers and a chance of something different. Perhaps a better future than this existence, a chance to live, to thrive and not just survive.

So, they all moved along with him as it gave their lives a purpose. Besides, their clan was too small to hold anything or anywhere permanent right now. Better to stay mobile.

They moved slowly in daylight hours and only after the ground ahead had been scouted by Steel and his wings. Mainly they now moved in the twilight of dawn and dusk, to avoid monitoring by those with military grade observation tools, or snipers.

The two wings moved backwards and forwards between Steel on point and the main clan to keep them informed of the need to change direction, stop, go to ground, or hurry up.

Gunner was used to bringing up the rear guard to make sure they could not be attacked from behind. He was astute enough to keep an eye on the main clan but maintain an all-seeing eye on the terrain they had covered using his monocular, along with the deep flanks either side. He was eagle-eyed and had clearly been trained well in field craft during his time in the real military.

It was not Radar who slowed them down, it was the baggage trolley. The all-terrain child's buggy brought by the newcomers. The clan had pimped it up to create a method of carrying their slightly larger kit. It was easy to push, was well oiled and greased and was as silent as it could be. The clan took it in turns to push along, whilst others kept watch all round.

The buggy held camouflaged tarpaulin sheets that provided weatherproof cover when they had to bivouac in the open, a cooking pot, large frying pan, assorted cutlery, and a variety of provisions from their scavenging and hunting. In addition, the spare machetes, a grinding tool and a small hand-press for rearming the shotgun shells. Everything was carefully wrapped and securely packed so that it did not generate noise to alert unknown enemies in their vicinity.

Each clan member had their own assortment of backpacks, side-packs, and slings for carrying their personal gear, armament, ammunition, and food on the go.

On average they managed about ten miles a day, sometimes more, sometimes less. It depended wholly on the terrain, who or what was in their line of travel and the weather.

Sometimes the weather halted them for days at a time. Not that anyone tried to measure time in days, dates or even years anymore. It was all about seasons, the weather, and the terrain. Dawn, Dusk, Sunset and night-time.

Holed up in defensive positions in the middle of the day, they only moved when it was safe to do so and in the poorer light of dawn and at dusk. They relied heavily on Radar's uncanny ability to detect other human beings, even when they were concealed in holes, behind walls and in the undergrowth.

He said he could see their heat forms... whilst that raised a lot of questions, it was not something Radar was prepared to discuss with them at this time. Despite many attempts to engage him on the subject. He would just ignore the question.

What was clear, was that the damage to his face was caused by something dramatic and strange that had led to him assuming new abilities. However, Radar would just not talk about it.

So, warned by Radar and Steel's scouting, they skirted miles around fortified camps and took great care when they were aware of any other reconnaissance groups in the vicinity.

They would go to ground and remain there all day if necessary. Very occasionally they would take out a scout or scouting party if they felt they had the advantage, and it could not be avoided. However, to do so, could mean a hunt and so they tried to avoid any unnecessary violence.

If that did happen, they would make themselves scarce with several forced marches away and into the wilderness - sometimes in the dead of night, relying wholly on Radar - but the older man would sometimes get tired and irritable. They needed to conserve his energy at times and would therefore stop longer and plan shorter walking phases to the day.

The clan were aware of how the Struggles had panned out. Armed militia and ex-serving military personnel kitted out with top of the range hardware had slugged it out for a long time. Hundreds and thousands died in the fixed battles, in the skirmishes before and after the battles, or the hunting down of retreating forces. All in the name of accumulating more hardware and eliminating the competition for the reducing number of resources available.

Some of the camps were like small castles, with heavy fortifications holding a series of strategic firing points with heavy ordnance. Their purpose, to hold and protect livestock, stores, and armouries. They must have been in possession of sustainable resources, including a good water supply, otherwise they would not have been worth the effort. They also needed labour, most of it forced. A new era of slaves.

Passing trade did not exist anymore. Those places always had their own scouting patrols out just to be sure and best to be avoided at all costs. Sometimes mounted, they could cover ground swifter than a party on foot.

Horses were rare assets though. Most of them had been hunted down for food by the city folk expanding out into the rural farmlands. It was only the powerful clans, with good fortifications and sustainable food and water that could afford such luxury.

It was pointless trying to engage with them. The white flag of truce had long since been trod into the dirt. Communication between strangers was at the end of a barrel or a long-distance shouting match behind good cover and a preparedness to invoke and inflict extreme violence.

Therefore, large, and well-defended encampments were always given a very wide berth.

It was rare to encounter anyone as evenly matched as themselves, which made the night-time advance by the intruders even more remarkable....

Chapter Four

2031 - Fight for Roasted Sheep Camp

After the hurt sound and the rustling of the bushes. Silence fell as the intruders paused to take stock. Raven thought *"They must have seen Radar sat by the fire. They may be driven by pure hunger. The smell of the roasting sheep fat was intoxicating, and its aroma spread far and wide."*

Perhaps they wondered where the clan had gone to? How many were in the clan? They may have sensed they were walking into a trap, after the sound of one of Steel's snare traps had echoed around. Perhaps it had reduced the size of the enemy by one? It could not be known at that time.

Their movement forward though, was now slower than before. However, the lure of the cooking food must have been too great. Clearly wary of the snares now, they checked as much as they could by touch before moving forward.

Then a slight shape movement in the silhouette of the trees and bushes and Raven knew they had arrived.

She easily held one of the two long-barrelled shotguns in a prone firing position, noting that Gastro was doing the same on her right and Med cradled the sawn-off shotgun, on her left. She caressed her husband's bayonet and placed her machete on the ground next to her.

They all knew the drill. They had to wait for Raven who would be the first to fire. That would be the signal for all the guns to be fired continuously until the ammo was expired. Radar called it "Shock and Awe." Then they would wait for any volley or single shot returns, then they would wait once more. That was their standard operating procedure.

They were to wait for the screams.

Looking up, Raven noted one upright human shape emerging slowly from the fixed silhouetted skyline, then a second, then another. They were about forty feet away and probably focussing attention on the figure of Radar sat still by the fire some forty or fifty feet behind her.

Knowing that to wait any longer could leave Radar at risk of an arrow, a bolt, or a bullet, she gently moved the barrel of the gun and aimed towards the leading and most central figure of the approaching group. Those around her sensed the moment was upon them.

Already set for both barrels she squeezed, and the stock rammed hard into her shoulder. The immediate retort of the shotguns and handguns either side of her were also fired and the expected burst of Gunners automatic weapon but just the one magazine that he sprayed across a narrow arc. It was indeed pure shock and awe. All their firepower was discharged in less than five seconds.

It was brutal.

Some rounds zipped around her as those intruders who survived the volley fire, made a game effort to shoot back but the main clan stayed low as they waited for the screams.

Steel had seen the volley fire from his clan's defensive position, left his crossbow slung on his back and grunted satisfaction at the close pattern of firing to deliver the shock and awe demanded of them by Radar. Then he waited for his signal and there it was. The muzzle flashes of those remaining alive. He and his wings could now visualise their targets and leapt at the figures still standing or kneeling. All three of them slashing left and right with their machetes.

It was all adrenalin and action but no words. Their attack pattern was deliberately mute and swift. It caused more panic in the enemy that way.

Death and dismemberment were delivered without mercy. The victim's scream's causing panic in those still alive. No way of knowing who they were in that moment. Steel and his wing had a clear responsibility to kill and stop the intruder's attack. If the stranger's intentions had been good, then they would not have approached in the black of the night as they had, cradling their weapons ready to use.

It was all over in moments, the screams of the dying and dismembered intruders just attracted the main force who jumped up and swept in from the front, slashing and hacking at anything that still moved with their own machetes. The attack was as swift as it was vicious.

Then it was time to take stock.

Steel and the wings faced the direction from where the intruders had approached in case there were any more that Radar may have overlooked but there were none.

The intruders were all dead, apart from one who was staring up with one remaining eye and struggling to breathe through what was left of his mouth. A machete blade had caught his skull and taken half his face off before embedding in his shoulder and neck. Removal of the blade would see him bleed out.

Steel took the opportunity to question the intruder but had to lean close to hear what he had to say in answer to some simple questions. A tweak of the blade embedded in the intruder's body being sufficient to get something akin to the truth.

There were no others. They were a small scavenging party from a much bigger and powerful clan who had taken up residence in a fortified farm many miles away. They were enroute back to their encampment empty handed and spotted the glow of the flames. A target and an opportunity to bring something back with them from an otherwise wasted field trip.

From distance it only looked like it was one or two people and they felt confident they would take whatever they wanted. They had hurried when they smelt the cooking meat and walked straight into the snare. Steel made a mental note to better conceal their cooking fires in future.

The only valuables they had were what they carried on the scouting mission. There was no baggage train or trolley. Though they had dropped backpacks behind a rock outcrop some way back when they decided to make an unencumbered approach. Steel knew it was impossible to find in the dark and would be something he and his wings could investigate at first light.

Information gathered, Steel swiftly withdrew the blade and the one-eyed intruder gasped and shuddered as he bled out and his life was extinguished.

Raven was thankful that all their clan wore light Kevlar vests that had been relieved from a burnt-out military convoy on the motorway some weeks ago. The clan had camped out for two nights and three days and kept watch to check it was not a trap. Even then, it was only Steel who made his way in to investigate. All the food, fuel and water had gone, as were all the guns and ammo, including some heavy ordnance crudely removed from the turrets of the armoured vehicles.

However, all had not been taken. Some of the drivers and crew had not been stripped of their uniforms. An oversight of some description, which meant the clan, except for the newcomers, all sported camouflaged outfits, the tops over the Kevlar armour they gratefully scavenged that day. Along with belts, bags, and some tools.

The armour provided good protection from projectiles and slashing, stabbing wounds. Though she doubted that anyone of their clan would have survived a slash down the skull.

Helmets were a rare thing to find. Those they did were because of their owner had taken head damage and what was left was of no use anymore. Their clan all tended to wear soft head coverings, depending on the weather.

Raven was also thankful as Med had clearly taken a round in her chest and she lay winded back on the defensive arc, as the burnt hole in her jacket demonstrated. Raven stepped over to Med and waited for her to catch her breath. Then she beckoned for her support to check all the clan members. It would be a waste of time checking the now dead intruders.

Then she went back to the campfire to brief Radar. No clan casualties and amazingly no wounds either. A surprise to come away from such a brutal encounter unscathed.

There were six dead intruders, four males and two females, all stinking to high heaven from what may have been a long patrol. Not a bad shout from Radar after all. One of them, a lanky and underfed youth was hanging from the tree by the snare. It had cut clean through his windpipe and throat, stopping only at the spinal cord and he must have bled out almost immediately given the blood-soaked clothing.

The rest of the clan ran through their own scavenging ritual of checking pockets for ammunition and gathering up the weapons and any useable boots, clothing, belts, or bags from the bodies.

Boy and Girl took the opportunity to gain some decent boots and swapped them out for the tattered trainers they were both wearing. They also took the least damaged smocks to kit themselves out in camo like the rest of the clan. The bullet holes could be sewn up later and the blood soaking would soon dry out and discolour in time.

The main clan retired back to the cooking fire, whilst Steel and his two wings dragged the bodies a few hundred feet away and lay them unceremoniously into a pile in a hollow. If anything did come scavenging in the night, it would take place far away from the camp.

It was not unknown to encounter big cats and bears since the zoos and private collections had fallen foul of all the looting and hunting for food. Packs of large feral dogs and the occasional wolf pack were also out in the field and more of a nuisance than a threat.

However, best not to get isolated in such company and something that Steel and his wings out front and Gunner at the rear, always kept a wary eye out for. They did also provide a decent meat substitute if a good clean and silent shot could be delivered.

What other carnivores did survive, stayed far away from human's but a dead body would put up a smell of decomposition long before it could be picked up by a human nose and therefore best to drag away from camp. No need to import any further risks.

Back at the fireside, the clan placed all the scavenged goods on the ground in full view of everyone. Then Raven oversaw the allocation or choosing of what was there.

Two handguns and several pouches of 9mm ammunition. Ten knives of various length, some with sheaths, a bow and quiver of hunting arrows, a crossbow and pouch of bolts, along with some catapults with bags of steel ball bearings. A surprisingly good haul in the circumstances and obtained without any injuries to the clan. Job well done.

The piece de resistance was an unopened packet of surgical wipes and two packs of ketamine/fentanyl/morphine combat jabs (one of each) that Med pocketed straight away.

Raven allowed Gunner to take the lion's share of 9mm ammo but made sure that the two handguns were available with at least one spare clip each. Steel shook his head, not his style. Radar was asked and declined a gun once again before Med and Gastro picked up the handguns for additional back-up. Gunner already had a pair of handguns as his backup weapons.

Guns were not going to be an option for the newcomers until they had been fully accepted into the clan. They knew that and did not seem overly put out. However, at Steel's nod, Boy selected the bow with quiver, with Girl picking up the crossbow and bolts, along with a catapult and bag of ball bearings each.

The knives were shared out one each across the whole clan, with the last two, more like carving knives, being placed into the baggage trolley. Raven nodded as their new, if tattered and battered camo outfits of the teenagers gave them more of a uniform identity with the rest of the clan.

With the spoils of the action distributed, the clan's attention once again turned back to food.

Radar had not sat motionless whilst the fight took place, he had poked and turned the sheep on the makeshift rotisserie of a strong branch over two x-frames of bigger branches. Partly to show he looked unaware of the intruder's approach and to maintain the pretence of being oblivious but also because he wanted the sheep to cook properly and not burn on one side.

"Nothing worse than trying to chew burnt mutton and he didn't want to make himself or anyone else ill by undercooking one side. Logical really!" Thought Radar.

Gastro used a clean carving knife to dismember the mutton joints and hand something to each member of the clan. They ate, cleaned their weapons, and re-filled the guns with ammunition. The empty shotgun cartridges were pocketed for re-filling by the little hand-press when they could. It would not be tonight.

Gunner picked up as many empty 9mm casings as he could. They would be used in a different way when they had an opportunity to set up their small armoury. He was experimenting with making grenades he could throw and was collaborating with Steel who was considering creating something akin to an improvised explosive device, or IED as they were more commonly known.

Despite lots of discussions, neither had made any progress other than collecting bits and bobs of metal, which they wrapped and stuffed into their back packs.

Steel wanted to add ordnance to his perimeter defensive measures if they were required to hold up for longer than a night or create a semi-permanent defensive position… but he was struggling with creating a reliable mechanical trigger to detonate the devices.

Gunner also wanted to make his own ammunition but had not got the means to do so. For now, he carefully wrapped and bagged the good shell casings that had not been stood on for some future use. Waste not, want not his mother had always taught him.

Once they consumed their fill, the fire was extinguished. They would not need its warmth tonight and it would allow what was left of the sheep to cool down.

Before they set about the rota for guard duty that night, Steel addressed the whole group. Radar could not stay awake all night and the clan needed to make sure they remained safe and divided up the night watches accordingly.

Steel wanted to share with everyone how well Boy and Girl had performed in their flanking move and subsequent attack. They each received congratulatory messages from the whole group, and it was Raven who walked over to each of them in turn to hold them by their shoulders and told them it was a job well done, that they were progressing well in their probationary period and to keep it up.

The teenagers took the plaudits proudly before Boy moved out of eyesight with Steel to make the first guard duty and Girl tucked herself up around hers and Boys backpacks and pulled a waterproof cape around her and over her head, then fell straight to sleep.

Chapter Five

2031 - The Chief

The clattering sound of a steel bucket being dropped and bouncing around outside immediately woke him and as his senses switched on, he realised he had already gripped the gun that lay beside him on the bed and held it ready to be used. An instinctive reaction.

He mused that it was those intuitive reflexes that had saved him more than once and got him here to this, the most important part of his life.

Lying still he heard a slap and a voice cry out. *"It would be the milkmaid,"* he thought. *"She was a clumsy fool but evidently a hard worker and a solid lay in the hay. She had her uses."*

Swivelling round on the bed, he sat up and rubbed his free hand across his pale skinned face to try and wake up but realised he needed the support of water to do that. He stood, holstered the gun, and walked over to the dresser, poured some water from a large jug into a bowl and washed the sleep out of his eyes. Then he rubbed his wet hands over his shaved head, before towelling them dry.

Pulling the curtain to one side he could see the puddle of milk spilled out on the ground and slowly seeping into it, drawing a cloud of flies into the soggy mess but no sign of the milkmaid or who had slapped her.

There was a knock at the door.

He waited a moment and then said "Enter."

In came his second in command, a leathery featured, big man in combat fatigues. "Morning Chief are you ready for the early report?" he asked.

The Chief continuing to look out of the window, smiled and asked, "Was that the clumsy idiot of a milkmaid again?"

The big man looked uneasy and replied "It was Chief. She stumbled carrying a full pail of milk on her way to the dairy. I gave her a slap on the arse and sent her back to the barn to milk the other cows and start again."

"Aye" said the Chief, "that was the right thing to do" and for a moment was lost in thought looking out of the window as the sun rose from its early position on the horizon and lightened up the whole room, he was in. His office, his bedroom, his planning room, the centre of the new world, it was his everything.

Who knew how hard it was to grow stuff and keep your people fed and watered? He wondered if God had considered all this when he created life on earth. The minutia of daily life. Managing livestock, ensuring clean water, growing crops, and creating a new and better society.

It all seemed to be a far cry from where he had been just a few years ago. A young captain leading a crack reconnaissance unit, used to being placed as a spearhead as part of major assaults, where he had been incredibly successful.

He was known by the name of Richardson then, first name William. Bill to his friends.

Using all his knowledge to fight the good fight, kick arse and win the day. Bill Richardson had managed to keep his unit together and most of them alive, despite some hairy battles as the country went from being a military power to almost nothing.

He had seen some terrible things. Gigantic bombings and missile attacks that destroyed large swathes of the military infrastructure, and of the civilian communities. Pitched armoured battles and then hand to hand fighting for the barest of food and all on top of the pandemic. The Plague that had kickstarted this whole thing, this fall from grace and all the devastation that came thereafter.

However, he had remained alive. His combat teams thought he was indestructible, and he had a plan. He would rise above the filth and squalor created by others and would lead his people like the Messiah. Out of harm's way and into a new world. A new order.

Over time he had gathered others around him. Some had been drawn to the leader who could not be killed. They came from both civilian walks of life and from other military unit's. Others had been captured and given a choice. Join us or face the consequences of not.

As Captain Richardson he had been exposed to new and more agile ways of working within the military and across civilian organisations, long before the Plague and the Struggles. It introduced the concepts of autonomous Chapters and Squads within a Tribe and the opportunity for a Guild, where tribes could come together for common aims.

A system of management that suited his objectives perfectly.

The power of the tribe is intensified by the creativity and delivery of the different squads, responsible for their own outputs. Bill had seen how this could help form the backbone of their new order. Their new civilisation at New World homestead, as he liked to call it.

He had instructed his combat troops to lose the rank and insignia of the old. He was no longer to be known as Captain Richardson, Bill, or even sir. They were now a tribe and he was their Chief.

No place for the weak. They would eliminate what was wrong with the old society and make a new one. A new world created by the winners and with no place for losers.

Every person had a place in the tribe or if they did not, they were used as forced labour or fed to the pigs when they were of no use anymore. He would ensure that the new society would be better than the old. More efficient. More effective. Minimise the waste.

He believed that they were like the pioneers of old. Finding new ways to make things happen. It made him feel proud that he had this chance to make a difference but there was still so much to do.

A "harrumph" of a cough came from the big man and roused the Chief from his musings, and he looked across at his devoted number two. They had fought side by side. Protecting each other, supporting each other, and had become brothers in blood. The big man was their Warlord.

Formerly a paratrooper, Sergeant Redding, was a leader of airborne raids when planes existed. His prowess with a gun, with a grenade and with a knife was legendary. He managed security across the whole tribe.

No-one but the Chief knew that his real name had been Otis. Same colour of skin but certainly not the vocal match of the old soul singer Otis Redding, from the previous millennium. Warlord ruled his squads with an iron will and no one ever crossed him and lived.

The Chief focussed his attention on his blood brother, who waved his hand to indicate they should both sit at his campaign table and said, "Yes Warlord, brief me."

The pair sat facing each other and Warlord updated his Chief on what had been going on since night fell the day before.

There were still three scout groups out on patrol. One of the others who had brought in the last group of survivors and were now locked in the stockade reported that some of them now seemed to be ill.

A fact that brought the Chief to full attention and he stopped the briefing there, quickly made ready and went out with Warlord to investigate.

The fourth scout group had been preparing to go back out on patrol, but the Chief held them back. He was not at that moment interested in the production rates that Warlord was about to brief him on.

A good yield from the wheatfields, milk production was on target with their next stage butter, yoghurts, and cheeses ready for the winter. The pigs were well fed, and the beef herd was in a new pasture.

However, Warlord realised that this was not the moment to continue the briefing and went with his Chief to check the stockade.

Chief was alerted to the sound of coughing before he even got close to the stockade. The wooden and metal palisade that contained the prisoners, the hostages and where all new arrivals were placed until they had been assessed for their suitability and usefulness.

He could smell the Plague before he even got there. Several people curled up in balls rolling about the floor outside coughing and spluttering, with one or two others lay still in a small heap, presumably where the others had thrown them. Probably to get them out of the bunk room where they could no longer infect them. However, the Chief knew right then that it was too late. The stench told him that.

It was scary how quickly the Plague could take hold, how easily it was passed from person to person. The swift incubation rate that matured in only a few hours before leading to an inevitable and painful death.

The remaining people wailed and screamed to be released. A mixture of men, women and children and Warlord's security squads looked to him for direction, but Warlord remained impassive. He knew what would come next and it would be delivered by the Chief, not him.

Chief said "Don't waste ammunition. Use bolts, arrows, and spears. Kill them all and set fire to the stockade. Then I want to see the scouting squad who brought the infection in. I need to know that they are okay and find out where these survivors came from?"

"Chief" was all Warlord said. It was an acknowledgement of the instruction and he then moved off to relay the deadly message to his teams.

Those in the stockade had nowhere to hide, other than in the bunkhouse. Most were killed scrambling to get inside the wooden bunkhouse. Though it offered them only the briefest of the sanctuary that they needed, it did not last.

It was like killing rats in a barrel. Bolts and arrows flew with unerring accuracy at those who remained outside and were cut down in seconds.

The security squad on duty did not go into the bunkhouse to finish off the last few. Not wanting the risk of infection, they just set about lighting some straw and twig bales to lay on and around the wooden building.

Chief remained until the bunkhouse was alight and the last remnants broke out from the smoke-filled interior to the fresh air outside and the instant death of the bolt and the arrow, fired into them without mercy.

Satisfied that they were all dead, Chief instructed that the stockade was pulled down and thrown into the flames to create a massive funeral pyre. Then the remaining bodies were unceremoniously thrown into the flames from the now glove and mask wearing security squad.

Only then, when the great plumes of smoke billowed into the air did the Chief walk purposefully with Warlord to the scouting squad, due to leave camp and commence their next long-range patrol to find survivors and scavenge for resources.

The scouting squad leader was acutely aware of what had taken place at the stockade and waited in trepidation of what the Chief would do next.

He need not have worried. His reputation and standing with the Chief were good. He wanted to make sure that the squad leader and his team were all well and wanted to know more about the survivors that had been brought in the day before. Where had they come from? What had they said and what they were like?

The squad leader reported that they had intercepted a small caravan of families making their way along one of the old roads. It had been an easy ambush, eliminating the armed ones and then gathering up the women and children, with their meagre belongings and herding them at gunpoint back to the Homestead.

Satisfied with the report that the scouting squad leader had provided, that there was no further risk, he waved the scouting party out on patrol. Then he turned back to the main farmhouse with Warlord for the briefing.

After taking only a few steps, Chief stopped and then decided to walk the perimeter of their fortified camp first and get the briefing on the way. He beckoned Warlord to join him and continue the brief. So, they walked and talked.

The stockade was almost square in the middle of the fortified encampment and it was not lost on the Chief that everyone would now know what had gone on. He would need to reassure all those he met that they remained safe. It was necessary to maintain good morale and ensure they had the means to survive the coming winter.

It was not enough to have fortified the farmstead, they needed to ensure that they had sufficient food stocks and fuel for the winter. They needed to ensure their survival was part of a sustainable operation. Their new order depended upon it.

The main house and annexes provided sufficient accommodation for all members of his tribe. All the women had nominated men with whom they shared beds. Every room but the cooking area and bathrooms were kitted out as bunk rooms and everyone had a bed.

Over time, Chief expected the population to increase by natural means as well as by immigration. He needed to make sure that there were no hindrances to making babies and creating new life.

Which reminded him that some form of nursery and education facilities would need to be constructed and a teacher designated. *"All in good time"* he thought, as they were added to the lengthy list of things to do that filled the Chiefs mind.

There were plans to extend out into the barn next, once they had naturalised the newcomers, when there was no need to keep hostage family members. He needed them to be held captive to make sure that people did their duties. Once everyone had been welcomed into the tribe, had a duty and a place then there would be no need for hostages held in captivity. *"It was an orderly process"* he thought.

However, maybe that could wait now until next spring. They would get by with what accommodation they currently had. When they did, a nursery and school room could be added. So much to consider when you were the chosen one. The Messiah.

Chief paused for a moment, sighed at all that responsibility and then carried on walking.

Warlord reported on the farming matters that he had originally meant to do before the need to eradicate the plague bearers. Then went on to say that the wood stocks were now at a level above what had been planned in terms of winter fuel and the lumber squad had turned their attention to cutting down the big tree trunks to create building materials.

As Warlord continued, they paused at the side of the battle tank that faced out onto the approach road that wound its way through the valley to the farmstead. Its turret and long barrel permanently facing anything that came at them down the road in a threatening stance.

Its imposing figure belied the fact that there was yet insufficient power coming from the solar panels rigged up on the farmhouse roof, to charge the tanks batteries. Nor enough time to maintain and lubricate the mechanics of the engine and at least get the turret swivelling again.

The tank was a relic to a time when such a fine piece of armour would get the attention of anyone on a battlefield, its only use now was an armoured machine gun post. Its gunner gaining the protection of the steel turret and manually turning the machine gun swivel mount around a wide firing arc on top of the turret.

If the batteries could be charged, then at least the turret could deal death and disaster on an unimaginable scale to thwart all but the hardiest of attacks. There was a good stock of high explosive ammunition contained within the tanks and the main armoury.

The fence line ran out from either side of the armoured beast and contained a mixture of battered vehicles from military and farming backgrounds, welded together in parts or sat on top of each other, to form an impenetrable defence wall, behind which the tribe could defend their resources.

Some of those vehicles had been theirs when they arrived, others salvaged from attackers who had tried to take them on. Some still had machine gun cupolas fitted on them and they usually provided the posts where the guards could maintain watch. The heavy machine guns in the mounts were also a formidable deterrent.

Chief checked both their waters sources, the well and the stream. Part of the stream had sluice gates fitted to divert water to a small wheel that in time would not only mill the wheat for bread but would turn a small turbine and generate electricity.

The tiny but tough little Engineer and her small squad of technical people had made drawings of what they needed and handed them to each of the scouting parties. Chief had no doubt that they would have farm-wide electricity in no time at all.

As they passed, he gave Engineer a morale boosting grip of her shoulder as he told her how pleased he was at her plan. She smiled proudly, as did her small team. She was still staring proudly as Chief and Warlord disappeared out of her sight.

Chief was pleased to see another batch of ducklings chugging round the small pond, which would expand the number of eggs being produced along with those from the chickens. When he got round to seeing Farmer and her squad, Chief was able to repeat back all the numbers that Warlord had provided him with and congratulated her on the productivity of the milking, grain production and her plans for cheese, dried meat, and hardened loaves for the winter.

Farmer also said that the fruit harvesting had gone well, and she expected to barrel up apples and several other items of produce as preserves. She went on to describe how she was liaising with Cook and her squad to maximise the greenhouse for growing herbs and spices. Cook could throw them all together and create mouth-watering meals on a grand scale for the tribe.

Finally, the Farmer reported that their small corral of horses was all sound, had all been re-shod and were available for patrols should they be required. Chief thanked her and said that he was holding back on the horses for now as so few of the security squad could ride properly, having never had the need to before.

It was yet another thing in the plan that needed to come to fruition. Horse riding seemed such an indulgence right now. However, he could see the benefit to longer distance patrolling that they would enable and made a mental note to create a training programme with Warlord for every one of the security squads to learn to ride.

The Mechanic reported on the level of fuel remaining in the tanker they had constructed an earth bunker around for protection and the state of their vehicle fleet. Two large, armoured personnel carriers, each with double swivel mounted machine turrets on their roofs, the two jeeps and the truck. All in fine working order should they be required.

The mechanic was a short, wiry thing with a big afro cut. She was also responsible for the armoury and reported that all was in order in there. Sunk under the ground in the barn that doubled up as their workshop and garage.

The Chief discussed the plan to clean out the tanks engines with Mechanic and both agreed it was a secondary task right now but was an integral part of her plan.

Finally, he completed a circuit of his New World homestead and spoke to almost every member of the squads who were present and awake. Noting that some were off duty having managed the night shifts and would be asleep. He was generally pleased with what they had created and told them all so.

What did not please him of course, was what he had lost and what he stood to lose next.

Clearly there was now a shortfall of labour from the stockade. He needed those hands to lift and shift the building materials, till the fields, pick the fruit and herd the cattle and sheep.

He also feared that those newcomers who were now out on patrol, only did so because their children had been held hostage in the stockade. Would they return. If they did, would they understand why and what he had instructed?

Whichever way he looked at it, Chief could not draw any positives from the situation and discussed his concerns with Warlord.

Quest

Chapter Six

2031 - Archery Club Surprise

Out in the wilderness and away from any signs of habitation, the clan continued their quest.

Since the firefight at Roasted Sheep Camp, the next few days had passed relatively calmly, with no encounters with any other humans. It was still summer, and the weather was even.

Steel and his wings had scoured a wide area at dawn and returned with the intruder's backpacks and news that the bodies had been scavenged by carnivores during the night, including the hanging youth. Though they had heard nothing in the camp nor was it detected by any of the guards. A sobering thought.

The backpacks carried the reward of additional 9mm ammunition, for which Gunner was pleased and a ramshackle collection of capes and bedding. Some of which they swapped out but mainly left at the firepit where the now carved up roasted sheep had been cooked. Most of the takings were of no use to the clan. There were some crossbow bolts, bags of ball bearings and a couple of arrow-filled quivers, all of which found a home in the baggage buggy.

The scouting party had been travelling light and clearly, they were returning to their own camp empty handed. May be that was another reason they made their risky approach. To bring something back rather than nothing. The clan would never know and did not really care in any case.

Chunks of cooked mutton were distributed to create food on the go for the clan and they set off on their quest once again. Gunner indicated he was going to take several long static watches as he was concerned about the noise from last night's firefight. In addition, they may be missed from the unknown enemy camp, if they were due to report in.

The lost party could initiate a chase and they all knew what sort of risk that could impose.

The clan were heading westwards, as directed by Radar, towards the coast. There was a place on the edge of the land he had said that would provide some answers for Radar and help the clan to move on.

It was on the third sunrise after the Fight at Roasted Sheep Camp that the clan saw any sign of life.

Steel had come across some cultivated fields which stretched for some distance, along with some well beaten tracks that looked like they were made by vehicles. Two big signs that the clan needed to detour. Cultivation needed labour and vehicles demanded fuel.

They figured that to retain that sort of thing would require a large and well-armed defence force.

They had been following animal trails, just below the tops of a series of hillsides, mostly covered by trees. Good cover for their travels but once Steel saw the organised fields below him sent back Boy to tell the main party to halt, whilst he and Girl reconnoitred another route out into the wilderness.

It took two whole days of extended hikes to walk away and around, before Steel was satisfied that the ground over where they would travel showed no signs of human use.

This was something they had got used to and did not generate any frustration and if Gastro, and wings had, it would not have been much change from their usual dour personas. Radar was the calmest. Clearly things going round in his head, he spoke less and less on their travels and stops, as he seemed to be inside himself.

It was some seven sunrises after the Fight at Roasted Sheep Camp that they discovered they were being followed.

The sky was beginning to clear, and the clan were waiting for Steel or the wings to call a place where they would halt for the middle part of the day.

It was Gunner who tagged it, what looked like one or two smudged faces peering out from a wood and clearly looking for their trail. He backed off some distance, then hurriedly caught up with the baggage buggy group and they went to ground and formed a defensive arc until one of the wings or Steel called back into the main group.

It was Girl and she cleverly identified there was a problem and covered the last few hundred yards very carefully and fully aware.

Raven briefed her and she retreated the way she came, at the same speed and with the same covert movements to recall Steel and Boy.

It was not long before Steel arrived. Got his briefing from Raven and slipped away to scout whoever was tracking them, leaving his wings to direct the main group to a good defensive position higher up the wooded hill that gave a reasonable degree of visibility in most directions. *"A good place to defend!"* thought Raven.

Whilst Gunner had spotted the chase, he knew that there was no one better in their clan of investigating without being seen and created his own advance observation point ahead of the defensive arc, as Boy and Girl deployed to cover the clan's rear.

After some time, Raven oversaw a methodical move up the hillside, with Boy or Girl leading the way and overlapping each other to make sure that if they had to fight, there was always more than one clan member in a prone fighting position as the others crept forward.

It was all carried out at a good pace and without any panic. Something they had practised and trained for many times. With Gunner once again taking up a rear covering role until they reached a spot, they knew they could defend. Then he joined them.

Radar, however, just harumphed and then tramped up the hill like he was out on a hike. He could not see anything that would stop them and demonstrated his disdain at the cautionary tactics of the others, with his erect form striding purposefully to catch up with Boy and Girl.

Raven shook her head at Radar but continued with the military hillside manoeuvres. Old habits die hard. They had kept the clan safe. She mused that Roberto, her ex-para husband, would be proud as punch if only he could see her.

Steel covered some distance before going to ground in a prominent spot. Wedged between the trunks of two trees that seemed to be entwined in a public display of lust. The accompanying foliage gave his very still and camouflaged form sufficient cover to use the clans highly prized monocular field glass.

The monocular was a small work of art and allowed him to see both distantly and what was in his natural vision just by shutting one eye and then the other. A long shroud ensured that it did not reflect the sunlight, unless pointed right at it.

Steel slowly moved the monocular across a narrow arc and picked out the animal trails, gaps in the boulders and trees that formed natural thoroughfares. He knew those would be the routes taken by their pursuers.

He was there a while before he picked out some activity. The merest of movement at that. A branch gently pulled to one side to provide a better view of the terrain ahead no doubt.

Steel monitored that and the area around it intently but could not see anyone at all. The branch remained pulled back, but the chaser or chasers were being extremely cautious, and he thought *"Kudos for Gunner for even noticing anything wrong."*

As he focussed his attention on the bushes around where he had seen the branch pulled back the calmness was rudely interrupted with a swoosh and a thud as an arrow embedded itself in the tree trunk next to Steel and he dropped immediately to ground and leveraged himself backwards from the tree clump to a secondary position he had already identified. With the monocular hanging from his neck and dragging on the ground.

It shook him up that someone could launch a projectile at him without him noticing it, but he knew he had to analyse the situation quickly or he would be at risk of losing his life.

The arrow had come at him from the left. Not the way he was facing. Perhaps the branch being pulled back was just a diversionary tactic. Like a magician or a thief. Look here what is in my right hand, as the left produces the dove or steals your watch.

Steel tracked his vision away from the arrow to the direction it had most likely come from and it was then, when he looked back at the arrow once again that he noticed it was different. It had something attached to the shaft. He had a bit of a "what the fuck" moment. However, he did not move. It could be a trap and so remained as still as he could.

He stayed there for most of the day. He thought it was too dangerous to move. He stayed awake and alert. Scanning the area around him as covertly as he could.

Though he remained vigilant to any visual movement, his mind did drift back to when he worked as a gamekeeper. He sometimes held positions like this, waiting for poachers to show their hands. His patience and observational capability were legendary on the game reserve. He also thought about the loss of his son. It was quiet times like this that affected him the most. He knew that he could not dwell in that melancholy place and focussed his attention on the job at hand and waiting like the gamekeeper he was.

His old role could be a lonely one that spanned unsociable hours. It had suited his need for isolation when he needed to but it could be a solitary existence when he was out in the field. Though he did miss the company of his small family and even fewer friends having the occasional beer. It was the loss of his wife when Rufus was so young that panged his heart first.

It had been exceedingly difficult to look after a toddler and carry out his duties. He had not taken his son with him in those early days, as he was just too young. It was only at the advent of the Plague and subsequent Struggles that he had let Rufus accompany him. More out of necessity as he made strides to separate himself and his son from the ravages of what was going in the towns and cities.

It was therefore not long enough to give him a better skill set than the ones he possessed when their camp had been ambushed. It brought a tear to his cheek that melted into the sweat that was building up on his head and face. Steel knew it was his fault that his son had died. No-one he could blame. It stiffened his resolve to stay alive. Sit out this tense standoff.

The sun rose high in the sky and shone its light and heat downwards and Steel began to feel uncomfortable as sweat beaded on his head and trickled down his face but still he did not move.

It was late in the afternoon as the sun bade farewell to the day and the cloak of darkness began to spread did Steel begin the retreat from his position. He did so carefully and slowly. Constantly scanning the area around him as he extricated himself from the open space.

Once he was clear of the area, he took on water to slake his thirst and shoved some food on the go into his mouth. Then he speeded up his jog cum walk and headed for the point the clan began their dispersal move.

It was Girl who identified his approach sometime later and clicked her fingers once as Steel got near, to let him know where she was. Steel tapped her shoulder once in acknowledgement of her concealment skills as he passed through the picket line of protection and headed towards the centre of the defensive position to brief Raven.

Over more cold provisions and refreshed by water drawn from a nearby stream the clan debated the circumstances of the chase. They concluded that their pursuers were not in a headlong rush to get to them. They could be related to the scouting party they had wiped out or just as easily be from a separate group. Perhaps from the people farming crops.

It was hard to work out with insufficient data and therefore they came to the decision that they needed to find the unknown people before they found the clan. The clan would therefore separate into two groups.

Gunner and Gastro would remain with Radar and the baggage in the current defensive position as it offered good views in the daytime and they held sufficient ordnance. Besides, they had the power of Radars vision with them.

The perimeter defences were beefed up with a range of snares placed by Steel and his wings, the locations of which were then briefed to the rest of the clan.

At first light, the false dawn, the following morning after a difficult night of guard duties, Raven led out an expeditionary force.

Accompanying her were Steel, the wings and Med to go and investigate, gather data, and work out a plan. The outcome may be to carry on running. Stand and fight. Or do something else. It was the something else that was causing concern to Raven and the clan debated it.

If the chasers could find them and hunt them down, it would be a constant pressure that they could do without. It could lead them into blundering into something ahead because they were constantly looking backwards over their shoulders.

Furthermore, the clan had no idea on the size of the party chasing them. It could go pear shaped very quickly if they were outnumbered and outgunned. Radar was unusually silent and offered no opinion on anything.

Led by Steel, the expeditionary group moved out in the eerie light of the false dawn. When the night sky starts to lighten but the sun has yet to rise. Accompanied by a low ground mist and a very still air, they needed to move lightly and careful not to make any unnecessary noise.

It took quite some time before they reached Steel's last observation point away from the entwined tree trunks. Raven could see the arrow through the monocular and noted that it held something wrapped around the shaft. Was it a message of some sorts? Hard to say.

Raven deployed the clan members into a short-spaced arc, and they approached the arrow pierced tree with great caution and used every point of concealment as they could. It was Steel who made the final move towards the tree over the last thirty or forty feet.

Without looking at it, he slowly reached up and plucked the arrow down from the tree. Maintaining his all-round view of the surrounding terrain as he did not want to be shot.

He retreated slowly back to the protection of the arc. There he handed over the arrow to Raven.

It had a leather parchment attached to it by twine. Raven unrolled it and read the short message, written in pencil. "We want to parley" which she showed to Steel. He raised his eyebrows.

Raven said that she could not see a way out of this unless they did find out the intent of the chasers and asked for a pen.

Med produced a Sharpie, used as a triage tool in large scale injury situations or combat to write on the wounded for others to follow up. Though in their case, there was no-one to follow her up, but she carried the indelible pen everywhere out of habit from her time working in hospital trauma cares.

Med rubbed out the pencil message with her hand and wrote "Okay, when and where?", got a nod from Raven and rolled up the parchment and attached it back to the arrow.

Boy was called forward and under direction from Raven, fired the arrow back into the lustfully entwined tree trunks. Then the whole group backed off out of arrow shot distance. Took up another defensive position and waited. What they saw next completely shocked them.

The ground around the tree moved and stood up.

First one, then another until a total of five ghillie suited figures showed themselves, all carrying bows of different types. The clan all clutched their weapons and prepared to defend themselves.

Ghillie suits are a whole level up on camouflaged kit. With lots of leafy branches and tufts of grass wound into a cape of net around the person, their head, their arms, and their weaponry They were virtually indistinguishable from the undergrowth and shrubbery around them.

What was exceedingly scary was the group had been within arm's length of their defensive arc when the arrow was returned to the tree by Boy.

One of the walking bushes took a few paces to the tree. Plucked the arrow. Opened the parchment and in a male voice shouted that this would make a good spot.

Raven, unsure as to how many armed bushes and living grassy mounds there really were, shouted back that this was not going to happen.

The figures remained stood up and the voice continued by saying "We could have cut you all down at any point from your scout arriving yesterday, until right now.

We deliberately gave away our position to your rear-guard to alert you and then the black man in the tree. We also watched your scout as he sweated out during the light and observed him make his way back to your hilltop position.

We could have killed either of them then or any one of you today but chose not to. Now do you want to meet in the middle of this field for a parley or not?"

Raven weighed it all up and decided that a parley would at least discover what was going on, even if it meant the whole situation going sideways. She made the decision to raise her hands and walk forward, after telling everyone to be on their toes but whatever that would achieve at this point was debatable. What if there were other ghillie-suited killers surrounding them even now and completely disguised.

This was a killing field if the walking bush strangers made it so. Therefore, Raven walked forward but the sweat was trickling down her face, her neck, her back, everywhere really…

The talking bush theatrically placed down a camouflaged short hunting recurve bow, raised his hands to match Raven and walked towards her at a similar pace.

The remaining bushes holding a mixture of crossbows and wicked looking recurve hunting bows, all painted in a variety of green, brown, and black shades remained impassively where they were.

No other bushes made a vertical appearance or looked threatening right now.

Raven and the quite tall male bush met in the middle of the hillside and stood about ten feet apart.

The silence was broken by the bush. He pushed his hood back to reveal quite striking Scandinavian looks, in a rugged face under a mane of blonde hair. "My name is Ernie, but the company call me Point, nothing to do with the sharpness of the arrow tip but my skill in taking point when we are on the move. You are?"

"My name is Raven."

"For the black hair?" interrupted Point.

"Sort of." said Raven "What do you want?" she asked abruptly.

"It's a long story." began Point.

"We have time, I think." countered Raven.

Point shrugged and started off "We used to all be friends at a community Archery Club. We competed together and socialised as families. When the Struggles began, we pooled our resources and tried to protect our families and our belongings, but it was untenable."

"Soldiers came with guns. We all lost loved ones, some more than others. Those that remained were pulled into one of the Militias who wanted silent killing skills in their scouting parties. Our families that remained were held hostage, whilst we went out on patrol."

"Were held?" asked Raven.

"Yes." Point continued, "In a guarded stockade. We were on a long-range patrol looking for resources when we found out that the stockade became plague infected with some prisoners brought in by others to act as slave construction labour and within twenty-four hours, every person in the stockade was dead or dying", he paused and then continued.

"It was set on fire, whilst some of those dying, were still alive." He looked away for a moment and appeared to shoulder a sigh and then returned to the moment and to his explanation.

"We only found out as we passed another scouting group on our return to the fort. With no hold on us, we decided to move away. That clan is not a good place to be. Limited resources that are rationed out and those in charge rule with a vicious streak. It is not a place for us."

"They speak of higher things and creating a new society, but it uses slave labour and is not something we want to be part of."

"We retraced our steps back out into the wilderness and heard a firefight in the night. The sound carried on the wind. When we investigated the following morning, we saw you decamp in the distance and move on. Checking the bodies, we discovered it was the patrol that had passed us days before when we should have returned to the camp. The people who had told us about our children."

"They were not our friends, and we were intrigued by your field skills and your organisational capabilities to defeat them so easily. We admired your avoidance approach and watched you skirt some of the cultivated fields."

"We thought that a parley may provide an opportunity to discuss a merger with your clan or if not, will leave you to your own devices."

Point carried on talking "Our field skills are good, and we rarely lack food. We are used to being mobile and can look after ourselves. We have no interest in your resources but do want to know what is driving your clan westwards. That is the question and hence the parley."

Raven nodded slowly, "I am going to walk backwards to my clan and confer." It was a statement, not a question and she began to step back. Point remained exactly where he was and just watched her back away.

Back in the defensive arc, Raven whispered the outcome of the exchange with the talking bush, who she said was named Point, and explained the suggestion of a merger and their query on our clans' purpose.

There were different opinions in the clan, but it was Steel who provided the candid statement that made their decision easy. He was shaken by their abilities and knew then, that if they had wanted to, the clan could have been wiped out by the strangers much better capabilities.

Steel could see the benefit of smarter trackers, creating a wider scouting path and if their ability to silently bring down any game, then it would add value to the clan in terms of the provision of food. In which case, it was almost a no-brainer.

As with any newcomers to the clan, there would have to be a period of trust building and they would all have to be on their toes to spot any hint of deceit. So, we need to agree on a practical method of them joining us, with a need for caution. This would be the largest change in the clan's brief history.

Raven mused for a few moments and then rose to walk back to speak with Point.

She explained their thinking with a heavy reliance on the need to build trust. Something that had to be earned, not just spoken about. Point agreed, nodded and then he stepped smartly away to speak to his other armed bushes and shrubs, whilst Raven stood by and observed.

It seemed that their minds had already been made up, even before this encounter. Perhaps as they tracked the group down. How near had they got? Why had Radar not seen them? She would discuss this with the old man later.

Point and the other four bow-toting ghillie-suited figures walked over and introduced themselves to Raven and stated that there were no others. Though it didn't stop Steel looking around warily as they all spoke.

Point introduced three middle-aged ladies, Count, Fletch and Whistler, and a young teenage girl called Bullseye previously a potential Olympic prodigy with a bow, the daughter of Whistler. All that was left from a suburban Archery Club and their families. Some seventy or so people all told and now just five survivors left. Loss on a scale that Raven recognised, and she could measure that in their faces. *"They look just like us"* she thought.

The introductions continued as she brought over Med, Steel, and the wings.

They moved off in agreement with the newcomers holding centre, Steel and the wings fanning out ahead as they knew exactly where the baggage group was. They all headed off as a unit, with Med and Raven taking the rear-guard.

On the hilltop it was Radar who noticed the group returning larger than it had left, which put both Gunner and Gastro on full alert. They both surrounded themselves with every available weapon that they had and prepared to fight.

As the extended group approached, Raven called a halt and made her way through and in between the newcomers and raised a hand to indicate all was well, as she continued walking towards the defence position on the hill.

Radar rose to meet her, and she explained the circumstances that had occurred. Radar just nodded sagely. Then Raven asked him why he had not noticed them following us and should not have been as surprised as she looked, when he said he had.

Raven looked perplexed but of course without saying anything Radar could not detect that, only the silence, so he continued, "Yes, I did see them, but their actions were cautionary, spectating, not attacking nor approaching with menace. I suspected they were not going to attack us, so I thought I would wait and see what happened next."

"And you didn't think to mention anything?" challenged Raven.

Radar chose his words carefully and replied, "They have not been the first group to track us in that way, but they are the first to sustain it. Others have drifted into and out of my peripheral range without doing any more."

"How do you know it wasn't just the same group?" demanded Raven

Radar breathed slowly in and exhaled just as slowly before stating "Their heat colours were different."

"What?" said the now shocked Raven "You need to explain!"

The old man took his time replying, "This is hard for me to explain but I see heat shimmers for humans and animals. Their colours are all different, almost like a fingerprint. I just know they are all different and not the same as..." then he tailed off.

"Different than what?" shouted Raven but Radar just shook his head and sat down.

Point could see the angry exchange from his position lower down the hillside but was too far away to make out what was being said. He took it that there was resistance within the clan to admit any more members and waited patiently for the outcome.

Raven then spoke with Gastro and Gunner, who relaxed their belligerent postures and lowered their weapons, then she walked down for a one-to-one chat with Point.

"Problems?" he asked but Raven just shook her head and beckoned everyone over and when they had all arrived, addressed the group.

"Radar knew the newcomers were observing us" to which Point took a studious look at the old man sat down near the trunk of a tree up the hill, as Raven continued "but he chose not to tell us, as he believed their intentions to be without malice. Therefore, under the terms we agreed, you can join with us and let us continue with the introductions." Then she led the mixed group up the hill.

Several conversations began between the clan and the newcomers. Steel was particularly interested in the ghillie suits and the newcomers demonstrated how they used them, including how they managed to "loose off" arrows and bolts from prone fighting positions, a skill that literally dumfounded Steel and he wanted to know more.

Gastro wanted to know if the newcomers had arrived with gifts, such as toilet roll or wet wipes, which generated some nervous laughter as they all swapped stories of cleaning bums with leaves and wiping dirty fingers on the grass or rinsing them off in the streams.

It was a good icebreaker to the tensions that had built up throughout the previous day and night. Left hand for bum and right hand for food seemed to be the consensus.

"Who could have guessed that talking about taking a crap and wiping your arse could be so important and interesting?" Said Gunner.

Point pulled Raven to one side and asked what she meant by the references to Radar, but she just pointed him in the direction of Radar and said, "Go ahead, ask him?" so he did. He walked over and crouched down next to Radar, introduced himself and began a conversation. They spoke for a few minutes before being joined by Raven.

She arrived halfway during the conversation "... and you can hear them?" enquired Radar.

"Yes, I think so" answered Point. Then silence.

"Hear who?" questioned Raven but got no reply from either Radar or Point. "You need to tell me what is going on?" she demanded.

"I don't know" replied Point, "I have always been able to hear murmurs of voices without being able to make out the words. My mother told me I could hear the voices of angels when I was a child, but others ridiculed me, so I kept it to myself and never told anyone again."

Point, seemed to be struggling to explain but continued, "The voices got louder sometimes and were completely silent for years. I struggled with my mental health over it for extended periods of time before coming to terms with it. I joined the Army and for years I forgot all about them.

It was during the spread of the Plague and the entire time of the Struggles that I began to hear the voices again, sounding truly angry but without ever being able to make out what they say." Then he looked at Radar and gave him a nudge.

Radar sighed and said, "I can see them."

"For fucks sake who?" said an angry Raven.

"The angels, the others, whoever they are, I can see their heat shimmers, which are totally different from humans and from animals."

"Oh, my lord!" said an exasperated Raven, flopping down on the ground "and you only tell us now!"

Radar wafted his arms about as if to explain further but did not.

Point tried to calm Raven down by continuing his story and was nearly waved away by her but pressed on. "I think that is what drew me to lead my scouting group to join up with you. I didn't know why until I spoke with Radar just now."

"Radar?" was all she could say but he did not answer and just sat by the tree. Lost in his own world.

The entire mixed group of clan and newcomers by now had all crowded round, drawn in at first by the angry exchanges but completely silenced by what they were hearing.

Then Radar began to explain.

Chapter Seven

2031 - The Others

Radar had been part of an elite military reconnaissance unit, trained in all aspects of armed and unarmed conflict and covert operations. He was known as Mike O'Neill in those days and a captain in the unit.

They had been trialling some advanced ocular kit that had consisted of a wraparound visor with some clever built-in technology. It provided Virtual Reality (VR), Augmented Reality (AR) with Artificial Intelligence (AI) to detect and pinpoint communications. They also provided thermal imaging that enabled the placement of friend or foe data into the picture.

The thermal imaging gave away persons trying to conceal themselves, in undergrowth, behind walls on occasion, and in ditches, in a fully three-dimensional (3D) picture. They were also experimenting with links to satellites to bring additional information into the mix.

The Virtual and Augmented elements of the kit enabled the visor to project objects onto the battlefield around them that sat, in real time, as if they were there. The AI was able to analyse the data and provide the wearer with response options, liaising directly with technology back at the unit's Head Quarters to record and replay as required.

State of the art equipment that forward units could use to detect and then take down enemy positions by calling in air support or long-range artillery and missiles.

Sometimes the VR/AR would cause all the view to turn to hues of lighter reds and yellows but would return with a "Technical Tap" or smack on the helmet. The kit could be quite unstable at times.

The government had intended to deploy the unit into some difficult regional conflicts that were underway around the globe, but the Plague had arrived whilst they were still on trial, and the world went into a nosedive of calamity and death.

It was during the Plague that Radar, when he was Captain Mike O'Neill, reported the unusual occurrences. Different colour heat shimmers. Humans and animals have darker reds, oranges and blue hues that help to demonstrate things like hypothermia and give operators the ability to differentiate between humans and animals, and whether they were alive or dead.

The heat shimmers that Captain O'Neill saw were all silver... no heat. That data was being reviewed and analysed back at HQ in real time and by their off-line AI systems.

The Struggles were in full force when his unit was deployed by helicopter to a city centre location to observe the activities of some silver shimmers. They seemed to be moving amongst large groups of people, at transport interchanges and shopping centres, getting close to people without being seen.

His HQ believed they were the source of the Plague and were continuing to spread it in some way.

This was also the time when the Struggles began to lessen as the bigger factions had killed most of the opposition off and were reduced to smaller militias fighting for the last remaining resources.

It was during the subsequent observation by Captain O'Neill and a colleague wearing the same VR/AR/AI visor that their presence seemed to come to the attention of the shimmers and one suddenly appeared in front of him. Making him jump.

Then there was an explosion and both O'Neill and his colleague were thrown backwards and into a building. Other explosions followed, then gunfire and the sound of screaming was all he could recall before he blacked out.

When he came to, he was partly pinned down by debris and began extracting himself from the rubble. Looking around everything was depicted in the red haze that the VR/AR/IR emitted when it was in fault and so Mike raised his arms to remove the helmet and visor, but it was not there.

He could feel his hands touch the side of his face without encountering the obstruction of the helmet or the visor and it shocked him.

With trembling fingers, Mike continued feeling around his face and got even more concerned when he felt the gouges of cauterised flesh where his eyes had been. Whilst he was able to snort out some dust and debris, he was not quite sure how he managed it as most of his nose seemed to have gone as well. Then he began to tremble as the adrenalin charge was doing its thing.

There was no blood or ooze, which he thought was strange, just a vast sore area of skin that had been seared in the explosion.

Even more weird was the fact he could still "see" the heat shimmers of humans beyond his immediate position and the surrounding terrain. The building was almost demolished entirely.

His colleague lay next to him but had clearly fared worse, it was not just his eyes missing, it was his entire head. The heat shimmer of his remaining form beginning to fade into blue as the heat ebbed from his lifeless body.

He could not though, see any more silver shimmers. The remaining human shimmers started to glow blue as he realised that he was the only survivor of whatever had taken place.

Radar explained that he could not be sure if it had been an Electro Magnetic Pulse bomb that had detonated nearby, a tactical nuclear weapon or something the silver shimmers had initiated.

All he did know was that he had been blinded but could still see and he needed answers.

Both their firearms were damaged and he realised they were useless. So, he had set off to trek back to his Head Quarters out west on the coast. Without transport it was going to take a long time.

First, he checked on his other comrades, but nothing was left of the helicopter or its flight crew when he got near to it, just a pile of mangled metal and bits of body parts hither and thither. There were some tattered packets separated from the standard military ration packs they always carried with them on missions. He picked up what he could.

He had no idea how long he had lain in the building, or for how long he had been walking. He managed to scavenge some food here and there to supplement his ration packs but survived mostly on water from streams and he was getting thinner and weaker all the time.

That was when Steel found him and concluded that "The rest you all already know. That I can see stuff in a weird way.

Then today Point has explained that he can hear voices and it could be that those voices are the communications of the silver shimmers. I just don't really know."

If he could have seen the detail on the faces of the dozen people around him, he would have seen them all catching flies. Mouths agape, they just stood there motionless. Lost in their own thoughts.

It was Gastro who broke the silence with a "Shall we have something to eat then?" he enquired, and it raised the levity a little with some nervous laughter and Steel regained his composure with a stated need to set out a guard rota and create a stronger perimeter defence than the one hastily put together when they arrived.

Then he stalked off with his wings to affect some additional snares and traps around the lower parts of the hilltop.

The snares were located at planned or random locations depending on whose opinion was sought and whether you were Steel and the wings, or the rest of the mixed clan.

Chapter Eight

2031 - Warlord

The Chief noticed Warlord looking and acting perplexed. He was not sure why. The construction of a new stockade and bunkhouse had commenced. Productivity across the whole camp was positive and ahead of target. A surprise given the drop in the numbers of labourers but everyone else had put in double shifts to get them back on target and Chief viewed that in the positive light that it was. But Warlord still looked at odds, so he went across to him and asked his close friend what the matter was.

Warlord said, "Two of our scouting squads were overdue and I am concerned. One of them was the crack team of archers who could blend into the wilderness with acute levels of concealment. The ones whose children were held hostage in the stockade."

"Perhaps they have found out somehow? However, how could they know what had happened? Unless of course, they had used that concealment to get inside the fortifications and had witnessed what had taken place. It was difficult to comprehend."

The level of trust that Warlord placed into each of the scouting squads was high. With the archers of course, it was the leverage of their young children's safety that was at risk. "So, what has happened to the other scouting party?" asked the Chief.

Warlord said, "That was something I need to find out."

Taking one of the remaining scouting squads and sending the other one out on a parallel course, Warlord led them in a series of walked sweeps in the wilderness that surrounded their camp and, in the areas, he knew they had been sent to patrol.

He did not need to go far. After only a few hours and several miles, he saw buzzards circling in the air and decided to go and take a closer look. Signalling to those around him, they headed over to see what was attracting the big, winged birds.

Warlord was not shocked by what he found, only surprise that one of his teams could have been taken down the way it had been.

The carrion birds were circling because a pack of feral dogs had taken possession of his scout's carcasses. There was not much left of them as they arrived, and the hounds scattered after two were felled by arrows. Warlord had instructed that no guns were to be used unless they came under attack. He wanted to carry out this investigation as quietly as possible.

Most of the scout's bodies had been left in a pile in a hollow, some way from the remains of a campfire and a sheep that had been barbecued over it. Its tell-tale skull picked clean by carnivores and the buzzards that were close by. As were some tattered backpacks and bits of kit that had been worried by the feral invaders and spread around haphazardly.

Warlord conducted a wide sweep of the area and found the location of a vicious firefight and nodded at the spot where he could see the residue of firing points in a tight arc, someway from the fire. He shook his head and made a frustrated "Tch" sound as he realised his scouts had not taken proper precautions in their approach.

Then he saw the skeletal figure, well just the head and torso, dangling from a steel wire noose from a sapling tree and reflected on the skill taken to construct such a device. Then the persistence of the carnivores who had taken the arms, legs, and abdomen of the skinny wretch of a figure remaining.

Warlord noted that his scouts had all been taken out in a single action. They had been that close together and he shook his head once again in dismay. All their training and drills were to approach the enemy in a wide skirmish line so that they could not be taken out in a single fusillade.

Warlord's thoughts momentarily took him from this situation. He was a leader. A giant of a man, he could move swiftly and employed all the training that being part of an elite airborne unit had provided. As Sergeant Otis Redding, he had been used to being the first boots on the ground of a hot landing zone and the last to depart if they were being extracted by air. He was fearless and tough.

He had pledged his allegiance to the man he now called Chief and his sole friend in these difficult days. They had met during a challenging combat situation during the Struggles. The command to which they both reported to had disintegrated in a series of vicious assaults and firefights. They had each saved the others life in numerous encounters with the enemy. Whoever the enemy of the day had been.

It was during some well needed downtime that they had lamented on the lack of good leadership, the collapse of society and all the things wrong with the way life had been before the Pandemic, the Wars, and the Struggles. They agreed in discussion that if they got the chance to make a difference, do something that changed the way things had always been, then they would try and do so.

It was why they had taken over the farmstead earlier in the year. A brief firefight with what looked like a well defended spot in a valley. Protected from the worst weather by big hills, the isolated site suited them for several purposes. Those who had not died in the battle were given the choice of becoming labour and part of the solution. Those that did not, became forced labour or were killed.

The soldiers had arrived as a mechanised unit. A single battle tank, all that was left of a full squadron with supporting personnel carriers, anti-air missile crawlers and heavy mobile ordnance. As they had run out of fuel, those armoured unit's that could, were hauled into a barrier that gave the farmstead some additional firepower and defence from assault.

Over the course of the summer, the Chief and Warlord had sent out scouts to recruit new tribe members. Some had come willingly and had been assimilated into the tribe. Others who resisted were killed and their valuables taken to help the collective. A few skilled people had been drawn in by threats of violence to their children, who had been held hostage.

The longer-term strategy was to move away from forced labour and violence to hold what they had and evolve into a superior society where everyone in the tribe was trusted, had key responsibilities and accountabilities, and become part of the solution.

It was only a matter of time before they could thrive and live off the land, creating a new self-sustaining community. Their New World.

His attention was drawn back to the present when their tracker alerted Warlord to the sets of imprints and damaged fauna departing the fireside. Something on wheels and many footprints. However, the surprising thing was that the tracker identified two separate groups. One probably travelling a day or so behind another.

All the signs pointed westwards. Towards the coast.

Warlord decided to return to camp and brief the Chief on what he had found and share with him his thoughts. He shouted out that they would return but before then took the time to bury their former comrades. It would not be good for morale for their partners and the rest of the homestead to see them in this state. Better to bury them here.

Some items of use were retrieved, webbing, damaged backpacks that could be repaired or used to repair other things and the carcasses of the two dead dogs were strung up on poles, quickly fashioned from nearby branches and carried back with them. No need to waste good meat.

Then Warlord said some fine words about the loss of their comrades, as they all stood around the graves. Then they headed on back to the farmstead.

****

Later that day he sat at a fire with the Chief, who was poking a long stick into the embers and watching the sparks float up from where it was stirred. Neither man spoke for some time.

Eventually it was Warlord who broke the silence. "My reading of what we found today is a separate group. Clearly well-armed, that took out our scouting party who did not deploy the skirmish line we teach everyone. It was a mistake that cost them their lives."

The Chief continued to worry the burning timbers with his long stick as if by stoking the fire, it would divine something to him.

Warlord continued, "The defenders of that camp were not only well-armed, but they were also skilled and had placed perimeter defences of snares, one of which took out a scout on approach.

The bodies were then methodically stripped of valuables and what was left was dumped. I did not like to find them like that. Ripped apart by feral beasts. Not the way soldiers should end their days."

There was a small "WHOOMPH" as the Chiefs poking finally produced a response from the fire and a grunt issued from the Chief but still, he did not speak.

So, Warlord resumed sharing his thoughts, "The tracker concluded there were seven or eight in the defending party and that they were followed by at least four others in a separate group. I figure that could be our five archers, the specially gifted ones from that family group we took in. The ones whose kids died in the stockade......" he tailed off as his friend, the Chief, looked up at him and with a single word interrupted Warlords flow "And?" he questioned.

"And we can either write them off and carry on about our business, or we do something about it and seek them out. Take what they have in revenge for our loss." Then he left it there for the Chief to review.

"I see it that we have three losses and two questions" said the Chief. "Firstly, the forced labour," (neither of them ever referred to them as slaves, though that is what they really were) "is a loss. The leverage over the archers and their failure to return, is another.

Then the slaughter of our comrades at that camp is the third. Can we carry on with our project being so many hands down, is my first question?"

Warlord gave it some thought and provided a considered response. "We will not be able to send out as many patrols anymore and that may restrict and reduce the spoils that arrive, in terms of human resources and valuables. We may not be able to bring in the rest of the harvest with the labour we do have. The tribe are tired after covering double watches on guard and then rebuilding the stockade this last day or so.

We do have just enough food and fuel for us to see out the forthcoming winter if we maintain the current rationing levels.

Rebuilding the stockade means we have insufficient construction material to convert the big barn into more accommodation. Though, with fewer people in the tribe, the need to do that right now, is questionable.

So, to summarise. Yes, we can continue with the project but at a slower rate and with tighter margins than we had planned, and we may all have to tighten our belts further, so to speak. We can start to grow again next year."

The Chief nodded in acknowledgment of the perspective and then said, "My second question arises from this.

If the archers decide to throw their lot in with this war band, then they could be able to mount an attack on us. To disturb our new society project. Take things from us and I do not like having that threat out there. Looking over my shoulder all day thinking when they would attack. They are the only surviving group who know who we are and more importantly, where we are. I don't like that.

So, my question is, can we split our tribe to leave sufficient guards back here while we set out to avenge our comrades and eliminate a threat?"

Warlord slowly nodded to indicate he understood the point of view but paused a moment or two before he responded. Not all airborne guys were gung-ho and oblivious of the clear and present dangers and he took his time in replying.

The Chief knew that his trusted friend, his blood brother would not jump in heavy footed. He knew that it would be a considered response and so he waited patiently.

After a minute or so, Warlord spoke. "My security team are all veterans of many firefights. They are well trained and well-armed, but our numbers are down a good quarter. We can field a total of thirty-two, and that includes you and me.

One or two of the non-combatants in Engineering have worked under fire but Farming and Cooking have none. We would need to split the security team and leave enough back here to guard what we have at New World homestead.

We take the remaining working vehicles we have left for a swift assault. It will however deplete our vehicle fuel to deliver this mission. But by taking a motorised approach, we can carry heavier ordnance than if we were on foot and it would be a quicker pursuit.

I would not choose the horses because so few people can ride properly, and we would need to haul some form of baggage train and that will slow us down. Therefore, a motorised deployment to bring our selves justice and bring back prisoners for forced labour and take what valuables they do have. If we do go after them, that would be my reasoning."

The Chief nodded. Not just in agreement but because the big man's proposal echoed his own thoughts.

"Alert the Mechanic. I want three of the vehicles fully fuelled, leave the truck and one of the jeeps here.

Plenty of ammo for the mounted machine guns and you select what additional ordnance you think we need.

Also, make sure we have full body armour for everyone who travels. Those archers are deadly.

Separate your security team into two, leave one half here and nominate the camp leader whilst we are away. Tell Cook we want provisions for a week. We will depart in the morning."

Chapter Nine

2031 - Hilltop Camp

Throughout that day on the hilltop camp whilst the clan rested, there were many conversations and heated discussions on what they thought they knew and what they should or should not be doing.

Some individuals remained quiet, listening intently but not committing to any fixed or firm opinions. Weapons were cleaned, maintained, and checked again. Shotgun cartridges were re-armed in the little press and ammunition belts re-stocked.

Radar was asked to explain again but elected not to do so. He said he had told them everything, but Raven could not be sure. It was Point who engaged Radar the most, partly from the fact that both came from military backgrounds but also on the special abilities they both seemed to possess.

Raven produced their map and asked Point to mark out where the fortified farmstead was and any other features that the thought were relevant. Using one of the few pens they had, he put a cross where the despot lived. He didn't think he had much else to add to it right now.

It was agreed that "the archers" would buddy up with different members of the original clan. That would be the process of assimilation into their new and now larger outfit.

Bullseye as the youngest was paired up with the wings to group up the teenagers together and she would take watches with either Boy or Girl. A slim and athletic build, she matched her skinny companions in overall weight but just looked better for it. She was particularly chatty and would probably fit in well there and fill the gap in communications that being mute left.

The three teenagers opted to move off from the main group and carry out some archery practice on another tree on the hilltop. They seemed to get on well as Bullseye showed Boy and Girl her own methods and ranges of shot from a decent recurve bow, along with firing from prone, which really got the attention of the mute pair.

Later Bullseye would explain the pressure of taking tournament shots and how she thought that was the pinnacle of tension until the Plague came and then the Struggles started. She had to grow up quickly as all her friends and most of her family had died, in the torture of the pandemic symptoms or killed in the battles and skirmishes. Now she could aim, draw, and loose to kill almost without thinking about it. How the world had changed.

She said that she would never again respond to her given name of Nicola. Even though for years she had been known as Nikki. It was a name from a beautiful past and not the horrible present. Bullseye was her name because she could fire an arrow so accurately.

Count had previously been a Senior Financial Advisor with an accountancy firm. Her real name was Sarah but as she could clearly add up, she continued with the assumed nickname that she arrived with. Her flowing black hair and good looks rivalled that of Raven, if in a slightly shorter frame. She was also a good cook and so it seemed a sensible option to pair her with Gastro.

Together they would be cooking for a larger group and working on a basis of two heads are better than one, should help manage and deliver the provisions they gathered or hunted. They collaborated on a menu for the main meal that day and elected to go with barbecued rabbit and wildfowl, with a red berry and herb dipping sauce.

A former nurse called Joanne, Whistler had been the archers medic. As Joanne, she had worked in the Emergency Medical Admissions unit next to Accident and Emergency and was used to dealing with urgent remedial challenges. Now in her mid-forties she was shapely but still athletic, could run hard and recover quickly. She brought with her a very modest first aid kit and was amazed by the amount of medical equipment that Med had gathered from the clan's recent raids and encounters.

Joanne had a very matter of fact approach to life. Keep it simple was her motto and deliver it well.

They immediately swapped several medical experiences in the same way that military people do their "when-eyes" which go something like "When I was ...." And "When I did...." Which put them onto the same social standing as they compared their own skillsets and a variety of complex trauma cases that each had been involved with.

Joanne liked to deploy arrows with small bulbous pieces next to the arrowhead. They had tiny holes in them making the arrow whistle. She used them as a ploy to startle game and hold them briefly in position before the arrow hit their target.

She could also use them as part of pre-arranged signalling without alerting others to her location. Not a bad cook either, she was content for now to see how the Count Gastro catering partnership performed.

The continuing dialogue between Point and Radar would not lead to a buddying up for the guard rota and Raven thought it best that she partners Point on guard and other duties for now, which was cool with the tall ex-military guy.

Point clearly recognised Raven as the clan leader and maintained a good line of communication throughout the day with both Radar and Raven. His story seemed more complicated than he had thus shared, and Raven was determined to find out more.

Under agreement, Fletch was assigned to buddy up with Gunner. She explained that her real name was Abigail, Abi or Abz, depending on the company she was keeping. Carrying a slight limp from a previous injury when she broke her ankle, it did not deter her from the arduous task of tracking down her prey.

Her role in the Archery Club was to repair and modify the bows and she had already earned her nickname of Fletcher or Fletch, from the formal role that she previously performed. It was only a part time position as her main job was working as a Senior Marketing Executive in the old world. Though not much call for that these days.

Having someone who could repair and modify bows was indeed a good skillset to have in the group, even though Gunner himself shunned the silent weapons, preferring the firepower and noise of the semi-automatic sub-machine gun he toted.

Whilst he could admire the skills of those who could use bows or crossbows, he believed that the superior rate of fire out trumped the longer range of the arrow and bolt. Plus, he still got a big kick from firing the machine gun, with an effect almost bordering on sexual release but not something he ever mentioned in conversation with anyone, ever.

There was a general discussion on the benefits of the ghillie suits and it was Point who quoted from Sun Tzu, the Art of War "Be extremely subtle, even to the point of formlessness. Be extremely mysterious, even to the point of soundlessness. Thereby you can be the director of the opponent's fate" and got some expressionless stares from the likes of Gastro but it was Steel who encouraged Point to expand on this.

Point stated that formlessness and stillness is the intention of every ghillie suit user. Detection of any kind can tip the scales of success and failure. Sun Tzu, the famous Chinese war strategist wrote that to directly control the fate of one's opponent in battle, you must be unseen and unheard. It was as simple as that.

Gunner said that it was a dichotomy of Radar's Shock and Awe tactics, a matter that Point conceded in discussion. A time and a place for both, he said, when he received the description of the events at Roasted Sheep Camp that he had heard in the distance. A short and loud burst of firing from multiple weapons and accepted that it was indeed a deadly tactic. More so when the machetes were used to mop up any survivors, he could see the clear benefit of such shock and awe methods.

Point went on to describe how they made their ghillie suits and how each day they decided to hold what they were wearing or amend the content of camouflage. More branches from bushes or less. More grass or less. How best to blend in with the natural environment they were moving into or through.

Their suit design was simple and based around a waterproof latex membrane that enabled some protection from the weather conditions but conceded that it in turn created a problem for moisture control, which drew some laughs from the gathering. Everyone knew what sweat was.

What Point did explain was all the benefits of support to carrying out activities in the field, maximising concealment under a variety of terrains and not every terrain suited the ghillie. Therefore, the archers had developed a routine of being able to quickly don them or remove them, as required by the field conditions.

There was insufficient material and other resources to manufacture a ghillie suit for everyone and so it was added to their wish list of requirements, should the opportunity arise to stock up.

As the discussions continued throughout the day, Raven made the call to remain on the hilltop for one more night. She thought the benefits of bonding with the new clan members outweighed the security of remaining in one place too long. She wondered if that were a decision that could backfire on them or not.

There was sufficient game and local plants and herbs to make a good supper that night, cooked in a hollow on the hilltop and well concealed from view. Everyone seemed impressed with the red berry dipping sauce, which pleased both Count and Gastro.

Raven was shaken awake as the false dawn began to lighten up the dark night sky. She heard Point getting up and both went out on their joint patrol. The clan had decided to move off only after a wider sweep of the area had been conducted.

So, Point and Raven silently left the camp and moved out onto patrol. After a broad sweep of the area around the hillside, they reported back that the forward scouts could go out and reconnoitre the route ahead.

Steel and his wings took the point in the move westwards and the main group got to grips with the baggage buggy and set off after them.

As the group moved off west, Gunner and Whistler took the back door. The rear guard operated as a pair now and both took turns to hold long static watches with the monocular, making wide sweeps of the horizon as the other carried out a flanking move left or right, to widen the field of view.

The clan moved off. Spread across a half mile from front scout to rear guard and from wing to wing and Raven wanted to know about Point's story and simply asked him to share.

Point said that his childhood had been impacted by the whispers of the voices he heard. They had been there on and off from his first recollections and just assumed that everyone could hear them.

Well, it was until he spoke about it. At first to his mother, who reassured him that it was his special talent that he could hear the voices of angels. His schoolfriends were not as gentle and ridiculed him relentlessly until he moved school and made the decision never to mention it to anyone again.

For years he could not hear anything and believed it to have been a childish imaginary friends thing. Then during the Plague, he had been shocked to hear voices once again, when others around him heard nothing.

The voices then seemed truly angry, more than one sound seeming to argue with another. Those occasions came and went, sometimes separated by days and weeks, at other times it could be a constant diatribe for hours.

Never anything he could make out. Raven glanced at his jaw set in place as he tried to recall anything of importance to share.

Point went on to talk about his time in the armed forces and the military field skills he had picked up. His hobby during his service had been archery and when he left the military, found he could not just continue to hone his skills but found like-minded folk when it came to hunting and their little sub-set of the group that specialised in field archery.

After the ravages of the Plague and then the fighting, they tried to survive as a whole community group. However, they had been assaulted by several different gangs armed with guns, who had killed family, raped women, and children, as well as robbing their clubhouse whilst those with hunting skills were out in the wilderness finding game.

They had hunted some of those attackers down and taken revenge in some silent but bloody encounters. However, not everyone had been avenged. They made a big decision to leave their town and move out into the wilderness.

It had meant, that those who did survive, had skills that were in demand and when they were faced with a do or die situation, opted to join a militia group that were going to attack them. Their role in that group was to be a self-sustaining scouting party.

The militia leader, a hard man, and his big number two held their remaining children as hostages whenever they were sent out on patrol.

Now that those children had been killed by the Plague and the vicious murder by their guards, ordered by the leader. A man they knew only as The Chief. There was now, no hold over them and they were free to move on.

As a group, they had considered a revenge mission back to the farmstead that the Chief referred to as the New World. However, their security teams numbered well over thirty-five hardened soldiers and would be a tough nut to crack. More a suicide mission than anything else and so they had reluctantly decided to move on. It was during that moving on phase that they had discovered the clan.

Raven thought that it was a similar terrible story but a different method to those events which had drawn all the group together. They were all managing family losses, had learned to kill to survive and appeared to have higher moral standards than their opponents.

The sun began to rise and soon the clan would be stopping for their daytime break and period of rest. Gunner began his last sweep of the horizon with the monocular as Fletch re-joined him from her flanking patrol.

It was then that he spotted the dust cloud on the horizon and froze.

Chapter Ten

2031 - The Dust Cloud

After trying unsuccessfully to focus on what was causing the dust cloud Gunner handed the monocular over to Fletch to see if she could see anything detailed. As much as she tried, Fletch was equally unable to make out the source of the cloud.

Gunner spoke out loud. "The only thing I know these days that can create a dust cloud is a mass of people on horses riding in a column or a line of vehicles. Neither thing is going to be good for us for sure. We need to get back sharpish and tell Raven."

When they re-joined the clan, it had gone to ground. Raven already knew. Radar had caught the movement in his peripheral vision and alerted her. She and Point had spread the clan out in a defensive position and welcomed the arrival of Gunner and Fletch, who would provide more detail.

However, other than being able to state that it was a vehicle convoy or soldiers mounted on horses. There was little else they could add at that stage and felt that alerting the main clan and making themselves scarce would be the order of the day.

Point shared an opinion that it could be the same militia that they had left from and the group from which Raven and her team had slaughtered the scouting party. If it was, then this would be a pure revenge mission and did not bode well. It could be a ruthless and sustained hunt.

All thirteen clan members were called in to discuss their options.

Point briefed everyone on his knowledge of the fortified farmstead that they had departed from. A tidy armoured vehicle fleet backed up by a tanker full of fuel, which consisted of two eight-wheeled personnel carriers with double heavy machine gun mounts, two jeeps and a truck. Their armoury contains mortars, rocket-propelled grenade launchers and an array of automatic weapons. The clan would be outgunned.

Motorised meant they could cover ground much quicker than the clan could on foot. However, those vehicles needed to stay on ground that could be tackled by their limited cross-country capability. It was debatable that the truck could, but the jeeps and personnel carriers were designed for just such a thing.

Standing and fighting on level ground, therefore, was an option that was immediately eliminated. No one showed any appetite to do that.

Scattering and moving off into different directions held some appeal but they could be picked off on the move, as standing guard would be made more difficult when they did stop. Furthermore, it would be even harder agreeing a rendezvous at some yet to be determined, point and time in the future. Not a sensible option.

Heading higher into the hills would be the preferred choice, to reduce the benefit to the armoured vehicles. Creating ambush points and fighting a guerrilla action as they continued their trek westwards would be the only way to survive. They would also have to consider varying the direction to try and confuse the chasing party.

However, combining what firepower they did have, with their ability to remain concealed in certain situations, offered them the best chance to survive. Doing so, would make it harder for the pursuers and try to reduce their numbers. This would be a war of attrition.

The only way to survive and to continue the quest. There was doubt though that all of them would make it through unscathed.

There was now a good light and normally when they would go to ground but not today.

They made a forced march up a hillside and it was after midday that Steel spotted the first defendable point on the route and one that would be difficult to flank without being seen. It was a ridge.

The clan would need to cross it anyway and he sent the three teenagers on over the ridge top to find a suitable route after giving them a careful briefing about not being spotted and to ensure that any route they discovered held limited risk of being overtaken by the road vehicles. However, they were also to be aware of much wider flanking moves by the vehicles, which could be carried out at great speed, for instance up a different valley or watercourse.

Satisfied that he had prepared them as much as possible, Steel sent them on their way. Then he sat down with Raven and Point to discuss laying out their defensive position. He was almost through with his briefing when Radar announced that he could see three vehicles.

Gunner got his monocular on the go but could still only see the dust cloud and deferred to Radar when he described what was approaching. It looked like a jeep in the lead, with two men in it and what must be two personnel carriers.

Radar repeated the vehicle description of two of the vehicle types that Point had provided.

He could see all the heat shimmers, of those stood in the swivel machine gun mounts and those in the protection of the armoured containers on wheels. Six figures in each carrier.

A force of fourteen and whatever armament that the personnel carriers could fit in.

They were motoring at some speed and then they stopped, whilst one of the crew got out and inspected the ground around the three-vehicle convoy. It was then, as the dust cleared, that Gunner could see them for the first time with the monocular.

This action was repeated several times. A fast drive, then a halt for a short period of time.

That was when Point stated that the militia tribe had an excellent tracker. It was he who must have identified their route and was following their signs.

It had not occurred to the clan until that moment that they needed to hide their tracks, but it would be something that they would try to utilise going forward.

Raven remonstrated with herself that it was a stupid oversight. Someone would have missed the scouting party they had destroyed and should have taken more care in how they left the site of the firefight at Roasted Sheep Camp. Damn it. But there was no time to dwell on the error. They needed a plan.

Steel and Point were in animated discussion when Raven walked over to join them. They were discussing ambush opportunities as they looked up towards the ridge and out to the flanks either side.

Once they agreed on the plan, the ten members were deployed into various positions and Steel began to lay snares as they made their way up the steep rocky hillside towards the ridge. They needed to get to a point where the armoured vehicles did not hold any advantages for their pursuers.

Gunner and Fletch maintained watch from inside a bush with the monocular. When it was Gunners turn to view, he was slightly shocked to be staring at a man with a similar monocular, looking directly back at him.

Then the cheeky bastard waved, and Gunner dropped the monocular in surprise before regaining his composure, picked up the monocular and looked back. Only to see the man put his forefinger to his own throat and move it slowly and theatrically across in the international signal of cutthroat. Meaning death. Brilliant.

The lens must have inadvertently pointed upwards towards the sun when they handed the monocular over. It is the only way they could have been detected. Gunner cursed himself at his sloppiness but Fletch calmed him by touching his forearm and conceded that it may well have been her and apologised.

Either way, with their cover blown, they would need to re-locate and set up their observation point again but first Raven needed to know. Fletch volunteered to make her way back and break the good news.

Chapter Eleven

2031 - The Pursuit

Warlord was driving the jeep sat next to the Chief. Tracker was one vehicle behind in the first of the Armoured Personnel Carriers (APC1) along with five lightly armed companions. They were spotting the signs and giving the go ahead over their mesh radio net. All the team had battery operated radio microphone headsets on.

The pursuit had been going for two full days, stopping to rest only when it got dark and slowed them down too much.

The team consisted of people from different squads. Ten were from Security, one Cook and one vehicle Engineer, plus Chief and Warlord. However, all were armed and dressed alike. Each were wearing full Kevlar body armour and that with the sun was generating a lot of body heat across the team.

When Tracker lost sight of the signs, they would stop and one of them would get out, check, and reaffirm the direction of travel. Which veered truly little from due west and easy to follow.

Their prey ahead had not taken any precautions to either conceal their signs or deviate from their intended direction of travel. He did wonder at that point, why that was so?

The Chief held a tactical field monocular that he used to scan the horizon for anything whenever they stopped, and the accompanying dust cloud cleared sufficiently for him to see.

It was when they were approaching the hills at the bottom of the mountain range that he glimpsed the tell-tale sign of reflection from another field lens and focussed in on the area he had seen it.

Chief was not surprised to see a person in military fatigues looking directly back at him and so gave him a slow wave so that he knew he could see him. He chuckled as he watched the observer drop his monocular and so decided to press home the point and gave him the cutthroat signal when the chap regained his lens.

"Give him something to think about. To worry about and prey on his mind." Thought Chief.

Then they continued their pursuit.

Warlord had offered a voice of reason, as they drove along, in that the direction of travel had rarely strayed from a due west direction. He commented to Chief that if that was the case, how much of a threat did they really pose if they continued to move at pace in a single direction.

Chief countered that it could just as easily be, that they are themselves, a small scouting party from a much bigger force that sits out west. Perhaps they were heading directly back to bring a much larger battle group to take them out in their farmstead.

He went on to say that this was the best course of action to take. Eliminate them from the battlefield now and stop the key messages getting back, whilst reducing the enemy's overall numbers. It still made sense to Warlord as well and so the pursuit continued.

Warlord slowed the jeep down as the terrain changed from being relatively level to starting a climb. It would not be long before their advantage of possessing armoured vehicles would cease and they would need to take the chase onto foot.

He debated the matter with his Chief as to which point, they could afford to leave the vehicles in a position where they could be safely defended and with a minimum of personnel.

In the end, they decided on a piece of flat ground in a clearing, just short of where the going got to be rockier. It was surrounded by a sparse coating of bushes and the odd tree. Not the sort of ground where they expected the archers could come from. It would more likely be the woodier hillside where there were more shrubs.

The jeep was drawn in at a broadside angle to the hill. The security squad slid from the APC's and they were both manoeuvred into place, side by side to the jeep so they made a block of armour. It gave all four swivel mounted machine guns a 360-degree firing circle around, like it was representing a gun emplacement out in the field behind enemy lines.

It was agreed to leave the Cook and Mechanic and two of the security squad to remain behind and provide a heavy machine gun presence and guard of the vehicles.

They were to remain vigilant for the time that the main pursuit was on foot. The intention was to return by nightfall, having completed or partly completed their task. Then they would fall back to a better position and review what their next steps were.

Chief and Warlord formed two separate teams from the remaining security squad members. Each of them had five hard and experienced soldiers. They opted to travel light and try and hunt down their prey and take them out one by one or piecemeal if the opportunity arose.

Each team carried one Light Machine Gun, complete with tripod supports and every team member held good reliable combat assault machine guns. They slung spare magazines and grenades into backpacks, and each indicated with a single word "Chief" to say when they were ready to go.

The whole thing from parking the vehicles to getting ready and setting off took no more than five minutes. It looked slick. It was slick.

To the watching Gunner and Fletch, now much higher up in the rocks it was impressive. If there was any doubt as to the competency of their pursuers, the organised way they had stopped, parked to create a heavy machine gun post, and then get ready to continue on foot, was mind-blowingly swift.

It was all carried out in almost complete silence as well, which made it even more scary.

The job of Fletch and Gunner was now to return, to join with their clan and brief Raven. But to do so in a way that alerted their pursuers.

To the watching Chief below, who could see the dust of the hasty move upwards by some of their prey, he was not deceived. He rightly assumed that this display was carried out to draw his team up in a headlong rush, but he did not.

There was still another five- or six-hours good light of the afternoon and evening. He wanted this to be methodical and certain of the outcome.

Wary of ambush, he indicated that Warlord was to lead up his team on a parallel course to his own, about fifty yards apart. They set off together. Two sticks of five, each person provided static cover as the team members overlapped each other. Standard routine in Recon.

Constantly glancing left and right, with their assault guns held at eye level and pointing towards the enemy. The two teams moved relentlessly uphill and noted any potential areas of ambush with clear hand signals to each other.

Within minutes they had reached the point where the targets observation post had been and took stock. There was still more ground to cover and a natural barrier ahead. A ridge. Chief thought *"If I were to defend this hill, the ridge was the obvious place to be."* It had not been in his view when he commenced the ascent.

Chief waved Warlord over and his team crabbed sideways, under overlapping cover. It was then that one of the team yelped as a snare caught his leg, just above his boot. They all froze and went to ground.

The snared man asked for help and Warlord inched over to him and noticed how deep the sharp snare had embedded into his skin. It must have tightened as he stumbled forward. He pulled out a knife and carefully cut the snare from its bonding point but could not get between the wire and his leg without cutting skin. He relayed this to Chief after asking if his comrade could still walk.

The grimaced nod he received was not convincing. Warlord thought again *"How nasty these snares were and wondered how many more were lay in wait for them on this hillside."* An unnecessary distraction that could affect their advance upwards.

He ushered his team over to the Chiefs until they formed a single unit, spread out in a defensive arc facing upwards, whilst Chief consulted his number two.

Chief stated the blindingly obvious that the ridge made a great defensive point. The realisation that the area could be littered with small booby traps was also a factor.

Had they had more soldiers at their disposal, he would have sent a motorised team round the edge of the promontory and into the next valley to cut off the retreat down the far side of the ridge. Then they could have pressed home an attack, knowing that the escape route would be closed off.

However, looking at it from this point, it would only take one or two people to hold the ridge, whilst the rest made good their escape down the other side. Then the enemy could slip away easily. It is better, from a defender's perspective, to leave a battlefield in ones and twos than it is with a larger group.

Warlord offered to scramble down and take one of the APC's around to the next valley and create a point to squeeze their targets toward. Chief considered the suggestion and then said, "Yes but take all the vehicles" and he continued "and one of the team from here. It will give you three drivers, two gunners and you directing play. In addition, we will not be too diluted trying to man three points.

I will take the rest of the team forwards and press on to create the squeeze. The wounded guy can hold a cover fire position from here until we can make arrangements to get him down."

"Chief" was all Warlord needed to say that he understood and would comply with his Chief's instructions. He tapped the nearest security squad member on the shoulder and said, "Come with me" and then held his throat microphone and let the vehicle defending team know that two of them were returning and to make the vehicles ready for moving off shortly.

Everyone else within earshot had heard the briefing and so nothing else needed to be said.

It was as the two of them separated from the Chief's group and began their scramble down the hillside, that the four APC guns down below began to chatter, and tracer bullets flew everywhere.

The machine gunner's voices shouting out and drowning each other on the radio net. It just served to urge on the two runners downhill and they slid and scrambled down in great haste.

Chapter Twelve

2031 - Ambush Below The Ridge

Point lay still and thought through what had happened. So far, everything had fallen into place as Raven, Steel and Point had predicted. The chasing group had separated, leaving a small team to guard the vehicles, whilst the rest continued the pursuit up to the ridge. The two armoured teams working their way upwards was truly an impressive sight. Highly organised, they moved swiftly and always had one or more providing cover.

However, Raven and her team, backed up by the three teenagers when they returned from their reconnaissance of the other valley would put up a stiff resistance and at the very least pin the hillside assault down, whilst the vehicle defenders could be eliminated by Point and his team.

The snares may well delay them too. Then they could catch the hillside assault team in a pincer movement with the archers making their way up the hill. That was the plan.

Point was concealed with his three adult archers in support, and it was now their task to take out the small group of soldiers with the vehicles. However, this had now been made harder by the way the jeep and both APC's had been positioned.

It had been anticipated during the planning session that there would be gaps between the vehicles, creating blind spots for the gunners and easier for the archers to stay out of range but being so tightly packed made it look like a single objective and all four guns created a 360-degree firing pattern around the defensive position. A much harder nut to crack then they had discussed.

The outline plan, if a little risky, was for the four adult archers to operate independently. They lay well hidden within bow shot in their ghillie suits. Set out in a widespread arc around one side of the clearing opposite the hillside. Lay in positions that gave them views of the target area and narrow firing arcs.

It gave the archers an opportunity to retreat away from the main body of soldiers if they elected to return down from the hillside. A simple plan and one that had looked deliverable when they put it together earlier but seemed much harder now that they were down on the ground beside the armoured vehicles.

The bow shot angles were not good as they thought they would be and most of the machine gunner's bodies were hidden in the cupolas of the swivel mounts. The defenders all wore tank-crew steel helmets and appeared to be in communication with each other on microphones. They were also wearing body armour, like the kit that Raven and the original clan members wore. This was going to be a tough call.

Point was considering at what point he would chance "loosing" an arrow from his prone position when the shock of all four APC machine guns firing at once froze him where he was.

The gunners were on the lookout for any movement of their former ghillie suited archer comrades or anyone like them.

The wait had them wound up tightly and it was the Cook who fired first. He thought he saw movement in the undergrowth by a bush and without any word or warning, let loose with the big half-inch calibre gun.

Whilst he had done some training with the gun, he had only ever fired it under command and a short burst at a fixed target. He had forgotten how the vibration affected his aim and so he continued to fire as he forced the tracer to aim at the point, he saw the movement. He only realised the others were shooting when he saw the interlocking tracer fire.

It was the Mechanic who fired next and so close after the Cook it would have seemed orchestrated. She, like the Cook, also lacked the discipline of a trained gunner and concentrated her fire in the same area. It was pandemonium.

Panic breeds panic and the other two gunners, not knowing exactly what was going on, followed suit and swivelled their guns round to focus on the same area. This was the opportunity that Point needed and he rose to his knee and loosed off two arrows in quick succession, aiming for the narrow gap between the top of the body armour and the helmet.

One of the two arrows fired hit the nearest gunner in the back of the neck, just under the helmet with the arrow protruding through his mouth and killing him instantly. The second bounced harmlessly off the steel helmeted figure as it collapsed across the rim of the cupola.

Then he "loosed" off two more arrows at the next gunner and felled another of the enemy with a similar accurate shot, except it went through the side of her neck and she collapsed down into the APC cupola. He lost sight of the arrow that missed its target.

Job done, he threw himself behind a bush and crawled rapidly away as fast as he could. It was now down to the other three to complete theirs.

The plan was to rendezvous on the other side of the bank of a stream. He was the first there and selected a good firing position before melting into the undergrowth.

All the time he was moving the shots continued to fire, eventually petering out. He waited for the other archers to join him. But they did not.

Away to his left, it was Whistler who had made the mistake that initiated the firing. She had been lay cheek down on the ground, as she had been taught and had practised. It gave her a view of the targets, the bow on the ground and her draw arm on top. Plain arrow notched and partly drawn taught.

She had seen one of the gunners tilt a water bottle up for a drink and thought this was her opportunity to take out the enemy. Unbeknown to her, it just happened that another gunner was staring intently at the undergrowth and as she drew the string slowly back, must have shown movement because the ground around her erupted in a hail of bullets.

Whistler was struck in both legs and she knew immediately that she was out of the fight but fired her arrow anyway. It caught the throat of the gunner that was her target. The narrowest of gaps. However, that was the last she knew as more bullets tracked across her body and it jerked about like a demented puppet, creating a bigger target for the other gunners, who continued firing long after she died.

Warlord was tearing down the hillside shouting "Check, check, check" into his microphone at the waste of ammunition being poured into the ground around the vehicle defensive position. Then he saw the ground rise and saw one of the archers loose off a total of four arrows to take out two of his gunners from the rear. *"How the fuck do they manage that?"* he thought as he scrambled downwards.

Before he could stop his downward run and fire off any shots, the archer went to ground and out of sight, partly by his movement and the camouflaged effect of his ghillie suit.

The APC guns had stopped firing by the time Warlord and his companion skidded to a halt by the vehicles in the clearing. Then the two ground troops made their way around the cover of the APC and moved towards the area where the guns had fired.

The ground was covered in blood. Two of the archers must have lain in wait whilst Chief and Warlord kitted their teams out and made their way up the hill. The Cook had spotted something and fired off a full belt of ammunition. Maybe it was his lack of training, but he had struggled to pinpoint his shooting but in doing so had taken out one of their quarries.

The body was unrecognisable as it was ripped apart by the heavy calibre ammunition. A fair result but for what cost in ammunition. However, their tribe had taken damage and Warlord needed to know what resources he had at his disposal. Lives had been lost in the firefight, from both sides and there were other archers yet unaccounted for.

Count had heard her companion dying in the deadly enfilade of firing all around them. She knew that it was now only a matter of time before they would search the surrounding area and she would be discovered. So, she was determined to make sure she weighed in with a kill of her own.

Then into view came the big black man. The tribe's second in command. The one known as Warlord. It was he who led the security teams and she knew that it was the security team who had killed her son in the stockade, back at the camp.

Count's crossbow had been loaded with a vicious looking barbed bolt and she only had to move it an inch or two to take aim. However, Warlord was stood still and did not move fully into her line of sight. She would have to move.

To make a killing shot, she knew she would have to rise from her prone position but wanted so much to take the life of the murdering bastard in front of her. So, she did.

Count partly rose, took aim, and fired in one clean movement. However, she knew that by doing so, revealed her own position.

Warlord rolled over the body that was lay partly face down and noticed it was one of the female archers. It was then that an arrow just came shooting out of the undergrowth right at him and pierced him in the neck, right by his collar bone. He had tried to react, as he saw it, but the projectile hit him before he could move properly. He twisted sideways and fired his machine gun as he fell sideways. Landing heavily on the ground.

It was an instinctive shot. Firing a burst into the point the arrow came from. However, his sideways move meant it was not a killing shot as he saw the undergrowth roll over and blood spurt out of a wounded adversary.

Warlord immediately shouted out and over his microphone for no-one else to shoot and instructed them to take their enemy alive.

The team member on foot rushed forward to comply and threw himself onto the wounded archer on the floor. It was one of the women. She tried to struggle away but was already weakening from the loss of blood from several gunshot wounds in her legs. He punched her twice in the face to subdue her and then he was able to drag her towards the back of APC1 in between that and the jeep.

Fletch was the remaining unnoticed archer and she made the awful, though sensible in that moment, decision to remain concealed. Hidden from their enemy's attention she decided to wait to see when she should intervene and make a difference.

In seconds, the APC gunner had jumped down, opened the doors from the inside and dragged the wounded prisoner by the shoulders into the confinement of the armour. Closely followed by the staggering Warlord, assisted by the guy who had scrambled down the hill with him.

Once inside, they took stock of their situation. One dead archer in bits outside, and a wounded prisoner. That left three more archers out there somewhere and Warlord instructed the two remaining gunners to keep watch up top. One of them was wounded in the neck, as was Warlord.

He had the foot soldier bind the prisoner and then provide first aid to the wounds on the injured gunner, who was also the Cook and his neck.

It was a cross bow bolt that had penetrated his neck and shoulder, causing it to bleed heavily. He had probably broken the collar bone when he fell sideways if the pain he felt was about right.

Thankfully, the wound had not cut through his carotid artery. He knew that because he was still alive. He would have bled out by now if it had. There was a lot of blood though and it was making him a little lightheaded, so he sat down and rested his back against the inside wall of the APC. He then briefed his Chief on the radio net.

Point heard the second burst of gunfire and knew that was not a good thing. He decided to get on the move and began to make a wide loop away from the enemy and see if he could make his way back up towards the ridge and get a better view. Keeping an eye out for his colleagues, hoping that they had made a safe exit from the deadly vehicle enfilade but fearing the worst.

It was whilst making his evasive loop that he heard the terrible screams of his friend. It stopped him dead in his tracks. It sounded like Count, but he could not be sure. Then he heard her scream again and knew that it was.

Inside the APC1 the interrogation of the prisoner was not going well.

Warlord was resting his injured arm. The collar bone had been broken. The bleeding from the wound on his neck had been stemmed and he was leaning back onto a rolled-up tarpaulin to take the weight of his head, neck, and arm. That way, the pain was reduced.

The Cook and wounded Gunner were up top manning two of the heavy machine guns, leaving the Security guy and Warlord with the prisoner. Security was standing on the leg of the wounded enemy trying to get her to answer some simple questions. What is the plan? How many are there of you? Where is the main battle group?

The prisoner just screamed in agony and would not say anything meaningful. All it did was spur on the torturers assault and outside drove Point and Fletch wild.

Fletch remained motionless and observed as much as she could. The death of her friend Whistler had greatly upset her but not as much as the capture and torture of Count.

She knew then if she moved an inch, she would either join the dead or become another prisoner and that would be a waste of her life and the loss of another capable fighter in the clan.

So, she stayed as still as she possibly could and quietly sobbed as she could hear the distressed noises coming from inside one of the APC's.

Her role now was to gather evidence and so she listened intently to the questioning.

Chapter Thirteen

2031 - The Ridge

On the ridge, Raven had gathered her forces into good positions where they could all see each other but had good cover. It had been a challenge half dragging, half pushing and carrying the buggy up the hillside, but they felt they needed all their resources ready and able to go if they needed to.

Gastro, Gunner and Steel all held their weapons handy, and they were ready to go. She felt a little undermanned as the teenagers had not yet returned from their reconnaissance of the valley behind them. She did not want to break cover just to see if she could spot them. Therefore, held the defensive position without moving.

By now, she had hoped that the forces on the hillside would begin a retreat down to the vehicles and they could pick them off on the move but right now, they were all bedded down in good cover and she could not see a thing. It was a bit of a stand-off. This required patience.

****

It was the screams from down inside the APC below that finally changed the status quo.

Not knowing how many held the high ground, the Chief re-evaluated the situation. He asked Warlord for an update on the radio channel and was not pleased with the response.

His team below had two dead and two wounded, with one injured still with him on the hillside.

They could not now affect the pincer movement by heading into the next valley and he was concerned on the strength of the enemy on the high ground, along with booby traps.

If he pressed on, he could take more casualties and there was no guarantee the defenders would just retreat, they could try to hold on to the ridge. Inflict maximum damage and then melt away downhill and away.

He decided, therefore, to re-gather his forces into one team and made the call to affect a controlled withdrawal. A terse message on the radio net of "We are withdrawing to your position" was quickly acknowledged by Warlord.

The Chief then issued whispered instructions to those around him. The eight-man team would retreat in pairs, two by two. With four at a time providing cover. It was awkward with one team member limping badly, but it was still manageable.

They were, however, providing that cover by facing uphill and it left a weakness on their flanks that only become apparent when they came under attack from the lower edges of the ridge. On their left as they retreated down.

A pair of his team, half crouched in the fern covered hillside at the lower end of their withdrawal just fell to the ground and did not stand up. No sounds other than light swishes and Chief knew it would be those bastard sneaky archers and said as much to himself but was also heard by those around him and then shouted out loudly "Get down" and the rest of the team went to ground.

****

Bullseye, Boy, and Girl had checked out the valley as instructed and found a couple of different routes out that provided their clan with cover. It was on their return up their side of the ridge to rendezvous with Raven that they had heard gunfire.

Instead of returning to the top of the ridge as had been agreed, they carefully crept over the edge to see the remaining enemy force, back tracking down the hill in front of them. Using hand signals and gestures, they quickly agreed to take out two of the force as the archers would not be in view as the enemy tracked down the hillside. A rapid exchange of hand signals and nods was all it took.

Then as soon as they did, they would go to ground and hot foot it back over the ridge and return to the original plan and rendezvous with Raven and the rest of the clan. They all nodded in agreement, notched, and fired at the two figures closest to them. Boy and Girl aimed for one and Bullseye the other.

They did not wait around to check their success and did exactly as they had agreed. Went to ground swiftly and made good their escape back over the promontory and then sprinted up towards the rest of the clan, using the ridgeline on their right as protection.

****

Chief shouted out instructions that they would check out their comrades. The remaining 6-man team from the tribe, inched over and checked that one of their colleagues had been felled with an arrow through the throat and the other with an arrow and a bolt also through the throat.

Stemming his anger, the Chief noted how accurate those archers were and shook his head with reluctant admiration of their skills.

Chief said they would recover their comrade's bodies, dragging them downhill by the scruffs of their tunic necks and to also check that they were leaving no resources on the battlefield for their enemy to claim.

With two dragging, it left four to provide cover, which they did by scanning both flanks and the landscape above them to the ridge. It was a much slower move now as it required more observation before each pair moved off and hampered by one of them limping.

With no further attacks on their withdrawal, they were able to return to the sanctity of their armour and carefully stowed the bodies of their fallen comrades into APC2 alongside the bodies of the two others who'd been left to provide gunnery support and had been lost in the first action with the archers.

Four good members of their tribe who would not see the light of day again. Several wounded team members and a nasty wire to remove from a leg before blood loss and possible infection took hold.

Ensuring that all four machine gun cupolas were manned. The Chief left the vehicles where they were right now, as they were in a good tight defensive position. With instructions to keep a wary eye out for those ghillie suited assassins.

The Chief knew right then that he needed to get something positive from this action, this clusterfuck and turned his full attention to the wounded archer.

Chapter Fourteen

Interrogation

The archer was bound with her arms behind and her ghillie suit cut off. She did not need her legs tethering. They were clearly damaged and bleeding heavily from her wounds. The legs looked broken as they were bent out of shape and life was ebbing from her as indicated by the blood continuing to pool around her on the APC cabin floor.

"By gunfire or under questioning?" The Chief asked.

"Both" stated Warlord simply. There was no sympathy in his tone or his demeanour.

Count for her part was struggling to stay conscious. The pain in her legs was immense and her thoughts drifted into wondering if she would ever dance again but snapped out of that reverie as something was jabbed into her knee joint and she screamed out loud. A long piercing sound that dropped off into sobbing.

Chief holding the knife in place said, "Now that I have got your attention, you need to answer some questions and we can then get you fixed up" but neither of them believed that was going to happen.

Count realised that she was going to die in that metal can and decided to try and go as quickly as she could. That could only be achieved by answering the questions and then she could go to sleep, and the pain would end.

As she went into and out of consciousness, she could faintly hear someone screaming. It sounded so painful and horrible. For a moment, Count's heart went out to whoever that was. Then she realised it was her and joined in the screaming.

Chief kept jabbing the knife into her knee socket and twisting it to one side and then the other, before the whole joint collapsed and she bled out in front of him. *"Just another weakness leaving the tribe"* he thought.

The interrogation was severe. He knew that but the Chief needed to know stuff now and got the answers that he needed. A bit of revenge, payback for the loss of four of his tribe but not revenge for the loss of his scouting party.

Chief wanted to take a positive from what had become an untenable and negative situation.

There were insufficient numbers of fit soldiers left to form a decent pincer attack. He was mindful of continuing with the chase, where their resources could deplete further, and he saw no obvious victory.

He was also concerned that both he and Warlord were away from the home stead, which left it weaker without them. The longer they were away, the greater the risk.

The prisoner was giving up the information he needed to make the right decision. He used some old interrogation techniques of asking the same question in different ways, along with inquiries to validate certain elements of previous answers.

Sometimes just twisting the knife gently and with others, sawing and jabbing to agitate the nerves around the joint. It would be damn painful on the receiving end and he could see the fight and energy leaving her, with every wave of blood oozing from her leg.

Satisfied that he had heard all he needed to, he withdrew the knife from her knee joint and saw the relieved look on her face, as the sharp pains ended, and her eyes opened.

He moved the knife higher and then slit her throat with a clean move from left to right. She wore a sad and slightly surprised look on her face as she bled out with a gurgle and then died.

His mind made up. He spoke out aloud so that all his tribe members could hear. Those inside the APC and up top manning the cupolas.

"There is no battlegroup waiting out west and therefore there will be no revenge mission back to New World homestead."

"The clan were heading west to seek answers for a blind man who could see and one of the archers who could hear some things."

"All a bit mysterious and so farfetched it could clearly not be true. No matter how many times I asked that question, she stuck to the same answers. I do not believe such senses exist and have therefore discounted it."

"The enemy party numbered no more than thirteen and that has now been reduced to eleven now the interrogation is complete."

Chief opted not to dwell on the damage and reduction in his own team, the one that had left the New World homestead now numbered eight, with three walking wounded. One of which was Warlord, and he would not be fighting for some time until his injuries healed.

His mission was complete as far as he was concerned. No battlegroup to come back at them. They could return to New World and know that their future would not be interrupted by these vicious scavengers.

However, his losses were high. Four dead and three wounded. His number two would be out of action a while until his injuries repaired. But he could make the journey home and set about doing so.

Revenge had not been satisfied. Just two dead archers to show for all their efforts but it did no good to dwell on things like that.

New World homestead was safe, that was the most important thing, and he could continue building his new society.

"Ditch the body and then we can head home." Was all the Chief said, and everyone looked relieved and buoyed by the certainty of his command.

They shoved the dead archer out of the back of the APC then slammed the door shut as her body slid to the ground.

Then they set off in close quarter convoy, with all four machine gun cupolas traversing left and right in a threatening manner as they moved off.

They would bury their dead back home. Somewhere suitable in the home stead. Not fed to the pigs or burnt like the weak ones. They would be remembered as heroes. The Chief was silent and morose as they left but still felt purposeful.

He cleared his mind of the deceitful archers and the unknown scavengers heading west. They meant nothing to him now.

The flotsam and jetsam of society. They were not worthy to be part of his New World.

Quest

Chapter

2031 - Ridge Rendezvous

Back on the hillside, Raven ordered a slow move down from the ridge as the enemy retreated.

She had decided that a full chase would not be in their best interests. Their adversaries were clearly highly trained, as their swarm up the hill had demonstrated. They had a radio net and could communicate with each other much faster and be more co-ordinated.

Now they were withdrawing, she could see that same discipline being maintained as the group kept a constant watch on the Ridge line.

Other than lobbing some arrows in the air, they could not guarantee a kill and so it was best not to waste ammunition. Plus, the enemy had much better firepower from their wicked looking automatic guns. She also knew that to press home any attack, would invariably cost their clan lives that they could ill afford to lose. She chose a wiser strategy.

As they slowly moved down the hillside, from bush to bush, they saw Point scrambling over the edge of the ridge towards them, so Raven called a halt.

The story he told was horrific. "Two or all three ladies were dead or taken prisoner. The defensive position created by the armoured vehicles was almost impregnable. However, I managed to take out two of the APC gunners. Seriously wounded or kills, I could not be sure. I did see the arrows penetrate flesh but could not stop to observe any further." A sobering report from the big man.

As the information was sinking in, Steel alerted them to the teenagers, who had appeared lower down the spine of the ridge. Life seemed to move in slow motion for Raven, as she digested the news of their loss and watched the teenagers approach the flank of the retreating enemy unit.

Staring down, they could all see what the teenagers planned to do, and it was audacious.

It would be dangerous to call out now and would not be in the young archers' best interests, so all they could do was stop and stare. Then watch as the action unfolded.

The timing of the move was spot on. Three heads appeared just above the height of the gorse and long grass, two arrows and a bolt were loosed almost simultaneously taking down two of the soldiers and the three heads disappeared just as the other soldiers turned round to see where the flights had come from. It was impressive.

Raven and the rest of the clan watched in admiration, as the three teenagers made good their escape, over the ridge and out of sight. Both Steel and Point crabbed back up and over the ridge to greet their young heroes.

Down below on the scrubby hillside, the soldiers went to ground. Raven knew that if the clan had possessed longer range weapons, then this would have been the time to press home an attack from the higher ground.

They had no such weaponry however and could therefore only continue to observe the enemy's withdrawal.

It was slower now that they were dragging two bodies and one of them limping, *"Must have turned an ankle or something."* Thought Raven.

"Well done kids" said Raven in a satisfactory tone. "Well done" but it was only those around her who heard.

Eventually, the enemy party reached the armoured defensive position and were quickly ensconced inside the protection of the personnel carriers.

Raven called a move back up the hillside and over the protective edge of the ridge and there she convened another briefing. Gunner kept watch on the scene down below whilst listening intently to the clan debate just behind him.

"Three of our clan are down. We could either withdraw now and continue our quest westwards or press home a difficult attack. That was the simple choice we now face." Explained Raven.

The arguments swung back and forth. Point wanted revenge for the loss of his friends. Steel argued that the armoured defensive position below was too tough a nut to crack. Radar expressed his deepest sympathies to Point but stated that they needed to press on to the coast and find the truth.

It was whilst the debate swung from one to the other that their minds were made up. It happened when the vehicle engines started up with a roar and Gunner said, "I think they are on the move and...."

"And what?" demanded Raven.

"..... a body has just been thrown out of the back doors of one of the APC's" replied Gunner sadly.

They rest of the clan scrambled onto the ridge and took it turns to use the monocular. They could see a broken blood-soaked figure, crumpled on the floor in the clearing and what looked like a second one a few yards away.

It had been the first time they had used the monocular since the attack commenced. Gunner had not wanted to give their position away again.

They waited a while until the three armoured vehicles, gun turrets still swivelling, headed back East, and were lost in the distance before they commenced their coordinated move down to the clearing.

Point and Bullseye took the left flank lower down, with Steel and the mute Boy and Girl with him on the other flank, higher up towards the edge of the ridge. Raven and Med led the centre with Radar, Gastro and Gunner remaining high up on the ridge with the baggage.

It took a while for the clan on the move, to get down to the clearing. They had to be sure that none of their enemy remained in concealment, waiting to use their automatic weapons on the lightly armed clan but thankfully that was not so.

As they arrived in the clearing, all still primed and on edge, they all halted as they heard a disembodied voice. It sounded remarkably like Fletch.

The voice said in a very calm tone. "It's only me and I am about to stand up, please remain calm and no-one shoot me."

Point was the first to respond and jubilantly exclaimed "Fletch, stand up!" and so she did.

Emerging from the ground, the ghillie suited Fletch immediately broke down and sobbed her heart out.

Med rushed over to aid but Fletch waved her away and said she was unharmed.

Steel bent down and looked at the broken figure of Whistler, partly revealed from the undergrowth and ghillie suit combined. Her body had taken the full brunt of four heavy calibre machine guns and it looked dishevelled and disjointed.

No longer a person. A painful sight for all of them.

Bullseye screamed just once. A high-pitched distress sound and fell onto her knees. The shape in front of Steel was unrecognisable but she knew who it was from the bits of kit and the damaged quiver of broken whistling arrows beside her.

Girl put her arms around Bullseye in comfort as she quietly sobbed.

Steel knelt beside the body of Count and it saddened him to see the state the enemy had left her in. One of her legs was almost completely severed at the knee and he could only imagine what pain she must have been in before she died.

Point held Fletch as the words just tumbled out of her. She talked about the torture she could hear, the anger in the one they called the Chief and questions asked, answers provided, and the summary provided by the Chief before he called an end to it and they departed.

Composing herself a little, Fletch said "He lost four soldiers and that made him very angry." Steel nodded to the teenagers and Raven touched Point's shoulder, all without speaking as Fletch continued. "He told Whistler that he would keep his knife blade in her knee until she told him everything he needed to know."

Fletch looked around at the rest of the clan and raised her voice "She told him repeatedly. That there were thirteen of us. That we were following Radar out west to the coast to find answers. She mentioned the shimmers, but he didn't believe her." She broke down in sobs again.

After a moment or two, Fletch continued "He wanted to know that there wasn't a battle group out west that we were going to report to and bring back to take down their New World homestead."

A statement that brought a shaking of heads, or shrugged shoulders, of all those stood by her. "Once he knew that there was no risk to New World, he seemed more relaxed but still angry about the loss of four soldiers and that three of them were also wounded."

Point interrupted her and said "Overall, with the loss of the scouting party and the four we killed here today, their security team, or squad as they like to call them, must be down to less than thirty soldiers now."

"They have a wide expanse of a farm to guard around the clock and cannot field all of them at the same time. I want to go back and kill them all." His voice rose in anger "and take revenge for this today and our children they murdered before!"

Everyone was looking at him in a mixture of empathy and sadness, but it was only Bullseye who responded with any affirmative sounds and cried "I want to see them all dead. All broken like this…" and her voice tailed off into more sobs.

Boy and Girl both put their hands on her shoulders and Girl turned hers into another hug and the two of them knelt on the ground in an embrace for a while.

It was left to Raven who said, that as much as she wanted to take the fight to this enemy. This was not the right time to do it. It would take a long time to trek back to the fortified farmstead it would not be a simple take down. It would need a lot of planning and much more firepower than they possessed today.

She urged that the clan should complete their quest. Find out what lay ahead on the coast. Satisfy their hunger for the knowledge that Radar assured them would be there and then, maybe then. They could arm up, perhaps recruit others, and then go back and take their revenge.

Dusk was approaching and it was agreed that Steel and the wings would return to the ridge and escort Radar and carry the baggage down with Gunner and Gastro, then camp for the night some way from the killing zone of the clearing.

So that is what they did.

Steel and the teenagers also retrieved the snares from the hillside. Their standard operating procedure. Waste not, want not. They would be used again and again. It was Boy who found and then held up the cut snare and they all realised its mini success, with the limping enemy soldier.

A suitable place for camp was selected. Something that they could defend, and they set about seeing what they could eat, whilst re-laying out some standard defence snares around the perimeter. Then it began to rain.

The baggage arrived in good time and it took only moments to provide a camouflaged weatherproof covering for them all and a small cooking fire. A hunting party was hastily assembled, and they disappeared off to find some fresh meat if that was possible.

Whistler and Count had been wrapped in their personal tarpaulins and carefully place under cover with them but to one side. They would be buried in the morning.

"The rain would help soften the ground and make it a little easier" thought Gunner. He had gained a lot of experience in recent times but not a point he wanted to share out loud.

As the black of the cloudy night closed in, the hunting party returned with some wildfowl and two rabbits. Paltry fare but enough to provide them all with some protein. The baggage train tipped up some leftover green leaves from those things the clan knew were edible and they at least had something in their stomachs.

The discussion continued to range over their choices, as each gave their opinions on what the clan should or should not do.

It came down to a choice of two. Continue the quest after burying their fallen comrades or turning back and creating an opportunity to take revenge.

Point, Fletch, and Bullseye were firm in the view that they should return to the farm and kill the Chief, Warlord and as many or all the tribe that lived there. It was a position of hate and annihilation. Complete revenge and nothing else. Yes, they realised that it could end with all their deaths but it was what they wanted.

Steel, Boy, and Girl too wanted to avenge the deaths of the archers but argued that they should complete the quest first, then re-arm and return. They pledged that is what they would do and received nods of acknowledgement from Point and Bullseye.

Radar led with the view that they quest was the most important thing and he was backed up by Gunner, Gastro and Med.

They all looked at Raven to provide the opinion of their leader.

After a moment or two, "We do both" said Raven, looking around at her clan. "We support Radar and conclude the quest. Then we accumulate the right sort of armament and return to take revenge."

Gunner agreed and was quickly joined by Gastro and Med. They too would pledge to return for revenge but only after escorting Radar to his objective.

Radar thanked them all for their support and then he too stated that once he had got the answers he needed, then he too would return with the clan and do what he could in taking down the murderous Chief and his tribe.

Unanimity was achieved when the archers held a quiet and separate chat. Buoyed by the support shared by the rest of the clan, they too agreed to complete the quest and then lead the revenge mission.

Sleep did not come easy that night and the patrols were easy to wake as they each took their turn on guard.

****

It was during the false dawn that they started to dig the graves for Whistler and Count in the lightly falling rain.

The burial took place at dawn and was a short, sombre affair. That came after the removal of anything of value that could sustain the rest of the clan.

Their ghillie suits had been cut to shreds and were all but useless. Though Point salvaged some pieces for patching. Both weapons had gone, as were their good quivers and other spare ammunition. Off to supplement the tribe's armoury no doubt.

Bullseye took some personal effects. A ring carefully removed and a necklace that had snapped off and been left unnoticed on the ground. Tokens to remember her mother.

Once the brief ceremony was concluded with some words from Point. The clan made ready to leave and departed the funeral site in their usual well-drilled way.

Scouts out front and on the flanks of the baggage trolley and a rear guard. It was going to be a damp day today and they were already wet through when they set off.

They continued their quest heading west.

Chapter

2031 - New World homestead

It was a sorry looking convoy that arrived back at the homestead. Chief had pushed them hard, and they had driven on through the night to minimise the time they were out on the road.

The security squad was tired, some were wounded, and they were all covered in grime from the trails. It had been raining and the roads were muddy. It would not be a comfortable bivouac, so they pressed on.

The first aid kits were insufficient to remove the snare and that would need some attention sooner rather than later.

The Chief didn't want to hang about and besides, their dead comrades were beginning to hum as their bodies deteriorated in the heat of the APC's.

He urged them on through the night and the following day, which brightened up a bit.

it was late into the next day when they arrived home.

The convoy navigated the chicane entrance, which was immediately secured as they came in and all three armoured vehicles pulled up in the main square outside the accommodation blocks that had formerly been the farmhouse and crew bunkhouse.

Tribe members had been drawn to the main square by the sounds of motor vehicles. Not a usual sight or sound. Sighs and cries sounded out from those seeking sight of their loved ones as they realised, they must be the ones wrapped in tarpaulins and being gently unloaded from the back of one of the APC's.

Their grief needed to be expelled. The Chief knew that and stood by whilst each of the bodies was claimed by one or more of those stood around. After a suitable period of wailing the Chief called for attention and explained to everyone what had happened and why he had taken the decisions he had.

Some voices dissented and called for a larger mobile force to go and hunt them down. To wipe them from the face of the earth. Understandable emotions and Chief allowed them all to vent their anger, whilst both he and Warlord looked on impassively.

Then the Chief spoke. "It ends here today. We bury our fallen comrades and then we get on with the job of creating a better society. Patrols will recommence. We will do our best to recruit others to join us and we will thrive here in our New World.

Chasing after the scavengers and archers may achieve the objective of revenge but it could also lead to disaster, as we would need to split our forces. It could leave New World exposed to the risk of assault by others and we cannot afford to do that."

There were murmurs of assent and silent nods from several of the gathering, so Chief continued.

"Let us concentrate on remembering our fallen. We will feast for them and then we will turn to and get back to work. Back to creating the superior society we all want. That's that." He announced with some finality, turned, and escorted Warlord into his room for a private discussion.

****

Once they were alone, Chief and Warlord discussed a great deal. Whether they did in fact have sufficient labour after the loss of the scouting party, the forced labour and now the four fallen on the pursuit.

The wounded would not be a productive until their injuries healed.

Their debate went on for a long time. They concluded that whilst their overall numbers had indeed been reduced, it was not so low as to place New World in any immediate levels of risk, above those they had already prepared for.

The security teams would continue rotating around with scouting patrols to ensure they had some variety and keep them all sharp.

Chief would engage with Engineering and Farming to ensure that they were all on programme in preparation for winter and ensure Cooking drew up some decent menus for the next few weeks to keep everyone upbeat.

Clearly there was now less demand on the food stocks, and they could afford to lift some of the rationing restrictions for a while.

Warlord in turn would need to reduce the scouting patrols to just two at a time but would challenge them to go further afield in the search for suitable survivors to join them. Willingly, or as forced labour.

Chief said, "This would be a good time to train the patrols to ride horses and enable them to travel further and faster on their long-range patrols." Warlord nodded and made a note to add the training into the rosters.

Satisfied that their strategy remained on target Chief dismissed his friend to go and get some treatment to his injuries and took the opportunity to rest himself.

As he lay on his bed his thoughts drifted.

"God must have had similar setbacks when he created life and the world as we know it."

"I as the Chief will also overcome these challenges and ensure my tribe survives and create a new order, a better society than the world has ever seen before."

Then he fell into a deep and untroubled sleep.

Chapter Seventeen

2031 - Wooden Sanctuary

The Clan had decided to force march around the rocky peninsula and across the hills for two full days, the first in the rain and then the second in drying conditions as the sun finally reappeared.

They managed the risk of assault by unknown enemies by sending their scouts out much further ahead than they normally would do and were able to cover a good thirty or forty miles. However, it had been hard going in the soft and sometimes muddy ground, and they needed to rest.

Steel had spotted an industrial feature in the last valley before the hilly region ended. It looked abandoned but would check it out more thoroughly with a bigger team. Point, Fletch, and the three teenagers all went with him.

What they found was pleasantly surprising.

It had been a logging facility and consisted of several large buildings that had previously been offices and workshops, stores, and a large sawmill. In its heyday, it must have employed a lot of people to cut down, haul in and process the big trees from the wooded hillsides surrounding the valley.

Steel noted with some interest, the sustainability plan that had been put into place, with new plantations demonstrating different growth patterns of new trees. But he was probably the only one who saw it for what it was. He smiled to himself and shook his head as he thought *"That was the gamekeeper in him. Looking at the management of growth."*

Everyone else just saw shelter and the opportunity to dry out and do some scavenging. The six of them searched the site thoroughly. Whilst there were signs of a hasty retreat at some point in the past, it had not been ransacked as so many places had been.

They were able to assemble a large collection of useable things that would be distributed later when the clan rested. For now, they continued stripping anything useful from the various buildings and workshops.

Fletch announced that the fuel tanks were still relatively full, although there were no road vehicles that could be found. Only some plant and heavy machinery like bulldozers and earthmovers, grabbers and telehandlers.

There was also fuel in the generators, which had been turned off. However, it looked like it could start up at a single touch and would generate electricity, which was a big surprise. Not that the clan had anything that needed power, but it was nice to know it was there if needed.

The workshops were still full of tools and the clan were like kids in a sweet shop as they found a variety of useful bits of kit to maintain their weapons, sharpen blades and some wicked looking axes were also picked up.

A small sick bay was situated behind what looked like it was the main office. With no power to the fridge, the consumable medication in the fridge had all deteriorated to the point that it stunk to high heaven. However, there was a healthy display of packeted medication in a secure cabinet that became insecure when prised open by Steel.

The office also contained a radio transceiver but was currently powered down. No-one wanted to turn it on in case it somehow gave away their position.

Boy and Girl were sent back to escort the baggage trolley and the rest of the clan forward to the sanctity of the lumber facility.

Steel and Point decided that the bunkhouse offered the best location. It was set away from the other buildings and would therefore provide good visibility of anything or anyone approaching. The ground around had been pressed flat by the removal of trees and the constant comings and goings of heavy vehicles in their day.

Now it was all silent. Just the sounds of wildfowl in the woods and the odd bark or cry of an animal. Perfect.

The perimeter was large and harder than usual to secure and so Steel and his acolytes had to work hard on placing sufficient snares before he was satisfied and took the opportunity to join the hunt for their evening meal.

Raven looked around and saw that the clan were exhausted from their two-day slog and probably as much from the adrenalin exuded during the fighting around the ridge. They needed to rest. Recharge their batteries for the final push out west to the coast.

Small conversations were underway around the bunkhouse as they all ate the fine fare that Gastro had served up, on this occasion helped by his sister-in-law Med. They had their own private conversation underway, remembering her sister and his wife, her husband and all their children. Happier times when their families socialised on a regular basis.

Raven knew that this kind of discussion only led to a period of silence. It always did. Best not to look back too much as it only induced melancholy and sometimes it was hard to rise from it and concentrate on the challenge of the day, or of that moment.

So, she started a broader clan discussion by shouting across the small fire-pit in the middle of the bunkhouse to Radar. "How much further to the coast old man?" knowing that it would get people's attention. She rarely derided anyone, and it did raise a few eyebrows from their watching audience, but it got the clans attention. Which was her intention.

Radar was always on her wavelength. It was one of the key things that brought the two of them closer together. He knew he had to play his part and did so with aplomb.

"Ha, ha, old man!" Echoed Radar. "I probably am an incredibly old man. I try not to think about it to be honest" and chuckled, "It's not far. As the crow flies, I would say it was no more than three days hike at our normal rate. So maybe thirty miles."

"That's not too bad" replied Raven.

"As the crow flies" repeated Radar "but there is a big garrison town in the way. It used to house thousands of military personnel from different unit's, their families and all the businesses that sprung up to support the bases."

"Some industry, schools, hospitals, and such like. A sprawling mass of a place and we either must walk around it or through it. Either way, it will slow us down and it will not be without its own risks."

By now the discussion had got the attention of all the clan that were there, clearly not the two out on guard. Everyone wanted to know more. What could they expect?

Radar continued with his musing "I was on detachment away from the base of course when the Struggles were in full swing. I went on several different missions, travelling further and further away from our headquarters. Transported by helicopters."

"We still had the communications of course back then and were in touch with each other using enciphered radio equipment. The last time was investigating a whole host of the silver shimmers when we came under attack out on deployment. Sometime before we all found each other."

By now, everyone was hanging on every word that Radar spoke. This was easily the chattiest he had been in a while. Perhaps it was in the realisation that they were nearing the end of his quest. They all wanted to know more.

"The base had already weathered the big attacks from our national enemies and when the energy sources started to dwindle. There was a lot of damage."

"Most if not all the warships were sunk, only submarines remained operational. The jet fighters were all downed and most of the infrastructure was devasted by a series of nuclear and EMP warheads."

"Our base though, was a little different than the others. It had to be. We were operating at the highest levels of secrecy and it was surrounded by some high-tech defences. It was a lot like the Maginot Line that the French built."

"The Maginot Line?" said Raven.

Gunner interjected, "It was an early twentieth century line of defences, laid along the Franco / German border over a hundred years ago. Gun turrets inter-connected by tunnels, with underground armouries and pill boxes, spanning half a mile of anti-tank traps and such-like, big, flooded trenches back from the border. An impregnable barrier"

"Wow" said Raven, "Impregnable? How did the Germans defeat it?" She asked, knowing a little about the second world war that commenced in 1939 but wanting them to talk.

"The Germans just went round the end of it, where the border with Belgium started. It was a gigantic white elephant!" Gunner exclaimed.

"So how sure are you that your HQ is still intact?" asked Raven. "Wouldn't the assault just go round it like the Germans did almost a hundred years ago?"

They all looked at Radar and he sat for a while before he answered.

"We were a special forces unit. We had Amphibious, Air and Ground capabilities. Our base was located on a peninsula. The landward side defences ran from coast to coast."

"The main base was pretty much all built underground, with sea-facing defences guarding the harbour. Autonomous turrets facing outwards and upwards to provide sea, air, and land defences. Infra-red motion detectors linked to an Artificial Intelligent central control."

"Nothing to go around. It was like an island. Self-contained and held its own sickbays, accommodation, kitchens, dining halls, and control rooms."

"It did not need a lot of personnel to defend it because of the autonomous turrets. I do, however, know a couple of ways into and out of the fortress. We had to be able to go about our business without being detected."

"If it does remain intact, it will be a difficult approach...." He tailed off and of course, could not see the open mouths and fixed stares of the rest of the clan as they digested the news.

It was Raven who broke the silence. She felt she needed to.

"So! We have to navigate a garrison town and probable battlefield, with known or unknown persons still present, to gain entry to what seems to be an impregnable defensive position before we get any answers. Outstanding."

The rest of the clan continued to watch as Radar replied "It contains the answers. If we are to recover from this devastating period of our history, we need to know more about why it happened, if we are to figure out a how to recover from it. Without that I cannot see how we can really survive. Does everyone understand that?"

The counter argument came from Gastro of all people and supported by sister-in-law Med. Clearly both fed up with all the travelling and the fighting.

"Why don't we stay here?" countered the big man. "This would provide a good base for the future. It has endless stocks of timber we can use to make a palisade for a fort. Use it as a base to trade with other groups for food."

"Yes" added Med, "There is good machinery, fuel and a generator. It would be our way of starting afresh. There is also a good stock of medication such as penicillin, along with boxes of surgical wipes in sealed packets, bandages and other paraphernalia that I would just bore you with."

"Until another group, more powerful than us, comes along to take it away" countered Point, rising to his feet. "We have already experienced the wrath of a psychotic tyrant, with access to armoured vehicles. We cannot compete with that."

"I agree that if the world were a more stable place, this could be just the position to rebuild our lives and create a community. It just isn't the right time." Then he sat back down. His argument complete.

Raven then took centre stage and shared her opinions.

"It is true that this place has a lot of potential but in equal measures, it will take a lot of hard labour and effort to make this work. To be able to live here and not just survive."

"We should record an inventory of what is here and what is missing. What is not here that we would need. We then hide as much of the valuable resources as we can in case another group stumbles on it like we have. We record it on the map. Then when the time is right, we can decide if we want to return here or go someplace else."

"Secondly, we need to take stock of what we can sensibly bring with us from here and complete the quest with Radar."

"We need to have some confidence in a stable future before we consider settling down. Does that make sense?" she finally asked but no-one responded.

After a pause, she added "We are also committed to supporting Point, Fletch and Bullseye with their revenge. We can come back here and stock up with anything we need before we press on with that mission."

There were some nods of acknowledgement and others with perplexed looks on their faces.

Raven then said "It has been a tough time over these last few days. Get your heads down and we can set out a plan in the morning. Okay?"

More nods and people made ready to kip or go out on patrol or finish off cleaning weapons and restocking ammunition.

Radar made his way over to Raven and sat down with her. She was their leader and he wanted to demonstrate his support for her and gave her a hug. She kissed the top of his head and pulled him into a soft embrace as they both leaned backwards on to their packs. Radar resting his head on her shoulder.

"A lot to plan" thought Raven as she drifted off to an uneasy sleep, cradling the enigmatic and special man that Radar had become.

Chapter Eighteen

Battlefield in the future – in the year 2531

Deep underground and five hundred years in the future.

The sound of explosions could be heard in the distance, but she did not take any notice of them. It was so regular now it was becoming the norm, almost rhythmic and would seem strange not to hear them.

She continued to fix her gaze on the hologram in front of her. The Control Centre hummed with all the activity going on and the room glowed with a pleasant blue. A hue deliberately selected by their predecessors as it was deemed to be calming. Though the events of the day were anything but calm.

"The figures within the hologram looked small, almost like old fashioned toys but no-one had time for playthings in these times." She thought. It was all about survival and nothing else. Every ounce of energy was dedicated to remaining alive. That most basic of human instincts.

She watched a small group of their ancestors, picking their way across the wide-open spaces of the countryside. She noted with a small smile that their skin colours depicted the old ethnic divisions of the day. Browns, blacks and pale. Something no longer a feature down here. *"We all have the same skin colour, a most attractive light brown."* She thought.

Leader continued to watch the figures trek across the landscape. It looked idyllic if it wasn't for the circumstances those poor people found themselves in. *"Through no fault of their own."* She thought and then sighed.

She also wondered, in that moment, how many times this sort of thing had had impacted on people over the eons, with enemies at the gate, wanting only to kill and loot from those behind the walls. Take from them all they had, including their lives. Survivors then trekking off to find new land, away from their attackers.

The downfall of the Roman Empire and others in ancient times that had taken their place. The great campaigns of the Mongols, the British Empire where the sun allegedly never set, and the oppressive Soviet Bloc had all come to an end.

Then the new Chinese dynasties at the start of the third millennium when their astonishing growth in technology and business had seen them become the world's most dominant nation. How it had kickstarted their Asian conquests and creation of an Eastern Empire with their acquisition of Japan, Korea and other technology developing nations.

It seemed that humanity had only ever known violence, aggression and stealing from others.

Now history was being rewritten and for that she had to take some responsibility.

"No time for melancholy" she thought, as her mind snapped out of the reverie and looked around at her command team in the Control Centre. "Sitrep please Number Two" she instructed.

It would not be a sensible use of her time to consider the activities that her command had set in place. Her full attention was needed for the here and now.

The lean figure of her second in command rose from his seat in a fluid movement and updated The Leader with the situation report. "Defences remain intact Leader, despite the repeated attempts by our enemies. The so-called Alliance" and paused whilst a louder explosion rang out and caused some anxious glances from the faces of the rest of the team who had swivelled around from their monitors.

However, the Tech-Controllers remained connected to the displays, keyboards, and monitors by a series of thin hoses and leads plugged into orifices implanted on numerous parts of their bodies. They were after all, bred to be part of the system itself. Tech Controllers.

Number Two continued, "The energy walls are holding fast. The enemy does not seem to have any weapon to cut through them."

"Yet!" Interrupted Leader.

"Of course." Nodded Number Two in acknowledgement and continued "The traditional defences also seem to be holding up as well. There have been some anomalies with the automatic reloading of the weapons systems as some of the drone bots are nearing end of life, but the Mech Techs seem to be able to keep them in the game with additional maintenance activity…" he paused.

"Our concern remains around the personnel we have left….." his voice tailed off as they all looked at the Leader.

"It is what it is" stated the Leader, less firmly and confidently than she had wanted to.

She knew that they had brought this problem upon themselves and she as their Leader, had to shoulder the responsibility.

It was why, in that moment, that her command team remained silent but hoped to offer support with their concerned and stoical looks. However, the Leader only saw grim faces as she continued to know the current situation.

"What are our numbers like?" asked the Leader, looking directly at her second in command. Knowing that they had set in place such fundamental damage so long ago in their past, with ramifications that still reverberated across their community today.

When someone died in 2031, it impacted upon the people here today in 2531. Their direct descendants just did not exist anymore. Their losses today were gauged against the causation from 500 years before. A process that the Leader had authorised to try and avoid the hell that was now taking place around them.

It had left them with less then ten percent of the population than they had previously had.

"The numbers have stabilised since the Struggles long ago have petered out. We continue to lose the odd person, directly attributed to the plague and others to the sporadic fighting and killing by the small groups of our ancestors that do remain. That seems to be rarer though as each Sol passes."

Sol was the only measure of time that related to anything that had once been. A twenty-four-hour period in the ancient measure of time when the Sun rose and fell in a day. Now of course, there was no Sun, no dawn or dusk. Just the endless florescent corridors of their subterranean existence. The only dark needed for sleep could be controlled simply by turning a light off.

Leader mused over the fact that the world above ground had long been uninhabitable.

Ever since going underground centuries before, to avoid the ravages of the ultraviolet waves from the Sun, slowly stripping them of skin, of life, of hope as the Ozone layers finally gave up the ghost following decades of carbon abuse.

It had left a volatile atmosphere that had slowly changed the weather conditions.

Up top, on the surface, storms raged for most of the year. Tropical storms, dust clouds that swamped life, tsunami waves crashing over the land in a new cycle of destructive seasons. *A horrible place.* Thought Leader.

She reminisced that the surface had become untenable for humans up there and their ancestors had taken their skills and their technology underground. Tapping into the energy sources of the magma core and recreating civilisations in a subterranean world.

A perversion of Noah's Ark had descended into the depths, taking livestock, grain and above all, technology, down below.

Miners had been worth their weight in gold in those early days, as they used their skills to open new territories under the ground. Great caverns and underground warehouses had been constructed to hold the agriculture needed to feed the population.

Heat and light drawn from the magma energy convertors had been used to grow and cultivate wheat, barley, and other products. Grass and other feed for their dairy herds, sheep, chickens, and other farming chattels.

They had lost most of the livestock in those first decades, to the unnatural conditions and those that remained did so only for research purposes and kept alive in artificial environments. Insect farming, laboratory grown proteins and hydroponics had tipped the balance and gave them a balanced diet. It allowed them to survive down below.

The underground streams, rivers, and lakes acted as enormous reservoirs, but care had to be taken during any construction phase to avoid them or tap into them as required.

Leader recalled the many errors that were made in the early days, as those valiant pioneers had wrestled with the topography and the laws of physics. They had, however, persevered to create their underground regional conurbation.

Many had died in the attempt to carve out their new world. *"Others had endured terrible injuries."* She thought.

Each piece of construction had to be capable of withstanding the massive forces of nature, the continuous movement of tectonic plates.

Earthquakes had been their primary concern in the past. Managing and then harnessing the differing magnetic fields as they penetrated deeper into the rock. Along with exploiting the heat of the magma core.

Every tunnel, every hall, had to be constructed regarding to the pressures of the rock, the flow of water, or the bulge of magma which had provided all their energy sources as predicted by the scientists.

She knew that it had been fortunate that so many scientists and technical specialists had survived the early days and helped guide the more artisan members of the nation.

New transportation systems using magnetic levitation had been created to swiftly move people where they needed to be. Vast air conditioning shafts connected to suitable caverns nearer the surface brought basic oxygen into the network, where it was enhanced by other sources of air expelled down below, re-filtered and re-used with carbon dioxide convertors.

Vast industrial areas churned out the necessary building materials that were needed.

"We have not just survived down here," Leader thought, *"we have thrived."*

Some of their wealth had been diverted to creating the gardens of tranquillity. Designed to replicate the parks and gardens of their ancestors, with lots of foliage camouflaging the harshness of their man-made world. The gardens had been harmonised with hydroponics to create living walls that also produced food.

Using their technical knowledge, they had been able to trade with other nations across the devastated world and brought in labour and raw materials via the trading posts that were located at the borders.

Leader knew that those borders were heavily guarded by everyone. Located at the end of incredibly long, single tunnels that ran for thousands of miles. Primarily constructed by Home citadel, they were the places where diplomatic envoys met, delegations were entertained and trade between nations was conducted. *"A time of growth, of development."* Thought Leader.

However, friction had developed between those nations who had less capability, less assets, which in turn had led to a breakdown in relations and ultimately to the wars. Endless wars whilst each nation tried to take resources from another and used up vital reserves defending what they had.

The battleground commenced at the border posts at first. Once they were conceded, a variety of defences were created. Some tunnels had been destroyed to prevent access, but their enemies had tunnelled around them and Home were required to fall back and defend closer and closer to their citadel.

Conflicts were now fought on a three-dimensional level. Attacks could take place at any point around the 3D shape of any nation's citadel. Great care had been taken with the defences of each element of the underground civilisations.

Tunnels had been used to intercept others, get behind defences and wage war. It was brutal attrition that was slowly bleeding value and life from each nation.

The Leader mused for a moment on how they had got to this point.

Theirs had been the most powerful of citadels, which they named Home. Created primarily under the American continents, their citizens came from north, central, and south.

Combining their cultures and values had not been easy but they had persevered. Largely Christian. The church had been their common ground and science provided them with solutions to survive and then thrive. Leader briefly touched the small crucifix made of precious metal.

They possessed technology capable of cutting new routes through the ground in no time at all using matter/anti-matter boring equipment. Incredibly swift transportation systems and a well-organised society of equals, with each person undertaking a key role in the collective. The intention had been to create a utopian society.

However, there was an underclass of labour called "Patronne", a derivative of patron or supporter because that was their purpose. To support the growth and development of Home.

The Patronne were originally young people imported into Home from the poorer nations to carry out basic construction tasks, cleaning and tending the agricultural warehouses or working in the industrial centres.

Initially, the young people had been treated like slaves but following several social reform programmes over recent decades, they had been assimilated into Home society.

However, the Patronne remained the poorest of Home citizens and were easily distinguished by the elaborate facial tattoo's that their community favoured. Proud to be different, they had their own customs, beliefs, and way of life.

Home had traded successfully with other citadels from other nations for a long time. They did so from a position of strength. Garrisons of able fighting battalions protected a harmonious and highly productive community.

Holding the upper hand with leading edge technology, they had struck hard deals when they did decide to sell off some of their older technology to the developing societies elsewhere in the world. Though the others had little to offer the Home society, other than labour, but they did what they could. It was benevolent and in keeping with the society they desired.

However, those less well off, those other peoples were jealous of the success of Home Citadel and banded together to attack it and take those riches for themselves. They called themselves "The Alliance."

It was a hotchpotch, rag tag and bobtailed collection of religious zealots, fanatics, and hardened warriors.

All the fighting so far, had taken place with assaults from the west. Seemingly good diplomatic relations continued with their furthest neighbours, the enigmatic Eastern ethnic Group. The EG's.

Despite requests for help, the Easterners had intimated that they were not fighters. Though they did say that they would try to help wherever possible.

Other than some suggestions on diplomacy, they had not really helped at all. A passive aggressive posture that Leader had seen right through and believed that the Easterners were actively supporting the Alliance but lacked the complete evidence to prove it.

Home Citadel had easily defended those early assaults. Often outnumbering their enemies and certainly possessing smarter systems to detect, to protect and to repel invaders. Home had not used their power in those days to initiate attacks on others but just to protect what they had.

The skirmishes had seemed so senseless to Home citizens but after a while, the Leader did authorise reprisals. If only to deter future attacks but all that did was add fuel to the fire of a conflict that became a feud, a jihad, and a crusade. Depending on which argument was at the fore of the "The Alliance."

Then of course came the time travel accident. The catalyst of their downfall. Leader could only sigh to herself on the outcome of her decision to proceed.

The Tech Scientists had come forward with what looked like a carefully prepared proposition that offered an altruistic way forward.

Go back in time and create better solutions that could be shared with all and prevent the imbalances that had led to this war.

They had tried to make peace with their enemies and offers of reparations for real and assumed wrongs of the past, but it had fallen on deaf ears and the fighting had continued.

The Leader knew that wars like this only ended with complete and utter destruction of one's enemy. Scorched earth. Severance of blood lines and all that. Or by peaceful means.

The only examples of peace that truly lasted were those achieved by compromise, negotiation and finally agreement. It was why she had approved the Tech Scientists proposition.

A method of going back in time. "To mend the broken fences of our neighbours" had been quoted. The technology was based on holography. The ability to project a real-world image into another dimension. In this case time.

At first the primary mission objective had been to educate their ancestors. Tell them what would happen to the world if the uncontrolled damage to the environment continued. However, it had been noted from historical records that eminent people of the day had failed to convey those messages. How would a message from the future be received?

Home Citadel were the only society capable of creating the technology to harness holography in this way. Even so, the design had flaws that had not been apparent at the point the concept was approved.

Complex ciphers were in use by all the societies. To protect one's own data, with systems too numerous to mention that listened, interpreted, and analysed communications data from all around them. Their enemies had similar systems to protect and intercept the data of others. Cryptography and cyber security were a complicated business.

The holo-travel had therefore to be enciphered on transmission to prevent their enemies from knowing what Home Citadel were doing and interfere with the plan. It also required the travellers to wear a special suit capable of withstanding the travel through time and project themselves into the past. A one-piece outfit made from fibres created from new minerals found underground had been the safest solution.

All was not plain sailing and they had lost many members of their teams of specialists who had volunteered, in the early concept phase with poorly made suits and inaccurate placements. Some had died during the transmissions when they failed to accurately pinpoint local hazards of the past. Moving vehicles, boggy ground, and suchlike. Some due to the poor quality of their holo-suits.

The technology had been developed over decades.

Some personnel had not returned whole as some malfunctions with the holo-travel equipment, which could have been a permanent set back had other members of the community not stepped forward by volunteering to be trained. An indication of their commitment to the cause.

The technical issues were gradually overcome, and a programme of planned interventions was put into place. Whispers in certain ears was all they managed to achieve, which did create some dialogue but failed to stem the inevitable ecological disaster.

Careful mapping of historical data could place people in a location to a precise time slot by using complex algorithms. They had determined a point some 500 years previously. In 2030. Work was underway testing the equipment in the decades before that but the "pinch point", the optimum moment was selected as 2030.

Purposefully established as a time of world peace, a time when all of earths nations had come together to manage the deterioration of their environment. Accords were being put into place to minimise carbon production and many spoke with a similar voice with a need to protect their environment and guarantee the future of their descendants.

It was also ahead of the great oriental conquest initiated by the Peoples Republic of China in the late 2050's, which had blossomed into their Asian expansion at the start of the third Millenia.

Despite those good intentions back in 2035, some countries managed their contribution in a selfish way that created imbalances. That was the point of the project determined in 2530. Go back to the moment in history when better decisions could be made. "Mend the broken fences", said The Leader.

All the scenarios had been worked through. The atmosphere would become deadly when the ozone layers disintegrated, and humanity would only survive by descending into the depths. That was a fact.

The primary mission of education was abandoned in favour of preserving key blood lines in each of the continental areas. That way, it would help the way that each nation descended and with what technology, that was crucial to the imbalances experienced.

Sending key resources back in time, to coach, to cajole and to encourage better decision making had been the intention. Share the knowledge. Ensure that each nation was better prepared to descend into the earth's core and enter it as equals.

However, the system enciphering corrupted the signal in some way. A way that they had failed to figure out.

Home citizens carefully selected for their roles had been sent back in time, but the signal corruption meant that they were barely able to communicate or even to be seen by their predecessors.

It had not been possible to communicate with their ancestors. Whilst some appeared to hear it was not known how or why they could. Those things just could not be figured out. Without proper two-way communication, it would not be possible to create suitable interventions.

Great care had been taken to identify the many previous generations of leaders and those people who would make better leaders. They had mapped out the genealogy of races, of key groups and identified crucial individuals. With this plan, Home Citadel could even up the way of life for all, not just the few.

They would make better decisions than those that had led to inequality, to suffering, to resentment and create a better world. They could ensure technology was developed evenly and value distributed equally across nations. It seemed to be good plan. An altruistic one.

If only they knew then, what they knew now.

Somehow, thirty years after they began the holotravel project, some level of underground microscopic bacterial entity had been carried through into the past. So unknown to their predecessors and so powerful that it had initiated a pandemic.

A world-wide plague that killed people in their millions and had been the catalyst for war between nations and then between regions. They had dealt death to their forefathers in a way that could never have been anticipated.

Worse still. They had changed history. Their own past.

People died back then and the generations who should have followed them no longer existed. A horrendous side effect that had not been factored into their planning. It was a massive error.

Home Citadel was devastated. Vast numbers of people just disappeared overnight. They no longer existed because someone in their previous blood line had died. Either in the Plague, the Wars, or the Struggles that Home had to witness on the holograph.

Whole battalions of Home Citadel soldiers were no longer there to protect them, to guard the tunnels, to stop the enemy infiltrations.

It was almost catastrophic. Their enemy had enjoyed their first major successes. Overrunning the outer perimeter defences just because there was no-one there to stop them. Though they too had been affected.

The Alliance did not know exactly what it was but had worked out that their own ancestral lineages had been damaged in some way and that accounted for the massive losses to both sides.

They did know, however, that it was not of their own doing. A matter that added more hate to their mission to destroy Home Citadel.

The human losses also meant that there were fewer Techs to maintain the autobot services. Tending crops in the specially managed farm factories and hydroponic walls, preparing and distributing the protein meals. Cleaning the corridors and the carefully camouflaged air ducting and filtering systems. Their one link left to the surface, which needed constant monitoring and maintenance interventions. The Achilles heel of each citadel.

Home Citadel sent more missions to try and evaluate the disasters unfolding before their view on the holograph but the more interventions, the greater the loss of life to their predecessors and the impact in 2530 and into 2531 of the disappearing citizens was becoming untenable.

The more times the holo-travel was used, the more it spread the infections, the more people died, the less there were left to defend the citadel. The Leader had called a halt to further use of the holo-travel system until they got to grips with the problems of sanitisation of those who travelled back in time.

It could not have come at a worse moment. The Tech Scientists had just discovered a small military group in the past, who had the equipment and capability to detect the Home Citizen travellers but the timing of some sort of EMP warhead dropped on the area concerned, had interfered with the holo-cipher in some way and it had not been used since.

The brave Home Citizens had not returned from that mission either. They disappeared in the explosion.

"If only things had been different", mused Leader. Then she was shaken from her thoughts as an alarm sounded, indicating a breach of their last perimeter defences.

Chapter Nineteen

2031 – Steel Stockade

The Clan set off west from the lumber mill two sunrises after they had arrived. They were refreshed, re-armed and had a renewed purpose.

They had awoken with every single member digesting the points of discussion the previous morning and whilst some carried out a full reconnaissance of the lumber facility, the rest got to grips with gathering up and then hiding all the valuables.

Some of the mechanised plant was fired up and used to create a pit, which they quickly lined and covered with tree trunks. Then the earth was bulldozed back over to protect the cache.

A small team planned how they would cross the garrison town and gain access to the special forces HQ.

Gastro and Med served up a simple breakfast of fried meat and beans they had found in the lumber store full of cans. Soups, beans, corned beef, and other fine fare. A rare find and Gastro commented, just the once, that it would still make a good base at some point in the future, which generated a few funny comments in return.

The rest of the cans, medicines, tools, and other goodies went into the pit to be hid and used at some point in the future. Raven made sure they mapped out the facility and the location of the pit. Then stored that with their sole printed map.

Later that day, they pooled the knowledge of what the lumber facility held, in terms of assets. It would indeed make a good starter base and a potential home, but they all agreed the priority right now was to complete Radar's quest. Get the answers and then plan to return.

This would be a staging point in their revenge mission. Tool up. Return East to take retribution and then, maybe then, they could think about settling down. Still much to do.

The rest of the day was taken up making good their travel plans, another good dinner provided by the canned larder and some fresh meat, then it was off on the quest to the coast. A veritable feast of food on the go was distributed around the clan. Then they left in typical good order.

Travel West was not as fast as they hoped. It was due to several different factors. The going was tough to get through the forest, even utilising the logging trails and they ended up camping out for two nights before they emerged from the trees. They also took great care to hide the tell-tale tracks of the buggy, which also cost them time.

Using branches as simple tools, those on rear guard duties had the task of "sweeping" across their trail and covering up the tracks. It was an arduous duty and so took it in turns.

They had carefully worked their way along a trail that must have been used as the primary haulage route back in the day. Huge ruts where the heavy loads had chewed up the ground on wet days had to be navigated with care.

Once they were clear of the forest, they walked out onto flatter land that had previously been farmed but not for a long time. Steel, Point, and the three teenagers fanned out and formed a wide skirmish line as the advance scouts.

Gunner and Fletch maintained the rear-guard on this stretch, with the baggage trolley pushed by Gastro, Radar and Raven in turns.

There were man-made barriers to overcome on the outskirts of the town. Some very damaged roads and the debris of enormous convoys of military and civilian vehicles that had been destroyed heading out of town towards the forest.

Not one of them appeared to have made it out. In fact, the lack of presence of anyone and the stocks of resources that had been discovered at the lumber camp demonstrated that acutely.

Another mystery was the limited scavenging of the convoys. Clearly the human remains had all been eaten and it was obvious where some larger body parts had been dragged away by carnivores judging by the way certain bits of kit and clothing had been distributed.

However, by and large. The vehicles contained a whole host of prized assets to scavenge but the clan did not want to stop. They remarked on a short break that it would be useful returning to this site to pick stuff up. They marked it on the map. Then they continued their journey westwards, towards the coast.

Their movement was finally halted when Point came across a small, fortified encampment that appeared at one time to be a military air base. Though there were no planes, and the runways did not exist anymore. Just huge craters in amongst tattered pieces of asphalt that made them look like islands in a sea.

The fortifications appeared to be built of armoured vehicles and it looked quite lethal through the field monocular. Several tanks had been embedded into the fortifications, their turrets facing outwards. However, there did not seem to be any movement of people, either inside or around the encampment.

Steel had returned to the baggage group and they had called in all the scouts and rear-guard whilst an alternative route or plan of action was considered.

Radar was questioned as to what knowledge he had of the base and he could share no more than they could already see. It had indeed been an air base, specialising in interception. Fast jets capable of climbing to altitude in a swift manner to engage incoming enemy flights.

The lack of aircraft on the ground or in the bombed-out dispersal hangars could either be, they were shot down in combat or had been routed to another airfield somewhere else. It could also account for the lack of personnel as the ground crews would most likely have moved with them if they had indeed been relocated.

Steel reported that either side of the air base were devastated elements of towns and they all knew the risks of working their way through places like that. Easy for enemy concealment and potentially littered with booby traps.

The wide openness of the airfield meant that any movement in daylight would be seen by those in the fortified camp. Somewhat of a dilemma.

Raven called for a clan consultation to reach agreement on the next steps.

They all moved to a place of safety. A wooded area that had natural berms running at angles that gave them a good place to defend if they had to. It allowed them to be as a group again, as they had in the lumber bunkhouse.

One or two of the clan maintained a watch outward, whilst listening intently to the discussion going on in the hollow between the berms.

It was a simple choice in the end.

Which risk posed the greater threat. The one they could see in the fortified camp or the ones that they could not in the bombed-out towns. Therefore, the decision was taken to reconnoitre the fortified camp, on both daylight and at night.

Steel and Point would set off in the late afternoon. Take up an observation position and monitor the camp and report back next day.

The rest of the clan set about securing a perimeter around the berm, agreeing a rota of sentries, and bedded down for the night. Raven noted with a smile that the teenagers seemed to find solace intertwined with each other when they were not on patrol or on guard. It was good to see them getting on so well.

As dusk approached, Steel and Point set off. It wasn't long before they found a suitable vantage point.

Point used the monocular and swept it left and right across the terrain for a few minutes before handing it over to Steel, who followed suit. When he had completed his sweep, he turned to speak with Point.

"There is a lot of hardware forming a defensive barrier. I don't see an easy way in."

Point nodded and said "I agree. There seems to be a gate of some sorts on the southern side, and I have seen one or two people moving around but the place looks deserted otherwise. I would have expected to see a lot more soldiers than that."

"I will take the first watch" said Point, "You get your head down for a while, I will give you a shake when I feel tired."

Steel nodded once. Curled up into a ball next to his bags and fell asleep. *"It was amazing how he could just drop off like that,"* thought Point and continued his watch of the camp below.

Later in the night he handed over to Steel, who woke immediately he was touched and commenced his watch, whilst Point wriggled around until he was comfortable on the ground, wrapped his cape around him. It took him some time before he slipped into a deep slumber.

Daylight came and they continued swapping around from resting and monitoring as the sun rose and fell. Towards dusk, they carefully extricated themselves from their observation point and made their way back to the berm corralled defensive point that the clan had been based in for the last day and a half.

Gastro had roasted some wildfowl taken by the arrows and bolts of the teenagers, which provided a good supper with some of the tinned vegetables stowed in the trolley.

As darkness fell, Point and Steel provided their report to the rest of the clan.

The camp was heavily fortified but seemed to lack sufficient personnel to guard it properly. Whilst all its occupants wore the camouflaged uniforms expected, the "troops" seemed to be of mixed age. Teenage boys and girls, lots of females and only a few males. Their demeanour also seemed to lack the discipline often associated with the military.

In summary, it was made out to look dangerous but did not seem to pose much of a threat. Therefore, the clan could either pass it by closely, or even try to engage with its occupants.

Fletch questioned what the benefit would be of engaging with the camp defenders and it was Point who said that the defenders could provide intelligence on the garrison, the town surrounding it and any hazards they might have to navigate.

The discussion went back and forth before logic prevailed and as usual, it came from Raven.

"Yes." She said, "We could make our way past the camp, but it was clearly a place of resource and could provide aid or support to our quest, in addition to the intelligence."

It was agreed they would approach as a clan under a white flag and hope that the defenders recognised it.

The clan would be spread out in case the defenders chose to utilise their ordnance, but they felt it best to show their number.

If the fortified camp chose not to parley, they could continue as a clan, by giving the camp a wide berth and press on into the assortment of garrison towns.

This seemed a simple and sensible plan and they would mobilise it the following morning.

The clan broke camp at daybreak.

Most had been awake since the false dawn, preparing their bedrolls, bags and checking their weapons. A quick breakfast of beans, eaten cold and straight from the Lumber Mill cans. Then they were off.

Using their usual approach of a fanned-out skirmish line consisting of Point, Steel and the three teenagers, with the rest of the clan surrounding and taking turns to push the baggage trolley. Gunner and Fletch took up the rear guard.

Ghillie suits off, they moved out across the wide-open space clear of the surrounding roads and what was left of the town outskirts without trying to be covert.

They were spotted quite quickly by the camp sentries, who mobilised their fellow defenders by use of a hand wound air raid siren.

It rang out its eerie warbling tone that rose and fell for a couple of minutes until all the defenders had been alerted, had grabbed their weapons, and made their way to whatever position they must have been designated.

Then the sound fell away.

The clan had come to a stand, well out of range of only the sharpest of snipers and it was Raven, Point and Steel who made the final approach under the international flag of truce. Sort of.

Steel held a piece of tattered and almost white cloth strung from a branch and they ambled forward until they were in earshot of the camp.

It was then that a female voice shouted out "Do not come any closer! What do you want?"

Raven shouted back "We mean no harm. We just want to parley."

There was a short silence and the defenders voice shouted out again. "Stay there, some of us will come out to meet you."

After a short while the clan trio could hear metal scraping on metal and without seeing how, watched as several armed people exited the barricades, form up into a group of five in a spread-out wedge with a female at the head, leading three other women and a tall youth. With one carrying a pole with a small white flag on it and begin to make their way over towards the clan trio.

They were all wearing Kevlar body armour over their camouflaged outfits and well-armed with a variety of military machine guns. Both groups clearly recognised that the other remained equipped and so all kept firm eyes on each other.

The defending group were within about fifty feet and then they stopped. "My name is Carla" said a sturdy looking dark skinned woman, "What do you want to parley about?"

Raven introduced herself and waved either side as she said, "My name is Raven, these are my associates, Point and Steel."

"We are on a mission to access a base on the coast to get some answers and want to find out if we can expect to encounter any other defenders, hazards, or pockets of the Plague. That is all. We do not need any resources. Just information."

"There is a lot in that statement that I don't understand" said Carla, "Answers to what and why do you need them?" All said without introducing those around her.

Raven replied with as brief a summary as she could provide. How their clan had come together out of a need to protect each other and survive. How they had met Radar and his innate sensing capabilities.

She had already decided to be open and transparent but opted to omit the encounter with the lunatics in their armoured vehicles or the lumber facility to keep the messaging simple. If you could call it simple. She felt it would be the best approach on this occasion.

Raven said, "We know that it is not far to the coast, but this last element of our quest could be the most dangerous after all the battles of the War and the Struggles, let alone any aftermath of the Plague."

"We just want to know if you can tell us anything about the hazards we may face?" Asked Raven.

Carla and the other four defenders listened intently and asked some clarification questions about Radar. They seemed genuinely shocked and concerned, as well as being intrigued as to what it was, he could "see."

"Give us some time to return to camp, discuss these things and then we will give you our response" said Carla.

"Cool" said Raven, as both groups backed away from each other, before turning around and returning to their own people.

Raven briefed Radar and those by the baggage trolley. Steel loped around the perimeter of the group ensuring that the teenagers and rear guard were all up to speed. Then they stood, crouched, or sat where they were and waited.

It was some time before the faint sounds of metal screeching against metal could be heard by the clan and the same group of five came out of the fortified camp again under a white flag.

Raven mobilised her party of three, being joined by Point and Steel, still clutching the off-white flag, as they made their way to what had become a neutral meeting point in the middle of the irreparably damaged runway.

It was Carla who spoke first.

"We are intrigued by your friend who can see without eyes," then paused and glanced around her own group before continuing, "you are the first people to come here since the fighting ended. We respect the fact that you have chosen to parley and we want to engage. However, you must understand that we are nervous of your real intentions. Can you understand that?"

Raven looked at her face and saw the concern etched into it that Carla had verbally shared with them. She realised that she needed to say things carefully and in simple terms if this fledgling relationship was going to move forward in a positive way.

"Our clan is a mixture of families and we have children with us," explained Raven. "We have a paramedic and hold a mixture of skills and capabilities across our group. If there is anything you need help with, let us see if we can help you in any way. Then you can consider if you want to help us?"

Carla held her gaze for a few moments and then replied. "You can camp outside for now but you, the paramedic and your vision guy."

"Radar" interrupted Raven.

"and your Radar guy" continued Carla, "can come in for a meeting inside the camp and we can explain. The rest of your clan must remain outside and in view please?"

Raven nodded and said "That is reasonable. I will return with Med and Radar." Then she and her two clan members turned and walked back to the main body of the clan to explain.

Carla and her four companions waited patiently where they stood.

The rest of the clan, sat, squatted, or lay down in a group on the battered runway and in full view of the camp. Then Raven, Radar and Med made their way over towards the waiting group. As they walked, Radar quietly talked.

"They have no more than twenty people visible inside the camp and in the welcome party. Some of them are children as Point and Steel spotted on the monocular. There could be others as my view of the buildings is hampered by what could be steel walls."

Raven murmured an acknowledgement, and they continued their approach.

As they reached the welcome party, Carla said "We need you to lay down your weapons. They must remain outside until you leave. We cannot take any chances with strangers but do need your help."

Raven slowly said "Okay? However, we think it would be appropriate then for one or two members of your group to remain here with ours, as insurance that something silly will not take place!"

Carla stood and thought for a moment and then nodded. She spoke quietly to a tall pimply faced youth and a squat dark-skinned woman. Instructing them to lay down their weapons and walk over to the main clan group.

After the pair walked by, Raven and Med began to lower their weapons.

As the welcome group stared at Radar she continued "He doesn't carry weapons." To which some of them nodded as the small pile of weaponry was placed carefully on a dry piece of asphalt. Shotguns, crossbow, handguns, and knives.

Then Carla said, "Please don't be offended if we frisk you" and tall woman approached and patted the three of them down. Med held out her medical bag open for inspection.

The frisking was not that professional, but it did the job of reassuring the defenders that no weapons had been concealed.

"Follow me!" Announced Carla and turned on her heels.

The three clan members dutifully followed Carla through a crude barricaded gate made of vehicle doors welded together, with the remaining two defenders following up at the rear.

Carla ushered them into the first building. It was a large dining hall and cafeteria. A small welcoming party was waiting and a table laden with mugs, biscuits and pots of tea and coffee!

It stopped Raven dead in her tracks.

None of them had smelt or even seen coffee and tea in a long while, never mind biscuits. Even the lumber mill had not tipped up any coffee or tea. Radar however, uttered a low moan and headed directly towards the smell.

There was also a little bowl of sugar lumps. The biscuits turned out to be hard tack ration pack stuff but that didn't matter, it seemed like a luxury to the clan.

Radar was in raptures at the smell of coffee and none of them could wait to tuck in but waited politely for the invitation to do so.

"Sit down and make yourself a brew. Sorry the milk isn't fresh, we have no access to dairy products as such, only stuff from ration packs and such like." Said a large lady dressed as a chef.

It did not matter. The three clan members got stuck in and made themselves hot drinks, Radar assisted by Med when he found out there was sugar but clearly could not make it out very well on the table.

As they all sat down at various places around the large table Raven reiterated her previous messaging that they were on a quest to find answers to what happened. The quest was so they could learn from what happened. Move on and find somewhere to settle down if that were at all possible.

Carla for her part explained their circumstances, some of which were obvious to the clan, but it was best to listen, before making any comments.

The air base was indeed an interceptor base. There had been hundreds of sorties in the War, as they fought to defend the garrison town from air and seaborne attacks.

There had been casualties and when the runway was bombed out of use, those planes in the air were diverted to other airfields, those on the ground were partly dismantled and transported out by road to another airbase inland.

"We have witnessed fighting and massive explosions across the garrison town and could only assume the other military bases were taking damage as well." Explained Carla.

"Most of the air force personnel had either flown out or been part of the convoys transporting the aircraft away. Those of us that remained had defended the air base from some small attacks by militia groups during the Struggles."

"It has been difficult. Many died in the aerial bombings or from the Plague. Some without family, just walked out and never returned. Those that did stay have laboured hard to create the defensive wall around what was left of the airbase. The canteen and one of the accommodation blocks."

"The sad fact is that most of our group that did remain, have died defending the base during the Struggles." She paused for a few moments and then Carla went on to explain that all the other buildings had been destroyed in targeted attacks during the War and then the Struggles.

"The control tower, the hangars, hospital, fire trucks and the transport warehouse had all been obliterated. We assume so that the airbase was no longer capable of waging war."

"What vehicles did remain and were not able to be driven and had been moved into the defensive perimeter. We all recognise that it is a ramshackle concoction. We have put together expecting to be attacked over the ground.

Raven now knew that up close, it could be seen that the tanks were no longer useful and had just been planted there to look dangerous from a distance.

Carla continued, "There are several armoured cars that are located in a bunker next to the underground communications control centre. None of which we really know how to use. Some of us were drivers but not gunners. None of us have a clue how the communications equipment works. Besides, there is no power to it."

"The vehicles that had not been destroyed, now sit alongside a vehicle fuel tender. There is also an underground armoury." Stated Carla, which raised the eyebrows of Med and Raven, whilst Radar just cocked his head in a slight turn.

"The only energy source we have is from some solar panels on the roof, along with some vehicle batteries we have managed to rig together without electrocuting anyone. It provides light during the night around the stockade and inside the buildings but that was it. We do not have any heating."

"Down in another underground store, we also possess large reserves of ration packs, dried food, and other provision. However, those of us left now are family people in the main. We are wives, husbands, and children of the air force personnel who never came back."

Carla said " I am the only military trained person in the camp. The rest are happy amateurs I have been able to share some skills with."

"We had a bout of Plague. It didn't last long and we have no idea how it arrived at our base but it killed a lot of people, including the remaining military, apart from me."

"After that, we lost some more people to illness and minor injuries. We have such limited medical knowledge and lack of hospital facilities. It has led to unnecessary deaths."

"To be fair, the whole thing had seriously tested our resolve. It was only our Christian faith that had held us all together." Raven could see several defenders reach out to clasp crucifixes on necklaces, as their story was told.

"Part of the defensive wall collapsed on the eastern side into a metal jumble and a lot of the rest is quite unstable. It may look a formidable defensive position from the outside, but it was all show as far as we are all concerned." Something that validated Raven's own analysis of the situation.

Carla continued, "Accidents have occurred, silly incidents. Some of them became fatal, as I said, we lack the basic medical knowledge that would have been easily dealt with under different circumstances."

"No-one else has come anywhere us them after the aerial attacks ended and a few forays by some sort of militia group. They had tried to attack in the middle of the night and it was during those difficult firefights when they had lost comrades."

"Some smaller groups, in ones and twos had taken one look at the stockade in daylight hours and left. Your clan arriving out of the wilderness has been our first contact with any other human beings since." Concluded Carla.

Raven thought, *"It is hard to believe no-one remains in the garrison town but if that were so, it would make their penetration of the special force's HQ a lot easier than they expected."*

Carla then shared what was really their bombshell news. "This is not a place to guarantee our survival and we want to leave. We do not believe that there is a sustainable future here, as far as we can see."

"We have no idea of how we might survive a harsh winter without heating. Other than the dry rations and cans, there are few other consumable provisions remaining."

Carla said in an exasperated tone, "We had considered using the hidden vehicles but where would we go?

Raven knew then that they would need help to get out, despite their obvious riches. They could not or would not manage it on their own.

"Furthermore, we all feel that the fortified camp seemed as much as a prison as a sanctuary, despite the variety of resources down in the different underground bunkers. Its holding us here and we don't want to be here." Said Carla sadly.

Raven really wanted to know more about those resources, but it would have looked like that is all they were after and it could undo these initial warm exchanges.

There was one further piece of news that Carla wanted to share. It was about her son Jose, a twelve-year-old boy.

"My son fell from a vantage position when on guard during the wall collapse on the eastern side just a few days ago. We think he has broken his leg."

"We have neither the expertise nor the medication to help him." She said sadly, looking down. "This sort of thing has been fatal in the past and I feel completely helpless." Then began to sob quietly.

This brought Med to her feet and her practical best said "Let me help. Show me where he is!"

Carla stood up and led Med out of the cafeteria and across the way to the accommodation block, whilst the rest of those present introduced themselves to Raven and Radar and started to ask a lot of questions, most of which could not be answered.

"What is happening in the outside world?" and "Who is left in charge of the country" which Raven thought *"That is quite naïve considering what has happened this last year or so."*

"It didn't really make any sense."

Radar in turn wanted to know what was contained in the communications centre and the other bunkers. It was he who led the discussions in the cafeteria and Raven piped up with odd comments to validate what he was saying.

He told them in painstaking detail about the shimmers, which surprised Raven a little, *"Perhaps now he has told the story once or twice, it has made it more normal for him to talk to others!"* She really couldn't tell. What was obvious was the reaction to what he was saying.

Raven could see one or two people move beside each other in a gesture of support, or fear. It was not easy to tell the difference as they all looked aghast at what Radar was talking about. One visibly shivered.

****

Over in the accommodation block, in a side annexe, Med found a young boy in a vague state of consciousness, lay sweating on a bunk. A girl was beside him damping down his face with a wet cloth. Med carefully lifted the blanket and saw his disfigured leg and the swelling flesh around it.

Med looked questioningly at Carla who spurted out "Jose screamed when we tried to reset the bones and I have held back from trying again." Med shook her head and Carla gave a helpless expression but didn't speak.

The paramedic knew immediately that it would be a challenge to set the leg with all that swelling, with little hope of saving it. Without antibiotics there was a risk of infection, gangrene or sepsis and a painful death.

Med had considered bringing some of the medical supplies from the Lumber Mill and briefly regretted that before reminding herself that they had all agreed to travel light and fast. Weight was an issue for everyone, and she knew she could return there and so did not bother to bring any. That wasn't any help right now though.

All she had with her, were the small cache of goodies collected from the fight at roasted sheep camp. One unopened packet of surgical wipes and two packs of ketamine/fentanyl/morphine combat jabs, along with some field dressings left back in the baggage trolley. Useful stuff to manage wounds in a firefight, unlike penicillin.

The wipes would be the only thing available to sanitise the wound if the boy's leg had to be amputated but she did not mention that to Carla just now. Best to take a positive outlook. Even so, she couched her words with caution.

"This doesn't look good" said Med in a pragmatic tone, "but I do have something to help knock him out and leave him resting whilst we re-set the broken leg."

Carla looked at her imploring her to continue. So, Med nodded and laid out her meagre kit. Then she briefed Carla and the girl, whose name was Joaquina and evidently the boy's girlfriend, to hold his feet together and head down onto the bed, respectively.

Med knew she needed to construct a makeshift traction pulley and needed a piece of wood and a strong bandage. She asked Carla but she was only able to produce a couple of broom handles and a sheet. Med snapped each broom handle across her knee. Then she ripped up the sheet to use for the traction and bandages for the splint.

They would not have the benefit of a post op x-ray to see how the bones lined up. It would be about Med's eye, gut feeling and luck that the sheet pull would impose sufficient stretch to navigate the swelling and get the bones roughly into place. After that she hoped that the arteries, veins, and nerve cords would all fall into place.

She used one of the combat medical packs. First, she jabbed him with the ketamine. Waited ten minutes and then jabbed in the Fentanyl. The morphine would be used later in the day.

Med tied the sheet around the boy's ankles, using the bed end as a fulcrum, then inserted a piece of the broom handle. As the other two held him tight, she twisted the material until the broken leg stretched out. Then she guided the Femur and Tibia into place with her hands and then manipulated the bones with her experienced fingers.

The boy woke and let out a long scream as the sheet was pulled tight and then fainted, but Med continued manipulating his leg until she was sure the bones were in a good position.

With the boys leg now straighter than when they started, she loosened the sheet, removed the broken piece of wood, and applied a makeshift splint using the bits of broom handle. Then she created some elevation with pillows from other beds and instructed the girl to maintain watch.

Taking Carla's arm, Med pulled her out of the accommodation block and back towards the cafeteria and began the briefing that she felt was necessary.

"These are tough times" she said softly but firmly, "The break may heal but it will take time and be very painful. I have only one more medical pack, which I will leave with you, but you must use sparingly."

"Even then, there may be infection and amputation may be required to save his life. I am sorry to have to say these things, but I am sure you know that I mean no ill."

"Gracious No!" said Carla, reaching over to tough Med's arm. "You have been a great help. We have neither the knowledge nor the skill to have done what you just did. I just hope it will be enough."

They walked back into the cafeteria to find several of the defenders wailing in tears and everyone with shocked faces looking imploringly at Carla.

"For fucks sake" thought Med. What now?

Chapter Twenty

2031 - They are not Aliens!

The cacophony of sound in the cafeteria was only ended when Radar shouted at the top of his voice "For the last fucking time. They are not Aliens!"

"Who aren't?" queried the arriving Carla as Med looked at Raven, who just shrugged and shook her head in frustration.

Radar continued with his voice raised "I have just explained that I can see the shimmers of people and animals. That for a period during the Wars and the Struggles, I could see other shimmers of human shapes, but we were not able to communicate with them."

"It is why we are heading to my old team's HQ on the coast where they were analysing the data I and others were collecting, so that we can find out what happened and why? That is our mission."

"These fools!", he waved his arms around theatrically, "have chosen to misunderstand what I said and think that we have been attacked by Aliens. Now they have got themselves all excited and upset."

"But could they be Aliens?" asked Carla.

"Raven let us just leave now. These people cannot be helped if this is how they think." Continued Radar in exasperation.

"This isn't the direction that the engagement was supposed to go" thought Carla. Raven shared her sentiments. They both shouted "NO!" at the same time. Which was enough to silence the cries of those gathered and shut Radar up as well.

"This is not why we asked you to come in here" stated Carla.

"And it was not our intention to frighten you" added Raven. "There is nothing we know that would lead us to think that we are dealing with....." she faltered, "things from outer space. That is preposterous!" she snorted.

"We have had to deal with gangs of looters and people intent on killing us." Realising that she had now strayed into territory that she had not intended to. She thought *"What the hell, in for a dime, in for a dollar"* and continued.

"We need to find answers to Radar's questions. We can do that in a day. Then we plan to head back east to deal with a problem group. For that we will need more trained people, better armour, and ordnance. It will be a difficult challenge, but they tortured and killed some of our friends and we must return to avenge them."

"It is our intention to choose somewhere that we can begin again. Start off a sustainable community. We just don't really know where yet." Then Raven pulled at Radar's arm and nodded to Med, "Come on, let's go!"

"STOP!" shouted Carla. "Don't leave us here. We will just fade away here. Dying one by one. That does not seem right. It has no purpose. Take us with you!" she blurted out.

Raven realising that this was a pivotal moment, said "Everyone sit down. I think we have all had just a bit too much coffee, got a bit giddy and maybe said more than we had intended to" and looked around her.

Some sullen, perplexed faces of the defenders, a stoical look from Med and jaw jutted out Radar, just stood there with his arms folded.

"Yes, let's sit down and talk some more" suggested Carla and that is just what they did.

They all sat down after making another brew and grabbing the remaining hard tack biscuits from the plate and shared some things that had not yet been said.

Carla for her part had a simple plan. Leave the camp for somewhere else. Anywhere, if it was part of a plan. The steel camp was a prison as far as their group was concerned. It could also be a target if other military factions came across them. These types of facilities must be listed in defence annals somewhere. The location was certainly not a secret.

The clan offered them a way out and escape from this prison. They had already discussed it and reached agreement very quickly before the clan trio were invited inside the stockade. They wanted to be part of the clan. Have some purpose to their lives.

Raven said, "With the greatest of respect Carla, your fighters lack the sort of military capability we would have expected."

Carla nodded and replied "Yes, that is a fair point. However, we have the strength of character. We are fit, healthy and could be trained. Besides, we have the armoury and the tanks. Well armoured cars at least, with small turrets, but still offensively strong vehicles."

"I agree that anyone with aptitude could be trained but it would not be a quick process." Stated Raven."

"Furthermore, this facility would remain a target and under risk of attack. Any training would have to take place elsewhere."

The discussion continued for some time before Raven offered a suggestion that a small team be created from the military trained individuals, Carla, Point, Gunner and Radar. With the rest of the clan remaining outside the steel stockade until they had completed a tour and itinerary of what was contained in the bunkers.

If it were acceptable, the clan could be issued with some additional hardware to take on their mission into the old HQ on the coast - not a problem if Carla's group did not want to let them leave with anything. It had not been factored into their planning and would be a bonus if it did.

On completion of the mission to investigate the HQ, they would return to the steel stockade and begin a demobilisation with Carla's team and move to a new interim camp for the winter, up at the Lumber Mill.

The facility had plenty of space for everyone, had clean fresh water and sources of energy. It was clearly not on anyone's target list (military establishments would always be a magnet to some groups for sure) as it had not been harmed by any of the fighting.

Together, they would see out the winter at the lumber mill. Train those who were willing and prepare to mount an expedition to take out New World Homestead at some point in the new year.

Raven said she thought it best to leave Carla with her team to talk all of this through as most of them were not present in the cafeteria. She, Radar and Med made themselves scarce from the cafeteria, were escorted over to the gate and left to pick up their weapons and re-join their clan out on the mangled asphalt runway.

Passing the odd couple of defenders who passed them by without any comments and picked up their own weapons before entering the steel stockade.

The clan re-gathered in a tight circle out on what was left of the airstrip. Positioned so that they could keep an eye on the skyline behind them and the steel camp in front.

Raven, Radar and Med shared their thoughts on what they had encountered in the stockade.

No-one was surprised at the mention of a cache of arms, ammunition, and suchlike, it was the imposition of expanding the clan with persons of unknown capabilities at this difficult time that caused the most dissent.

Autumn was indeed imminent, and it would make concealment of any revenge attack on New World homestead difficult but not impossible, if they could get everyone kitted out in ghillie suits.

However, it may only be successful if they left today and trekked hard to get there. It would take two to three weeks, possibly longer, to get to a good position in the high pastures above the farmstead. That was before any assault could be planned. A difficult enough proposition. With winter on the way, their timing could be out and it could turn into a suicide mission.

There was logic in an interim camp to re-stock, re-arm and train some additional capable individuals to add to their assault team. Clearly not all could go. Radar for instance would be incredibly useful on recon but would provide little help in a firefight. That could not be said of persons from the stockade with whom they had not yet met, let alone assessed.

There was the benefit of armour and the additional ordnance, but it needed to be checked out and driven back east without being detected. A lot to think about - some of which was incredibly positive of course but not without risks and concerns.

The debate rocked backwards and forwards.

It was whilst they were still in discussion that Bullseye alerted the clan to people moving about where the gate to the stockade was.

A small deputation of five turned up and began to walk over to where the clan was, which stirred everyone to attention. The deputation stopped at the same neutral position they had previously. As Raven, Steel and Point walked over to meet them.

Carla was quite direct and repeated pretty much what she had stated inside the stockade but included some of Raven's words.

"We would like to invite you into the stockade, to help us take stock of what we have in terms of military advantage and provisions to last the winter."

"We don't feel able to support you on the push to the coast but will send a guide with you," and nodded to the tall pimply faced youth beside her. "Hector here used to work off base in a diner in the town and can help you get to the not-so-secret, secret base on the headland."

Radar laughed at the not-so-secret, secret base reference but could not see the steely glare that Raven shot at him. She responded to Carla's proposal with "Just the military experts or all of us?"

Carla paused for only a moment and said, "You may as well all come in, we don't have any more secrets. To be fair, we don't really know what we have. I was an MT driver, not really a combatant. I just learned how to handle a gun and have done my best to help others in our family of friends and associates. Follow me."

At that, she and the small deputation turned on their heels and headed back to the stockade, which almost caught out the clan for a moment. There was a brief discussion and some concern expressed of a possible ambush inside the stockade. Then Raven called them all forward.

They still approached the steel-clad defences with some caution and not all at the same time. They strung out a bit and eventually entered the stockade in ones and twos.

Whilst their concern was justified, it melted away once they got into the stockade and those entering for the first time smelled the coffee, which did lower the psychological barriers somewhat.

There were some awkward moments in that first hour or so as introductions were carried out. It was difficult to remember everyone's names as there were too many for people from either group to memorise.

What did become apparent was the mixture of skills and capabilities amongst the group of defenders. Drivers, chefs, and some of the children were comfortable handling weapons but had hardly fired a shot in anger.

The stockade population consisted of eleven female adults, four male adults, ten teenagers and three young children. Not much from an air force camp that once contained over three hundred personnel and their families. Such was the devastation from the Plague, Wars and Struggles.

Raven thought *"it is odd that the stockade has never come under sustained ground attack. Just the bombing during the Wars and the sporadic attempts during the Struggles."*

Whilst it was not immediately evident, some of those who remained had struck up intimate relationships since their previous partners had left and never returned.

There was little space in the accommodation block, so the clan agreed to bed down in the cafeteria overnight whilst a small group made up of Carla, Point, Gunner and Radar made a tour of the underground bunkers.

Gastro found his counterpart amongst the defenders, a well-built and quite butch former air force chef called Bee and consulted with her on what supper might look like. The defenders were overwhelmed by the amount of game the clan had brought in with them. Canned meat had been their fare for such a long time, and it seemed a decent exchange to share the game and receive coffee in return.

It certainly helped to create some conversations between the two groups, but it was not a full guard down kind of thing. Just light and easy conversation. Each kept their personal weapons within reach, without being overt about it.

The underground tour went much better than expected.

On the downside, there was an array of complicated communications equipment, none of which anyone had any experience of operating. Besides, there was no power supply to it. That part of the bunker was contained within a steel lined bomb proof and reinforced concrete membrane. For now, they agreed to close and lock the door.

The military transport bunker was a bit of a goldmine, two 8-wheeled armoured cars with twin barrelled heavy machine gun turrets. Room for a dozen troops in the rear and a crew of three.

A half-track personnel carrier, lightly armoured but capable of holding twenty troops, along with a large equipment trailer. It was also mounted with a large calibre heavy machine gun.

Completing the inventory was a heavy-duty haulage tractor attached to a large, armoured fuel bowser and a separate bunded fuel tank that contained several thousand litres of fuel. If the gauges indicated the correct data.

Altogether, a road fleet capable of carrying the clan and the stockade defenders from here to the lumber mill and probably beyond to carry the fight in the revenge attack onto New World Homestead. Along with a lot of provisions.

However, the jewel in the crown was the armoury. It was huge. There were several parts to it, all separated by hefty steel blast doors. At the runway end it was all the ordnance that was required by the fighter jets.

Whilst the runways above had not survived their encounter with enemies, the jet planes armoury underneath was well-protected. Sadly, little of what was contained in there was of any use right now. So, like the communications control centre, it was locked up for another day.

It was the rest of the armoury that was of interest. Tripod mounted heavy machine guns, light machine guns, assault guns and countless boxes of ammunition for all of them, plus the heavier ordnance on the vehicles.

Boxes of grenades sat beside mines and mortar rounds. Mortar tubes and plates, shoulder fired anti-air missiles and rocket propelled grenade launchers.

Rack upon rack of assault machine guns. Lockers full of steel helmets and Kevlar body armour. Not the vest type worn by the clan, but the full kit worn by riot troops, with arm, shoulder, and leg plates. A veritable treasure chest.

Point and Gunners eyes lit up at what was held in there. They did not bother to try and count it and in discussions later in the evening, merely referred to it as "loads of stuff." Which was a fair description in non-technical terms.

What was surprising to the clan was the amount of ordnance in there and why it had not been taken when the last aircraft left the airfield by road. Perhaps they were to return and collect all the arms and ammunition but never made it back.

Carla and her team did not really know. They did talk about an expected return by their former comrades, wives, and husbands but it just did not happen. They had mourned for a long time over the loss of their loved ones and some still did.

Raven thought about the number of burnt-out vehicle convoys they had encountered on their travels west. The Wars and Struggles had been ruthless and fought relentlessly. No quarter given by anyone. It was of no surprise to her that no-one had returned.

Bee had taken Gastro and Med around her provisions store bunker and later they all shared the news on the amount of dried and canned food that could be gathered and taken with them when they did depart.

Med had called in to see Carla's son Jose, to see how he was progressing. It was not a pretty sight.

The swelling had hardly shifted, and Joaquina reported that he was barely conscious. Med knew that he needed penicillin, but their only source was up in the hills at the lumber facility.

Not a positive situation.

She returned to the cafeteria to brief Raven and left Carla tending her son for a while.

Later that evening Raven called a small group together to plan the next day's activities. The run across town and to the not-so-secret, secret base as it now seemed to be called. *"Everyone knew it was there. Hardly secret at all!"* She thought.

Carla and Hector from the stockade, Radar, Point and Steel, with Raven acting as the chair.

Her leadership style was flexible. Sometimes from the front, sometimes from the rear. It depended on the circumstances. She was a clever leader, and everyone acknowledged that.

As ever with these planning meetings there were options. Some less obvious than others but Raven had learned to let those taking responsibility for the activities to set the pace. Let them share their observations, concerns, and expectations.

Then it was fair to let those with doubts have their say, before she added her own analysis and synopsis by way of a suggested direction. A clever leader.

It really came down to a fundamental that they all bought into. The stockade would pack the provisions and a selected list of arms and ammunition down in the bunkers. The vehicle convoy would not leave until the clan returned from the mission.

To take any of the vehicles with them to the coast, would incur a delay in stocking them on return, in addition to any damage, losses incurred if they met any resistance could have a serious impact on their retreat to the Lumber Mill.

Furthermore, the sound of the vehicles could also alert any others to their presence and it was a risk best avoided. Therefore, they would not be using the mechanised armour to penetrate the town.

Radar also explained that all the bases' defences, if they still existed, would be monitoring the road approaches as well as the sea and air ones. They were all reminded of the Maginot Line effect of defences in depth. Radar still had to explain how they were going to navigate those and penetrate the base.

Hector clearly knew his way around the garrison town but had not left the base since the Wars and Struggles had taken place. Neither he nor Carla had wanted anyone to go into the town to explore.

They had holed up in the steel stockade, miles outside of town and hoped for the best. That their families and their comrades would return, and all would be better. That had not happened.

The outline plan was for the convoy to convey all the people and as many provisions and ordnance as possible, along with the injured boy. Should he survive the next couple of days. With the potential for convoys to return and take more of the bunker's contents out and up to the lumber facility if they felt it safe to do so.

The clan had decided to add some grenades from the armoury to their mobile arsenal. The buggy would not be taken into town. Only Point and Gunner were assault gun trained and even though neither had used them in a long while, still chose to add one to their own base kit. "A bit like riding a bike." Said Point, "You never forget how." Everyone else stuck with what they had.

The archers left their ghillie suits in the buggy and donned as much of Kevlar body armour as they could, from what Carla issued to them from the underground arsenal.

Weapons were cleaned. Bow strings were unstretched and stretched. Arrows and bolts fletched, then stowed in quivers and on clips. Spare ammo for the handguns, shotguns and the two assault guns were all cleaned, checked and stored in various backpacks, slings, and belts.

They would enter town with what they could carry as individuals. No bedding, capes or tarpaulins would be needed.

Radar then explained how they would enter the base once they got through the town.

Chapter Twenty-One

The Alliance in the future – in the year 2531

"HAHA!" boomed the deep voice of the big man, festooned with the facial and body tattoo's. The tribal markings that were a cornerstone of a culture and depicted bravery and courageousness. "We have breached their outer defences, it is now only a matter of time before we have our glorious victory!" he shouted as he thumped his fist onto the tabletop, causing it to reverberate.

Li Khan winced at the display of emotion and aggression. It was not really needed in this company. Strong leadership, devoted submission to the cause and inherent inscrutability of purpose was. "Of course," he said quietly and bowed his head.

It served the purpose of the Eastern ethnic Group, or Eastern as they preferred to call themselves, to support this assault on Home Citadel. Inside, he seethed. So many of his society and aligned nations had perished in the catastrophic storms that had swept in from the Pacific Ocean centuries before.

Great Tsunami waves wiping out many of their greatest conurbations before their technology enabled them to get below the earth's crust and the apparent safety from the failing environment above them.

They were all that was left from the great Asian conquests that had begun by the Peoples Republic all those centuries before but gradually taken over by the business intellect and savvy technology-led satellite nations.

Now known only as "EeGees" by the rest of the world. They had combined the immense populations from India, China, Indonesia, Malaysia, Thailand, Korea, Vietnam, and Japan, with the vast natural resources of Australia, New Zealand, and Antarctica to create a broad collective, with technology far in advance of their alliance compatriots and on a par, or even greater than that of Home Citadel in the West. Held together by the strength of their religion. Primarily Buddhism, their church was broad and welcomed Taoist, Islam, and Christian alike.

Eastern had maintained discreet diplomatic relations with the West via the longest tunnel border on the planet, under the Pacific, whilst secretly constructing a parallel tunnel hundreds of miles away that had not been detected.

So far as they knew, Home Citadel were unaware of many things involving Eastern. The tunnel being one and the Eastern support of the Alliance.

Eastern believed they had been left to rot by the rest of the world back in the day.

Nothing that had happened since had shifted that burning hatred to gain revenge. They would arm and advise the Alliance until the time came to take everything over and have all the resources in the world under their control.

This was their mission.

To remain secret and only show their hand when they decided to. The parallel tunnel under the Pacific was another secret, that was not known to the Alliance.

"What is your next step Effendi?" enquired Li Khan, looking directly at the Alliance leader.

"I care not for your feigned politeness Li Khan," said the big man with contempt.

"I have led a powerful army to the gates of the West to right many wrongs. Do not try to undermine the effort that has taken!" He spoke with such intensity that blood had risen to his face, highlighting the intricate facial tattoo's.

Effendi continued to stare at Li Khan intently until the slighter man bowed his head in acknowledgement and looked away at the third person present. General, the leader of the NPL, or Northern Peoples Liberation as their full title is known, or just Northern.

General looked down her nose at Li Khan and then over to their Alliance war leader and said "Yes, Effendi, you have led us well." She raised her well-manicured hand in a mock salute before continuing, "We are now entering the most difficult stage of this war. How do you plan to breach their energy defences without destroying everything?"

"A good question!" Thought Li Khan and he too looked questioningly at the big man for his response. Everyone knew the maths and science of the matter and the anti-matter that had created the energy beam walls. It was a delicate balance of co-existence.

All the nations had them, and all were aware that they only way to stop the beams was to hit them with the same matter and anti-matter mix.

However, that lethal concoction only served to combine and create powerful explosions that obliterated everything for hundreds of miles around. Up, down, and across.

It was not possible to breach them without self-destruction and it was by far, their biggest problem to overcome.

Remote detonation had merely destroyed everything, requiring costly re-tunnelling and massive delays. It was not an option they wanted to use.

Effendi stood facing the pair of what he regarded as weak leaders. People representing all that he hated about this world. Their technologically and supposed superior knowledge, their resources and what they had done, or not done in their past.

The Central communities had fared the worst before the loss of the ozone layer. They were mainly from the poorest nations. The war torn African and middle eastern and east European continents. It had taken sacrifice on a massive scale to literally dig down beneath the earth with their bare hands.

Rudimentary mask filters and antiquated breathing apparatus meant that millions died in the toxic fumed passageways and tunnels before they were able to purchase old technology from the West at vastly inflated values.

Paid for by slave labour.

So many children and young people had been sent West in exchange for the basic ability to survive.

Effendi represented a people that were angry with everyone for leaving them to fend for themselves and to lose so many friends and family members.

They trusted no one. Particularly the secretive people from the East and the old colonial masters from the North. None could forget how the Europeans had divided up Africa and the Middle East as though it was one giant cake for the invaders to eat. *"We have long memories."* He thought but did not say aloud and knew that he was leading a Jihad. A holy war. Allahu Akbar.

It was a great source of pride to Effendi to know that it was his warriors. His men and women who led the assaults on the West. Their fighting prowess was unmatched on this planet and they would prevail. Then they would sort out these weak nations that funded the war and emerge as the one true society in this world. *"To the victors the spoils"*, he thought, and he would ensure that his nation emerged as the victors.

"Unlike you." Effendi looked pointedly at his two companions and wafted his arm at them as he spoke. "We have people on the inside of Home Citadel." He paused for effect, then said with a firm nod "Who are going to power the energy defences down."

This made Li Khan and the General sit up and take notice at this new development.

"Please explain?" asked the General in her warmest tones and a wave of her hand to ask their leader to clarify.

"It was interesting!" She thought and wondered how contact had been maintained with any of the vast number of slaves effectively sold to the West for resources. She could only imagine the hurt, the pain they must have felt to let so many young people leave their nation, their communities, and their families. Sacrificed to make sure their nation survived.

"Nothing like the challenge faced by the northern nations!" she mused silently to herself. *"We had all the technology we needed. We had leading edge developed construction methods but all of that meant nothing."*

"Our predecessors had wallowed in their self-righteous belief that they knew best. Colonial Empires of the past and delusions of grandeur that they were better than the rest."

"It had led to political posturing and a hiatus on the work they should and could have completed before it almost became too late."

"For too long they had tried to impose their highly educated and knowledgeable approach to saving the planet, on the rest of the world. Telling them what they could do and not do."

"Imposing strict carbon limits and manipulating the price of carbon deposits, whilst failing to do anything about the clearly deteriorating environmental situation."

"It was years after the rest of the world that the ancient northern civilisations commenced tunnelling. Millions of people died before they could successfully mine down, as the arguments of don't drill here and don't drill there due to areas of national beauty or heritage, formed the major arguments of the day."

"It had made the northern people quite furious. They were angry because they were embarrassed and humiliated." Her face reddened at the thought.

"None of the areas of national beauty or the world heritage sites survived the first major storms that ravaged cities and the countryside alike. The futility of posturing had cost lives."

"The great Northern people were also angry that so few of their vast population had survived and only did so because of hand me downs from Home Citadel, purchased at high cost to survive. Leaders in technology, they had to give up and hand over to the West their leading-edge construction engineers and scientists. It had left them poor and undeniably incensed."

"Northern wanted revenge and to retake their place as the wise leaders of the world."

"In the meantime, they would support this ramshackle and bobtail alliance and win on the backs of the fearsome Central nations and the technologically superior Eastern ensemble. Then they would assume control and be world leaders once more."

She smiled and waited patiently for the big man to explain.

"It could not be as simple as flicking a switch and all those deadly energy walls would power down."

"Surely not?"

Chapter Twenty-Two
2031 – The Coast HQ

The clan along with Hector as a guide, were fully Kevlar armoured up. With black chest, shoulder, and back vests, complemented by black arm and leg plates, and wearing black steel helmets, made their way out of the stockade and towards the various garrison town elements.

They were ready for business.

They took with them their normal weapons, but each person carried a couple of hand grenades. Only Point and Gunner would probably use them, it was about spreading out the load and you just never knew when one was required.

They simply had not enough time to train with and use the array of assault weapons that were available, so it made more sense to go with what they felt happiest with. Though Point and Gunner did carry them. It would add significant firepower which they, at least, understood how to handle.

Each grenade had its fuse set for five seconds. It would just be a "pull the pin (count one, two), throw and duck down job" said Gunner. Keep it simple. Fewer mistakes that way.

It was an eerie walk into and through the towns. Not a living thing moved or made a sound. Something that they all noticed, and some commented on. Why would that be so?

The clan were spread out into two straggle lines, either side of the road. Taking their time as they encountered different hazards. It was the complete devastation that shocked them more.

Not a building stood more than a storey high on the outskirts, with debris piled up in a direction away from the centre of the town.

No sign of any human remains.

They passed what had been another military base, but it was hard to say what it had housed. Hector hissed "Tanks" but not one was in sight. All the buildings, including the reinforced concrete bunkers that housed the tanks had gone.

What sort of non-nuclear explosion could have done that?

The clan moved through what must have been ground zero. An enormous crater resembling something that could be viewed on the moon with a telescope. It measured hundreds of yards across but was not that deep. Massive scorch marks radiated out in all directions and not a building remained.

Then Radar directed them towards the route he had explained. Sometime later, they picked up the promenade part of the seaside garrison town and headed towards the beach.

The headland reared up from the beach with what seemed to be steep and unclimbable cliffs.

The devastation at the waterline was on another scale.

The sea appeared to be full of wrecks. Not just ships. They could make out parts of aircraft wings and what looked like upturned tanks in the shallows. Belly up, like dead mechanical turtles.

Still no bodies and surprisingly for a coast, no bird life either. Nothing. Only the crash of the waves hitting the beach and the grinding of metal on metal from the scrapyard in the water. It was not a pleasant sound.

Up on the cliffside they could make out some of the automatic turrets that Radar had warned them about. Embedded into the rock, with just a barrel and the barest sliver of armoured cupola surrounding them. Some were laser, other were missile launchers and heavy calibre guns in the rest.

Stretching out to the left were all the normal tell-tale signs of what a significant military base it had been. Surrounding it was the remnants had been of what must have been the "Maginot Line" of defences, most of which had been obliterated.

To the right, the beach tapered off towards the horizon with smaller rocky outcrops and hints of other bays beyond.

There at the end of the beach was the waste-water treatment entrance block, tucked into the cleft of the cliff wall. Apart from some fragment damage to the concrete, it had remained largely intact. *"Probably testament to its design,"* thought Raven.

A concrete block of a building with big rusty doors, peeking out from the rocks.

That is where the clan headed. Still strung out in straggle lines and keeping a wary eye out all around.

This was the point that Hector had agreed to escort the clan, but he didn't want to walk back through the ghostly town by himself.

It was therefore agreed that he would stay outside the treatment entrance whilst the clan made their way into it and act as a lookout.

The smell on the approach was exactly as Radar had described it. A totally overpowering stench of ammonia and excrement that was not created naturally but a clever trick to keep nosey people away from the entrance. The smell was foul and quite overwhelming. Exactly what it was intended to be.

Hector took up a position in some rocks about fifty feet from the entrance block and pulled his jacket up over his face to try and keep out the stench. Goodness knows what any previous beachgoers had thought of it when they were sunbathing.

Hector remarked that no-one ever came to this end of the beach and people continually complained to the town council to fix the smell, but they were never quite able to resolve the issue. *"No shit Sherlock"* thought Raven.

Raven could also see the covert camera's disguised as drains to allow rainwater to flow from the flat roof of the block. The rusty doors at the entrance were a decoy and just welded into place to make it look as though it was the way in.

Exactly as Radar had described.

The actual door was at the side of the block, accessed by some seaweed covering and slippery looking boulders, with a long drop to some wicked looking jagged rocks below. A forbidding looking place.

Radar said that it was all a sham, and the seaweed and rocks were not slippery at all. In fact, they were camouflaged friction pads and easy to step onto.

Once the artificial seaweed and non-slippery, slippery looking rocks were navigated. Around the corner of the block and out of sight from the beach, was the real entrance. Guarded by hidden cameras and automatic laser guns.

This was where it was going to get tricky. Radar said that the door was only opened from someone inside, or the biometric verification system.

The system primarily used a retina scanner for unique identification. Fine under normal circumstances one would assume but as most of Radars face was missing this was going to be tough, if not impossible.

There was a secondary fingerprint scanner, usually the validation once the retina scan was complete, as a two-stage process. However, if the retina scan failed would the laser guns fire, that was the question?

The retina scanner was built into a screw on the left-hand side of the wastewater treatment warning sign, with the fingerprint scanner on the right side, also disguised as a screw.

Radar was confident that the fingerprint reader would work on its own and he could get in. He told them a story about a night-time return when it was pitch black. He and his colleagues had emerged from the sea on a boat. Still wearing night vision goggles.

He had automatically looked at the camera and pressed his un-gloved finger at the same time.

The door had opened. It would have been impossible for the retina reader to see his eyeballs. He was not lasered, so it must work by itself. That was his theory.

"Time to put it to the test then" said Radar, in a matter-of-fact kind of way and approached the sign.

He shoved his mangled face in front of the camera after he had swiftly removed the bandage.

What he thought that would achieve, as his eyes and half of his face were missing, no-one really knew. It would have been a funny thing under different circumstances, but nobody laughed.

Then to everyone's surprise but Radar, the entire concrete wall smoothly and silently retracted sideways into the rock of the cliffs. It left a thin aperture that a single person could slide through sideways, having unslung weapons and back backs.

Radar issued a terse "Told you so" and slipped inside to override the door closing sequence.

Then a few seconds later, his head emerged from the aperture and he cheerily announced "Right, come on in then!" The clan went in one at a time. Slowly withdrawing their spread-out cordon on the beach as they moved inside.

The last in was Gunner and he gave a thumbs up to the wide-eyed Hector back in the rocks until he too disappeared. The door was not visible to Hector and it looked as though the clan had just disappeared into the rocks. One by one!

Unsure of the mechanics of the door or the situation they might find inside the military fortress, it had been agreed to leave someone at the beach end to keep guard.

Gastro and Med had volunteered to guard it as an escape route, or to raise the alarm should they see anyone approaching. Hector was aware and he was to keep an eye out along the devastated promenade and to skip over to the block should he need to warn his new colleagues.

The expeditionary force was led by Radar and included the rest of the clan. Raven, Steel, Point, Fletch, Bulleseye, Gunner, Boy, and Girl.

They chose not to use the robust looking industrial lift on offer but instead, climbed up the metal staircase that rose from the ground and disappeared into the darkness above. Another reason that Gastro volunteered to remain at the bottom. Being the size he is, he was not confident his aerobics were up to the climb. Besides, it was an opportunity to spend some short quality time alone with his sister-in-law.

It was a little unnerving, as the larger group carefully made their way up the staircase. Proximity detectors turned on ambient lighting close to where they were and extinguished the light below them where there was no movement.

Onwards and upwards they crept.

Whilst Med looked out of the aperture, Gastro looked up to watch his comrades moving in a slow lowlight glow. They went up the staircase until they were so small, he could not make them out as individuals. When they were out of sight he moved over to Sheila and gave her a cuddle, which she was expecting and turned to kiss him full on the lips.

It was only since the terrible events that had taken their life partners that the two of them found that they had unexpressed feelings for each other. Something that they had discussed many times on guard duties together since.

It was not yet a time to take those feelings to the next level. For now, they were like young lovers in their parent's midst. Grabbing a kiss and cuddle whenever they could. It was quite a turn on. Kissing but not doing anything else in case they got caught.

It was enough to kindle their love for one another in a desperate place and at a difficult time. They both let their kiss fade away. Then they separated and resumed their guard duties.

Up top, the expedition party stopped at the next barrier. Blast proof double doors in a landing that was also evidently guarded by cameras and laser guns. It was just as Radar had described.

The main group waited on the staircase whilst Radar made his approach to the doors.

This time, he picked up a rugged looking handset from a unit next to the doors. As he picked it up, it automatically started calling.

After several rings, a belligerent voice answered and said "Who is this and who are the crew cowering at the head of the stairs? Answer now or die?"

"It's me," said Radar, "Mike O'Neill. Captain of the VR/AR recon unit."

"Fuck me!" said the disembodied voice, "Come in!" as the big blast doors slowly swung outward and revealed a fluorescent lit entrance hall where several armed figures stood aiming assault guns at the landing outside.

Similarly dressed to the clan, in black Kevlar armour and the faces peering out of their black steel helmets. *"They looked just as grim as the clan."* Thought Raven.

It was a tense stand-off.

Both groups held their weapons cocked and ready to fire. It was a moment in time that could erupt at the slightest, so no-one moved.

"Lower your weapons!" Instructed Radar, in a military bark but nobody listened to him. Both groups faced each other and everyone remained armed and staring over gun barrels, bows and crossbows for several seconds and so Radar repeated his command.

"I am Captain Mike O'Neill, and I am instructing both teams to lower their weapons. We are here to help and find out what the hell is going on, not to attack!"

The stand-off was only broken when the same voice who spoke when the doors were opened, addressed everyone again over a loudspeaker system. "Stand down and that means everyone. Lower your weapons. Everyone wait there, I am coming down!"

"Coming down from where?" thought Raven.

It remained a tense situation for a minute or so before a dark skinned, diminutive, and bearded figure bounded through a set of double doors into the entrance hall and shouted, "What the fuck happened to you Paddy?"

Radar replied "Basher. You old sea dog!" and both men embraced.

Raven thought *"Paddy?"* as both men hugged each other for way too long that had people momentarily looking sideways at each other on both sides of the entrance hall and landing.

The two men finally held each other away and it was the little black guy who looked around and shouted, "Sling your weapons and follow me!" in both a statement and an instruction.

"Perhaps he only has one volume. Loud." Thought Raven as both teams took stock of each other in the confinement of the entrance hall, then began to follow the two men, Basher and Radar, arms locked as they both marched through the doors together.

Weapons were indeed lowered, but Raven noted that no-one had shouldered or slung them and recognised that the situation remained tense.

Beyond the doors was a large crew room. Tables, chairs, some sofa's, bunk beds and walls full of monitors.

"Beer, lemonade or Coffee?" questioned Basher to the room now filling with people.

"Everyone's got coffee!" thought Raven "but how come they have beer and lemonade. What is going on here?" she then spoke out loud, "We have some guys down on the beach level, keeping guard. We weren't sure what sort of reception we would find or whether there would be anyone lurking about outside."

Basher explained that there was no-one else outside or anywhere in the vicinity. Everyone had been killed, one way or the other. Raven said one of their group was a guide from the stockade on the edge of town.

It did come as somewhat of a surprise to Basher that there had been another group left from the garrison town that had previously numbered hundreds of thousands. Raven thought that a fuller explanation of Carla's team could wait for now.

It took a few minutes for everyone to make their way into the crew room. Some were sitting, most were standing, and the two groups were no nearer to reducing the atmosphere from the icy setting it had started on.

It was Basher who said "The rest of the clan are more than welcome to join the coffee meeting. Perhaps you should use the lift?"

Steel nodded, stepped out of the crew room and through the open blast doors. He was soon in the lift zooming down to the ground (beach level) floor. The lift control panel showed many more levels below that of ground and Steel raised an eye in astonishment.

Not quite as much astonishment as the look on the faces of Gastro and Med as Steel pulled the lift doors open and there was a moment when it could all have gone pear shaped. It was Med who broke the tense silence with a "For fuck's sake" exhalation of breath.

"No way to let you know in advance" shrugged Steel, "Call in Hector, there is no-one left alive in the town but us. Carla's team back at the stockade and the few guys and gals hiding out in here upstairs."

Gastro shouted out to Hector, but it took several exchanges before he had the confidence to make his way over and enter the HQ lift shaft. Together, the four of them rode up to its highest level at the blast doors.

Stepping out and into the crew room, they found a spot where they felt comfortable. Backs to the wall mainly.

It was Basher who instigated the warming by reminding all his team, who Radar was and what he had achieved with his technology led recon group.

Some of it was known by the clan but Radar, clearly modest, had erred on brevity previously and failed to mention some of his heroics, as his story was told by the eloquent Basher.

It certainly caught the attention of the base crew and clan alike.

Captain Mike O'Neill had served in the military for almost forty years, a proper veteran.

He was an expert in infiltration and had developed a thirst for using new technology in covert situations. His special forces training had led to many different critical missions and postings.

His experiences were without equal. The defenders too had heard of the legend that Paddy had become, and they were impressed by these additional stories that they had not heard either.

Basher had served with Paddy on several very hairy missions and special operations over the years but with his growing age, Basher had moved into leading and managing missions rather than physically going out on them anymore. He found it difficult recovering and having the right attributes to go again.

Basher had marvelled at his friends physical and mental strengths to keep at it in the field and regaled several actions and escapades that "Paddy" had got up to.

It only served to raise the respect that Radar was held in by the clan and Raven noted the nods of admiration that the defenders were now giving him, to know that it was a quite an extraordinary character they had in their midst.

Then Basher invited Radar to explain what had happed to his face and who were these fine people he had brought with him.

Raven thought that Radar responded with a bright but unerringly accurate rendition of their quest in fewer words that Raven herself could manage. As Radar spoke, Raven could see Basher and the defenders all take full notice of someone they clearly respected.

"The explosion that Basher mentioned threw me back into a building. When I came to everything appeared as if I was still looking through the VR/AR headset but I wasn't wearing any. What happened to it and to me I don't really understand. What I do know is that I can see shimmer images of people and animals."

Raven noted that the new people all displayed the same range of mannerisms experienced by the clan. Incredulous looks and mouths agape as Radar continued.

"The first person I saw who was alive was Steel..." The raised hand from Steel helped to identify him to the HQ defenders, as Radar carried on. "who introduced me to Raven and the rest of the clan."

"Together we have had a few adventures, the worst being a lunatic who tried to hunt us all down."

"We met new archery friends, some of whom were lost in the fight with the lunatic." The remaining archers, Point, Fletch and Bullseye all gave a muted wave to the gathering and received nods of acknowledgement from around the room as Radar completed his briefing.

"They have worked with us and more recently the good people out at the old airbase on the edge of town. We also discovered an untouched lumber facility in the hills that has a lot of potential for the future." Radar paused for a moment and then continued.

"Then we came here to find out what the hell is going on." With that Radar nodded to himself that it had included all that needed saying.

By the time he finished. Everyone had pretty much sat down. On the chairs and the sofas.

One of the defenders, a lithe oriental guy with corporal stripes on, was drifting around the room handing out cans of ice-cold beer and ice-cold lemonade to quench people's thirst.

Raven noted that no-one took up the offer of a coffee. Perhaps it was the cheap military instant coffee. Grounds would be as readily available as rocking horse poo at this moment in time and assumed it was more ration pack dried stuff. Pleasant enough but it clearly didn't compete with ice-cold sweet fizzy drinks or a beer.

When Radar finished, it was Basher's turn to provide an explanation of all the things they already knew about and equally, what was news to the clan.

It was not a short rendition and before he finished, another defender, wearing sergeant's stripes, a big tough looking girl with serious facial scars quietly distributed second cans to anyone who raised a hand.

The more that Basher spoke, the more the clan sat open-mouthed.

He provided a world overview, some of which the clan knew or had worked out for themselves but there was much more that they did not have a clue about.

The special forces HQ had been attacked many times. By air, by sea and by remote missile. Its automatic defences and impenetrable construction had guaranteed its survival. Some defenders had left the fortress to carry out missions against some of the land forces and not all had returned. They had decided not to venture out again. Their losses though, were quite light in comparison to the devastation experienced by the clan.

It seemed that the initial attacks were all concentrating on military bases, energy production and industry before spreading out to major cities.

The Chinese attacked first. It was both unprovoked and opportunistic. They attacked to their east and south, focussing on the US, Japan, and Australia. It caught the US by surprise.

In a simultaneous and probably orchestrated and unprovoked attack, the Russians went west and south, taking out the European NATO forces. With various tit for tat assaults by the Arab nations on Israel and into Africa. Various cross-border wars were fought across Africa and between India and its immediate neighbours.

It was a world at war.

Regimes were all trying to take advantage of the deteriorating civil situations in each country. Perhaps to remove a competitor for resources or a deluded attempt to take over the world. Whatever it was, the real intent was unknown.

Thankfully, the nuclear non-proliferation agreements of 2025 had reduced the number of major ordnance devices but the replacement EMP, thermo nuclear tactical weapons and the new and deadly Vacuum Bombs had still taken out each country's ability to wage war remotely.

As the clan looked perplexed, Basher explained that Vacuum Bombs, also known as thermobaric weapons or aerosol bombs, were used on a massive scale. A type of explosive that uses oxygen from the surrounding air to generate a high-temperature explosion. Also known as a Fuel Air Explosive, or FAE, it has a horrible impact.

Anything near the ignition point is obliterated and objects and people around are sucked into the maelstrom of the explosion. People and animals are briefly suffocated before being consumed in the blast. Each side deployed them as they saw fit.

They took out large formations of ships at sea, armoured battalions on the ground and were particularly deadly in built up residential areas.

Raven literally screwed up her face in revulsion of such a thing and probably accounted for the massive damage and lack of bodies, animals, and military hardware in the garrison towns, let alone the loss of buildings.

Basher explained that FAEs had been dropped into the garrison town at the instruction of HQ as it was in danger of being overrun, despite its defensive array. It had wiped out the last attackers. Those who came ashore.

Boots on the ground assaults had been achieved from beach landings and paratroopers dropped close to military camps but the death toll on both civilians and military were catastrophic.

Many had already died in the plague pandemic, then the wars had decimated those who were left. There were too few defenders and so the FAEs had been the last hurrah of the country's inter-continental ballistic missile teams before their last missile site had been taken out.

Fired onto their own bases at the coast to preserve the HQ.

The Struggles had played out on a much smaller scale world-wide as humanity turned upon itself. It had little to no impact on the HQ because there were no serious military factions left within its range. Few from outside of the area would have known it had survived.

Some small groups did try to penetrate the base grounds but failed to enter the HQ and moved away. Basher explained that they held back on using countermeasures to not give away their presence.

Using existing communications links, the HQ had remained in contact with some groups around the globe. Friends and former foes. However, those contacts had been reduced to just a handful as various factions rose, fought, and fell worldwide and regionally within continents.

The HQ held a small team of scientists and data analysts who have been monitoring the situation a long time.

Basher went on to explain that the team's analysis of world-wide communications had indicated that earth's population has reduced by over 95%, quite probably more. It is just not possible to calculate that right now with the limited systems still on-line.

Energy production, storage and distribution had been dismantled all over the world. There were no governments to speak of and no-one with the capability or possibly the inclination to wage any further war.

Some fiefdoms remain in different regions and lands, but they are small and confined to limited parts of the world where there are natural resources to exploit. "Warring bands of desperate survivors," was how Basher described it.

Lack of energy has brought each country to a standstill. Little to no transport and no industry. The world has been set back decades, if not centuries.

Basher paused to look around the room and said, "None of this would have happened if the others had not come to visit us...." His voice tailed off.

"The others?" challenged Radar, "When you sent to me to that Midwest place where that silver shimmer came right up to me. What do you know about them? There must have been data that was captured, and you must have analysed it. That is what you guys do here!"

Everyone looked at Basher, so he continued with his explanation, after a brief pause.

"These were things of national security at that moment in time. When we still had a national government."

Things that they had not wanted to tell Captain O'Neill but really needed more information about. So, his team had been directed to a mid-west town that seemed to be a centre of their activity.

"At first, it was believed that they were not from this planet." Said a sage Basher.

"Aliens?" Questioned Hector.

"No!" replied Basher turning to look at him and then went on to explain in a series of punctuated sentences.

"It is true that at first we thought they were not from this planet, but we never termed them to be aliens," he said, still staring at Hector. "Their form was human. They appeared to try and communicate with us. We just could not make out what they were saying."

"It turned out to be enciphered audio. Something we might use out in the battlefield. Although goodness knows why they needed to encipher it."

"It took a long time to break the system code. We had just cracked it when you and your team were despatched." He said, looking directly at Radar but then realised he would not see the look and added "Paddy" at which Radar nodded.

"All their communications stopped that day. We have neither seen them nor heard them since."

"What we can make out is they are from our future. They came back here to change history for themselves but in doing so devasted our world. It may well have impacted on theirs too, but we have no way of truly knowing."

"What we do know is they unintentionally brought the plague. Some form of bacteria from underground to which we have no immunity. All their communications contain elements of other conversations and it has taken time to piece them together and our analysis does include some assumptions."

"There must have been sort of merging of future and current technology at the explosion that took off Paddy's face. Sorry mate." He said whilst reaching out and gripping Radar's shoulder. "We just have no way of knowing how or why. Only that it is." He paused to look around at the wide-open mouthed audience that both groups had now become.

"Some of this must have been new news for the security detail" thought Raven.

Basher continued, "We think that they tried to help, to stop the plague they had inadvertently created, to stop the wars."

"We know this from the deciphered communications."

"They seemed to be aware that we had kit that could recognise they were there, but the explosion that nearly killed Paddy, seemed to bring that to an end."

It was Point who interrupted Basher by saying "But what about the voices I could hear? Are they the same ones?"

"Hard to know for sure." Replied Basher. "Some people claim to be able to communicate with the dead. It is not for me to comment on. Without the data, we have nothing to analyse or investigate. I am sorry."

Point nodded but he was still as confused about the voices as ever. What he had heard today merely aggravated the agony he used to feel, never mind about the myriad of questions now running through his mind.

Basher carried on, "It looks like we will never know for sure what they were trying to achieve." He turned once more to face Radar and said, "I am sorry to say that we thought you were dead Paddy." He continued to grip Radar by the shoulder "and I am so glad you are not" he said. Then he stopped speaking.

The awkward silence was interrupted by Raven, who asked "So, what do we do now?"

Basher looked at her and said, "A lot of that depends on what you want to do?"

"I guess so…" replied Raven "but we have a lot of questions to ask first. I think that will help all of us to understand where our little group fits in with the big picture, so to speak."

There were nods and some murmurs of agreement around the crew room.

"So how come you have ice-cold beer and cans of fizzy?" questioned Raven.

Basher laughed out loud and said "Ha, ha, I love your sense of priorities" then slowly shook his head from side-to-side whist still smiling. He went on to explain a lot more about what they had and why.

"The special forces HQ has an independent small nuclear power source that can be maintained for the foreseeable future. However, there is no expertise to do anything more than that."

"At some point, the HQ will need to deactivate it by drowning it. Not a worry right now but something that has to form part of a plan. The reactor sits down in the bowels of the base, below sea level."

"Through international communication, it has been revealed that a vast number of major disasters have occurred world-wide, following attacks on nuclear facilities."

"Meltdowns of different types of nuclear reactors must have occurred at most, if not all the world's nuclear generators. This has resulted in many no-go areas that will remain radioactive for hundreds and hundreds of years."

"The true extent of the damage may never be known for a long time as there are no communications in place with some of the countries that are known to use nuclear power."

"The HQ team maintain a listening watch and communicate with those countries who have been able to retain similar levels of technology, but we know that it is not every country."

"The limited verbal collaboration has deduced that If there is to be any hope for the future, the fighting must stop. Humanity must concentrate more on surviving and thriving. Otherwise, extinction beckons, which it would if nothing changes for the better."

"We need to engender an approach to providing mutual aid and assistance and somehow overcome all the hate and enmity that has infected the world, if we are to truly survive." Is how his sermon ended.

Then he turned to face Raven and spoke. "With regards to Raven's question about ice-cold beer and cans of fizzy pop." Basher looked directly at her when he spoke with a sort of smile.

"HQ is running out of consumables. The beer and fizzy stocks are all out of date and fading fast. Once the stock is gone in the HQ there will not be replacements unless someone can brew alcohol, make drinks other than plain water, or grow grain to make bread. We are just using it up before it wastes."

"The freezer and stores are almost empty. HQ has probably two- or three-months' worth of provisions. Possibly enough to last the winter if they can be supplemented. If not, then rationing them would need to be imposed to see HQ through the bleak months."

"Humanity needs some sort of return to some form of hunter gatherer and farmer to guarantee survival. Trading surplus produce for payment in kind"

It should not have been a surprise but looking around the crew room, Raven could see that everyone, including the clan and HQ base members, were all looking dejected.

Raven responded. "It is not our intention to remain here Basher or use any of your resources. Our mission was to accompany Radar, sorry Paddy, here so that he could gain some understanding of what happened to him."

"We have all agreed to take revenge on our lost comrades by returning east to find the crazy tyrant out in the farmlands. That will be a risky mission and there is doubt that we will all survive it."

"However, that idea was formulated in a desperate place, when we knew less. I think we will need to reflect on what you have said and as a clan, discuss that again before we do anything about it."

"In the meantime, I can say that there are more than enough dried provisions at the Steel Stockade to see both our groups through this winter. We just need to get ourselves organised."

"It is still our plan to evacuate Carla's team from the Steel Stockade and take refuge in the lumber mill for the winter. It has fuel for the generators and there is heating, lighting and basic but good, accommodation. It seems to be isolated from any other groups and will be a safe base for us."

"We just need a way of doing all of that, remaining in contact and planning for our future survival. A lot to think about."

Looking around the crew room, Raven could see that there were a lot of stoic looking faces, with most of them nodding in some form of agreement.

Basher said, "We don't seem to have as many enemies at the gates than perhaps we first thought of....." he mused for a moment and then continued, "Let's sit down and plan this properly."

"Our HQ team can support you in the evacuation and together we can take stock of what we have as combined resources. There are some vehicles here that have not seen light of day in a long time. we can use some or all of those." He turned to his security detail and said, "Corporal Yoshida?" the diminutive oriental soldier stood up and said "Sir?"

"Let us make everyone feel properly at home. Show some of the military guys" and he looked around at Raven, who pointed to Gunner and Point, "What we have here and agree a plan of getting the vehicles out to help each other."

Raven interrupted and said, "We also need some medical supplies to treat the young boy at the Steel Stockade."

"...and medical supplies" continued Basher. "I will take Paddy, Raven and Sergeant Martinez" pointing to the chunky scarred girl, "into the control room and we can make a plan for our next steps and alert the Doc!"

"The rest of you can introduce yourselves properly and show everyone around the base and brief the rest of the team as you find them at their stations."

With that he led the way into the control room, followed by Paddy, Raven and the big sergeant.

"So, tell me more about what is left at the airfield?" asked Basher.

Raven replied, "We are not absolutely sure. There are some pieces of communications kit there but no viable power source. Some military vehicles and bunkers full of arms, ammunition, dried provisions, and other military equipment."

"Whoever designed that base, made sure it would withstand a direct hit."

"I think it has to form part of our plan that you guys assess what is there and how it can be used?"

She stopped speaking as they entered the visually stunning control room. There were screens showing some satellite images and lots of communications bays. Some of the people sat monitoring or tapping away at keyboards wore military uniforms and others in a variety of civilian attires.

Raven thought that this whole image was a reminder of their past. Technology, heating, lighting, air conditioning, proper chairs, and workstations. Completely at odds with their recent times out in the wilderness. It was a world apart from where they had come from and where they would be returning to.

Basher introduced them and gave a brief explanation of what was underway and then ushered the four of them into a glazed conference room full of monitors and fancy Perspex screens which could display maps from within but could be written on using water-based pens, then wiped off again.

They mapped out the known locations from the dog-eared pocket map that the clan had been using. HQ, the Steel Stockade, the Lumber mill, some known sites of human activity that the clan had avoided, and the location of the despot known as The Chief.

Chapter Twenty-Three

2031 – Planning for a better Future

It took some time to take stock of what they had, what they needed to achieve and how each task would be delivered.

There was a limit on the amount of fuel they had, here at HQ, out at the former airfield and up at the Lumber Mill.

There would need to be multiple journeys and therefore to maximise the efficiency and effectiveness of the plan. Each journey had to be meticulously thought through to get people and resources from here to there, from there to there and back before the fuel ran out.

At one point Radar said, "This is like the riddle of trying to cross the river with a fox, a rabbit and bunch of carrots when you can only carry one item at a time and cannot leave the fox with the rabbit, or the rabbit with the fox!" but not everyone understood what he meant. So, he just sighed and carried on listening. Chipping in when he could.

There was a need to find out more about what was in the bunkers at the airfield, in particular the communications equipment. Send aid to the boy with the broken leg and share with them the opportunity for sanctuary at the HQ or whether they were set on pressing on up to the Lumber Mill.

A better assessment of just how many people could the Lumber Mill support over a winter and whether everyone, including the Clan, could winter in the HQ instead.

Raven said, "The sum of the clan and the steel camp comes to 39 souls. A mixture of family people and happy amateurs!", repeating the words Carla had used.

Basher responded with "I lead a mixed team of 53. Made up of 5 scientist / technicians, a medical team of 3 and a combat / security team of 45. A small but compact unit."

"Sadly, we have lost all our special services reconnaissance teams in the Wars and the Struggles. Paddy is the only one from a cadre of 20 air/sea crew and covert specialists to return to HQ."

Down in the depths of the coastal base, the team were shown a large underground military transport depot. Complete with two big articulated armoured fuel tankers. Four Humvee's, four large eight-wheeled transport trucks and four eight-wheeled armoured personnel carriers. Other than the tankers, all twelve vehicles were fitted with heavy machine gun cupolas on the cabs.

Point and Gunner had already whispered to each other how much they wanted to use them to take the fight out to the madman at the farm. The so-called Chief.

They were told that none of the vehicles had been used in a long time, so some of the HQ team set about digging out the keys, turning the engines over and working out what could and could not be used. As they did so, massive extractors turned on, blowing the fumes out of exhaust pipes fed out at different points and dissipated unseen across the cliff face outside.

There was a medical facility, including a doctor and two military-trained nurses. They spoke about mending some sprain injuries and fighting off some influenza outbreaks with use of antibiotics, but none had seen a real patient in a long time. They eagerly prepared themselves to aid the boy with the broken leg when they were told about him. A proper patient.

The lower floors were not accessible because of the nuclear reactor. There were layers and layers of concrete and steel, as well as the rock surrounding the natural cavern that had been exploited in its construction.

All the corridors, staircases and lifts had wall-mounted radiation detectors, linked to an integral alarm system that was also used for fires, attacks and other emergencies.

A cleverly disguised harbour, that also utilised a natural cavern, was protected by massive steel blast doors, camouflaged with imitation rock and seaweed formations on the outside. Narrow but wide enough to permit small rigid hulled, fast inflatable boats to pass through.

Up top in the crew room and at different points around the underground base, conversations were taking place between clan members and defenders about what they had heard today. What that might mean for all of them and their struggle to survive.

Opinions on some matters were subtly changing.

Right now, though, they needed to prepare for winter.

The Clan were determined to push back out into the wilderness. They all commented to varying degrees, on the claustrophobic nature of the coastal HQ. Even some of the defenders agreed that being outside and closer to nature was something they missed immensely.

Some of the security team wanted to do something more than sit on guard duties on the inside of a fortress.

It was Raven who called a pause to the planning stating the need to brief Carla and her team out at the airfield, provide medical aid to Jose but not waste the journey out there either.

Basher said he wanted to send over some communications technicians and some others to check out the bunkers. The doctor and one of the nurses, were already to go with a comprehensive medical pack.

Point, Gunner and Corporal Yoshida reported back that all but one of the trucks and one of the personnel carriers, had running engines and so a choice could be made on what sort of convoy would make its way out to the steel stockade.

However, the ramp from the garage was blocked by fallen debris from the devastation on the surface. It took all spare hands, one of the Humvee's fitted with a winch, and a lot of effort over time to move all the blockages out of the way.

Only then could any of the vehicles could leave the garage.

****

It was nearly dark when the four-vehicle convoy left. A Humvee and three trucks.

Raven knew that the arrival of military vehicles would cause a lot of consternation to Carla and her team, but she could see no way to avoid it. She and Hector sat in the first vehicle.

It took some more time to navigate the myriad of hazards and blockages on the road out of town. Some had to be hauled out of the way with the Humvee winch. Others were manhandled by combinations of military staff and clan members working side by side.

Thankfully, all the clan had decided to return to the stockade that night, along with a dozen or so of the HQ defenders. All were needed as the going would have been a lot slower without them all.

As they got nearer to their destination, and even over the sound of the vehicles, Raven could hear the air raid siren going off. They were still about half a mile from the steel stockade.

Seconds later, Raven called a halt and as agreed, she and Hector approached the stockade, both carrying torches. Hector focussed his on the damaged road surface, as they picked their way forward. Raven pointed hers up at the white flag on a pole that she carried.

Hopefully, no-one in the base would be trigger-happy.

Arriving back at the stockade in a convoy was not one of any scenarios that had been discussed before the clan and Hector left that morning.

To be fair, they had discussed several situations that could develop, including a fire fight, running retreat under fire, not everyone coming back and even no-one returning.

Military vehicles driven by headlight at night was certainly not one of them.

As it was, Carla had kept an open mind and made sure that those on watch were to be prepared for anything. Raven and Hector were recognised quite quickly, when they emerged from the leading vehicle and both were called forward to the gate.

No welcoming committee needed.

Raven briefed Carla on all the good news, without some of the world-wide bad news, that could come in the next conversation. The priority was to get the help in for Jose. Carla gave orders for both gates to be opened to let the convoy in.

The yard in front of the buildings was already occupied by all the vehicles from the bunker under the airfield. However, there was just enough space for their cousins from the HQ bunker and soon all the military vehicles found a home inside the cramped stockade.

Even though there wasn't much likelihood of strangers outside, no chances were taken. All the vehicles remained in the compound. The clan, plus the additional security team members from HQ were all bunked down in the cafeteria for the night.

Carla led, Med, the doctor and nurse over to the accommodation block to see Jose.

It wasn't a good sight that greeted them. Jose's condition had deteriorated in the day they had been gone. The swelling was worse, and Jose was unconscious.

Med could smell the tell-tale odour of rot. She hoped it would be the lesser of two evils. Septicaemia would be impossible to fight under these conditions. Gangrene would mean the loss of part or all his leg if he were to be saved.

The doctor confirmed that with a grimaced nod as soon as she saw and smelled the same thing.

Med took Carla and the attending Joaquina out of the bunk room annexe to brief them outside, in terms of what would happen next. Med told them that they both had to remain strong for Jose. The doctor would do what she could but be prepared for the worst.

Inside the bunk room. The doctor and nurse prepared for a surgical procedure. *"Not quite battlefield or combat surgery but not far from it."* Thought the Doc. The alternative was a difficult drive back to HQ where they had access to a much more sterile environment, but this was now a matter of time and a swift decision to save the young boy's life.

Any delay now would be costly.

Outside, Carla was in floods of tears. It was something she had already considered in her own analytical way. She was not stupid. Far from it.

Med said, "I now need to go back inside and offer my trauma care knowledge." Something she had already discussed with the doctor and the nurse on the way out to the airfield.

Over in the cafeteria the conversations about the future were in full flow. There was the great news on the availability of the facilities at HQ. Great news on the number of like-minded people seeking a better future and knowledge that they had the means to do so.

No-one bedded down. The discussions were full on. They had coffee. Full bellies and a great deal of concern on the health of a young boy in the next block. Someone that not all of them had even met but they were all caught up in the emotion of the situation.

It was some time before the Doc returned to the cafeteria but not before she had briefed Carla.

Jose's leg had deteriorated too far. Gangrene had set in and the only way to save his life had been to amputate his leg above the knee.

It had been a difficult operation, but they had deployed all their combat surgery knowledge to affect a clean severance of the poisoned lower limb. They had put him on a glucose and morphine drip, as well as a good dose of penicillin.

Med and the combat nurse would be sharing the bedside vigil on shifts with Carla and Joaquina.

There was a palpable sigh of relief from around the cafeteria and the discussions returned to the following days' work. To load up the trucks for the journey back to HQ and prepare a convoy for the road trip to the winter refuge in the woods.

Some got their heads down. Others stood watch. Many were lost in their own thoughts. Their own memories of how they had got to this point and the hope for a better future.

Chapter Twenty-Four

The Control Centre in the future – in the year 2531

The gentle blue hue of the Control Centre had now been replaced with a throbbing red glow, indicating what they all knew, that a condition of danger had been declared across Home Citadel and the alarms continued to sound.

"Silence those alarms!" instructed the Leader, "and get some more normal lighting back on!" then she continued in the same forthright manner, "I need an update. Number Two, what is happening?"

The second in command looked down as his hand-held display and looked back up again as if not believing what he had seen. Then he looked again and composed himself ready to speak.

"Well?" questioned the Leader, "Speak up man, tell us what is happening!"

Home Citadel's tall second in command cleared his throat and then spoke, "The energy walls have been powered down Leader." Then shook his head in disbelief and looked back down at his data pad.

"What!" shouted their Leader, "How the hell can this have happened?" she bellowed. "Get them powered back up immediately!"

"We are already on to it Leader. Some of the Patronne have overpowered the security team and taken over one of the secondary control centres. They have overridden our control from here to power it down."

Leader stared intently at her number two and said "They would have needed weapons to overpower the guards. Passcodes to enter and today's enciphered commands to have done that. We have been undone! What are we doing about it?" She questioned.

"We are already re-routing the command back to here and have mechanically shut them in. Security is preparing to enter and eliminate them as a threat."

"Yes." He said, holding his hand up in pause as he responded to a personal audio message in his almost invisible earpiece, then looked up to continue his briefing.

"The energy walls are back up but err... we estimate several thousand of the enemy have already made it through at a number of key locations around the inner keep Leader."

"They now outnumber us inside our own fortifications." Said the number two sadly as he lowered his head.

Some of the control room operators gasped as they brought imagery up onto the main monitors that confirmed the statement to be true.

There were running battles and skirmishes taking place all over the citadel. Hand-held lasers and projectile cannons were wreaking havoc on the Home Citadel citizens and defenders alike. No quarter being given by either side. It was brutal and horrific.

The monitors were lit up by explosions and bright flashes of energy burns, as the destruction of their complex was taking place.

Number two continued, "We….er, er" He stuttered for a moment, then continued, "We, are losing ground steadily and the numbers of our defenders have been decimated." He paused again.

"Leader. I fear that we are on the edge of defeat."

At that moment, Leaders own personal audio kicked in. It was her chief tech scientist and long-term partner, with an update on some calculations based on the devastation caused to their ancestors. The message was brief. "I know that there are far more important things happening right now, but you need to digest this Leader. It may help you in any negotiations with the Alliance."

The control room was a hive of activity as Home forces were gathered to protect vital installations and in particular, the control centre bunker, deep within a labyrinth of physical fortifications protected by automatic laser and projectile turrets.

Attack teams were being directed to interrupt the enemy's assault and all the time data was being transmitted on the power outputs of the shield walls, the productivity of the autoboot reloaders and the number of defenders still alive around the complex.

Their lives were identified by small blue lit spots on a chaotic looking schematic of the complex. As they died, the lights turned from blue to red. The enemy were showing as flashing yellow lights and it was demoralising to see their vast numbers against the small clusters of blues.

Leader turned her gaze from the main schematic maps and tapped her data pad to view the information provided, whilst listening to her lover and trusted tech scientist provide an audio briefing to support the information.

"Data has been gathered from the holotravel and hologram systems, as you required Leader. You wanted to know what the lasting impact would be of our.." she paused, "interventions on our ancestors that caused the pandemic known by them as the Plague and the subsequent Wars and Struggles" the scientist paused again.

"I can report that there was a reduction of 97.5% of the world's population. Some regions and countries have zero population, whilst some remote islands have remained completely unscathed."

"There is no industrial output, no air flights and the likelihoods are, that will continue for many decades, if not centuries."

"We have extrapolated that data forward to calculate what that means for earth."

"Without the original carbon emissions that would have been produced beyond 2031, global warming does not just halt, it winds back a whole 1 degree Celsius, plus, or minus a 20% tolerance on variable data patterns."

"Overall, it has had the most seriously positive outcome. It's almost a miracle."

"Earth returns to a better environmental and ecological climate that it has not enjoyed for over three hundred years."

"The population recognise the danger of producing too much carbon as their ancestors did and concentrate on utilising sustainable power sources. Solar, wind, river current and waves. It becomes a wonderful world that is balanced correctly."

"The polar ice restores, sea levels drop, and the pattern of extreme weather evens off."

"That means the world above us now is not one of storms and untenability to survive. It is a veritable oasis. Our air duct sensors are now measuring pure oxygen. They have never, ever detected that!"

"We have changed the world for the better. Our massive error has brought about a good thing. It is nothing short of amazing!" She concluded.

If her chief tech scientist has any visual link to her Leader at that moment, she would have seen tears welling up in her eyes.

Leader thought to herself, *"There will be no need for our ancestors to leave the surface and move underground. It will not lead to imbalanced societies. All this digging and tunnelling, the enmity, the war. It has all been a complete waste of time."*

"We have become a possible future that will not come to pass for our ancestors. We are down here playing out this struggle for meagre resources and eking out an existence, whilst above us, there is fresh air, clear blue skies, and clean water."

Just the thought of it created a pang in her heart. *"It was a heavenly place we had never expected to see."*

"We now have a chance of returning to a green and luscious surface enjoyed by our forebearers. Five hundred years on from when it started to get better."

Her tears of joy were interrupted when the Control Centre shook, and the immediate sound of a large explosion caused it to reverberate.

They could all see that parts of the structure had begun to fall inside of the control centre, small pieces of reinforced building material, as a rhythmic pulse gun began to hammer on the steel reinforced entrance door.

Chapter Twenty-Five

2031 – The Exodus

The first thing next morning, Jose was conveyed to the HQ in his own truck. Complete with attending medical staff and a small security detail.

He was still attached to several plasma bags via cannulas. Morphine, antibiotics, and glucose were being circulated into his body to help him through this first and quite critical twenty-four hours after the surgery. Helping his body fight the infection that had cost him his lower leg.

Raven had watched as Joaquina had pleaded to go with Jose and help him with his recovery and rehabilitation. Carla was not going to stop her and a quick radio call back from the trucks to HQ confirmed that it was fine with Basher.

The HQ had been without their families who had all perished in the War and Struggles. Basher thought that having some young people there would be a good thing. For team morale and for his medical team to have something to get their teeth into.

Saving the boy was only the first step. He would need help and a prosthetic if he were to become a useful member of their new world.

The truck had been padded out with mattresses and blankets to try and make the journey more comfortable. Even so, the crew were careful in the route they chose, retracing their steps from the night before, knowing the road ahead was clear of obstacles.

It was just a matter of negotiating the smaller of the holes in the road and not the gaping wounds of previous damage.

Carla had made the leaders decision to stay at the stockade and help prepare for the exodus. From what Raven and Radar said, she knew that Jose was in good hands. Besides, he had his childhood sweetheart as a constant companion.

The communications technicians were in raptures at the quality and type of equipment in the control room bunker. It contained satellite imaging software that the HQ did not possess.

It would not be possible to relocate it to the HQ right now. However, it could be used when a smarter power system could be installed. In time, it may be able to be moved. They would need to put a programme of work together to make it happen.

It had the potential to connect them to a different range of satellites and provide HQ with a wider set of tools and data sets to analyse.

Boxes of dried provisions and cans of food were loaded up onto the two remaining trucks. Enough for HQ to survive on over the winter without recourse to rationing.

Once that trip had taken place. All the trucks and the armoured cars from HQ would return to help with the exodus into the wilderness and make the lumber mill habitable for the winter.

The stockade was a hive of activity.

Carla liaised with Raven and together they arranged for all the things that would be carried up to the lumber mill were prepared for transport. Mattresses, blankets and other paraphernalia that would be of use up in the bunkhouse.

Canned food, dried provisions and as many cooking utensils were stacked up in the cafeteria and made ready to go. Bee and Gastro checked that everything they would take on this first trip was a priority.

There was a second pile of stuff being made ready for a second trip if it were going to be needed, or it could be packed into any spare space they had. It had been a matter of getting their priorities right.

There were some tensions in the cafeteria, as Gastro tried his best to explain the differences to Bee about being out in the wild versus the relative luxury of an air force base. Albeit a battered and quite distressed military establishment at that. There were some testy arguments of what was a priority and what was not.

All the vehicles had a once over in terms of fitness to move. Then the remaining two trucks left with the Humvee, packed to the roofs with foodstuff and returned to HQ. They arrived there not long after the truck carrying Jose.

Basher reported that he would be staying at HQ along with all the scientists and technicians, the medical team and twenty of the soldiers under Corporal Yoshida. Whilst Sergeant Martinez and the rest of the soldiers wanted to accompany the clan and Carla's people up to their new base and help them get set up at the Lumber Mill.

Martinez had promised to train the civilians to use the automated weapons. Help set up a suitable defensive perimeter and she held numerous discussions with Steel on some of his gamekeeper turned poacher skills, which the big Sergeant wanted to know more about herself and improve her own field craft. They made a slightly odd couple, with his wiry slight frame less than half the size of her muscular and athletic build.

Basher wanted to utilise the control centre bunker at the airfield and would task his team to come up with a method of how best to use it. Once the technicians had constructed a suitable plan.

In the meantime, with vehicular access now in place, the airfield bunkers would receive additional security patrols from Yoshida's crew. Who would leave a small detachment of soldier there to maintain a continuous presence? They would also be responsible for moving the useful contents of the airfield armoury to stock their own and more secure arsenal in HQ.

Yoshida and his team were pleased that they had something more to do than just look at monitors, exercise, and clean weapons. He went about sorting out new rosters for his people. He also had the task of sorting out the remaining two vehicles to see if they could be used in the transport challenge facing the exodus to the woods.

Once Jose had been safely ensconced into the sick bay and suitable accommodation arrangements had been agreed. The rest of Sergeant Martinez's team grabbed all their personal stuff and staffed up all the useable transport fleet from the underground depot. Leaving just two vehicles for Yoshida.

Then they made their way back to the steel stockade to support the move.

The convoy was a long one when it finally left the steel stockade. The pleasing thing was not much had been left behind. They would be able to convey all they needed in the first trip. The trucks were full of people and stores etc, but not overladen. The route was going to be a tricky one and they did not want to jeopardise it.

What had remained was resecured in the bunkers and under the control of Yoshida and his team.

The convoy consisted of 13 vehicles, plus the tractor and fuel bowser and a total of 64 people from the clan, the stockade and HQ.

It had been estimated by Gunner, one of the few with any real armoured experience, that it would take about 8 hours to get up to the lumber mill in the hills. In fact, it took longer. They had not forgotten about the bombed-out convoys blocking the roads in different places but had not counted on how much effort it would take to clear the way.

The convoys were stripped of all useable equipment and ammunition, for which there was just enough storage capacity left in the vehicle fleet.

Twice, they had to leave the road and use trails to get round major obstacles and that was before they reached the logging trail that would take them up to the lumber mill.

The net result was the threat of an uncomfortable night in the wild.

The clan were used to it and were quickly able to create sufficient areas for everyone to find somewhere dry to get their heads down.

Whilst Gastro and Bee set up some cooking fires, the clan went out on a hunting party before it got dark, leaving Martinez to arrange appropriate lookouts and guard watch rosters from amongst her team.

Steel was particularly pleased to take down a large deer, but it took him and the three teenagers some time to gut it and carry it down to the makeshift night camp.

As an unexpected bonus, the roasting venison drew a lot of attention. More so for those from the two military bases who had no sight or opportunity for such things and revelled in the BBQ kind of atmosphere. *"The only thing missing were some cold drinks, but you cannot have everything!"* Thought Raven.

It was a good evening of joviality as Carla and her people knew they were rid of their steel prison and they let their guard down a bit and engaged in lots of discussions with the clan and with those of Martinez's team who were not out on patrol.

It was a pleasant evening all round in the end, less uncomfortable than they had first thought. Raven noticed the friendly attention that Steel and Martinez gave each other and knew it was a good thing that her friend had found someone he could engage with.

Next morning, they continued their journey, which was a lot slower and harder uphill with the fully laden vehicles.

They finally arrived at the lumber facility mid-afternoon on the day following their morning departure from the steel stockade.

As agreed, Raven and Carla managed all the arrangements of who would sleep where. The 2-storey bunkhouse was not quite big enough and so they agreed to utilise an adjacent office building as well.

They made sure that the mattresses and bedding was clean and dry before sharing out to the various sleeping areas. Then got on with the task of ensuring they had heating, lighting, and getting the showers to work in the bathrooms.

It was all hands to the pump, and everyone got involved.

Martinez and Steel took on the responsibility to set out a defensive perimeter. There would be a temporary plan to put into place, whilst their more permanent solution would develop over the autumn months.

The armoured cars were spaced out to cover all the open areas from the high ground. Each had good fields of fire and some enfilade opportunities were created. Four mortar pits were dug, one on each corner of their perimeter, to create some longer-range offensive capability, along with connecting trenches.

They used as much of the mechanised plant as they could for this immediate task. A mini digger was useful for quickly constructing the trenches, whilst a much larger Caterpillar digger, with a 360-degree bucket, was used to create the mortar pits. The soldiers had done this sort of thing before and quickly set about the task.

Gastro, Med, Bee and a few others oversaw the decanting of the food and medical supplies.

One of Martinez's team was a combat communications specialist, and he was busy setting up their radio to a generator initially, before they had sufficient mains power and kept in contact with HQ on a series of set times throughout the day. Along with a separate emergency channel connected to a loudspeaker. That was left powered up constantly. It was he who set up the air raid siren that had been removed from the Steel Stockade. It would serve as a rally should any attack take place.

The valuable cache was dug up and re-stocked into useful places determined by Carla and Raven.

By the time it got dark they had populated the lumber mill. The canteen was alive with the sound of happy people. Gastro and Bee had put their testy debates the previous day behind them and their knowledge of mass cooking was put to the test. They came up trumps.

After supper, Raven called a management meeting in the one remaining part of the administration block that was not being used as sleeping quarters. They called it their team room.

It had wipe boards on two walls, that Raven was using to write down all the immediate and near future challenges. She explained that with a finite resource of 64 souls, some of them children, allocating tasks and work patterns would be a responsibility of this group.

Raven referred to it as their "Last Planner" and it would reflect the status of all their workstreams, the moment the team left the room. What remained was a snapshot of progress that anyone could see. It would only be amended when they met as a team. Hence the name, Last Planner.

It was good visual management tool that any member of the various teams could look at. It showed the plan and progress against it.

The process recognises that there are many inter-dependencies, not least the people element, it was about timing their efforts to maximise productivity. Each person, each workstream relied on the others to be complete so they could accomplish their own. That was the approach. Everyone immediately bought into it.

Raven explained that she used to use in construction project management from another time and place. *"Back before I lost Roberto"*, she thought but did not say out loud.

An outline of the camp had been drawn to show what they wanted to achieve. Next to it were the columns of responsibility and below it, the lines of activity.

Martinez spoke first. She said, "Our security is of paramount importance and it should be the first workstream to discuss." Everyone nodded, so she stood up.

First, she sketched a wooden palisade that would be erected around the agreed perimeter. She explained that it would still provide plenty of open ground before the trees started and would give them ample views all around the hilltop, should anyone approach with intent to harm them. *"Not untypical of our pioneering ancestors"* thought Raven.

"We need to roster security guard duties from across the adult population." Announced Martinez. "I will also commence automatic weapons training and suggest a firing range here, where it opens out over a rocky outcrop and faces away from the accommodation."

Martinez then added her estimate of how much timber would be needed. What was already available on site now and what would need to be cut down. An estimate of building time and the machinery needed to complete it. All drawn on the planner with the amount of resource and time needed.

"Looks like a fort" laughed Carla, "A wooden one instead of a metal one." She continued wryly.

Raven looked at the sketch and asked, "Why not?" and looked around the table at Carla, Point, Steel, Radar, and the standing Martinez.

Radar stuck up a hand and said, "We could call it Fort Lumber" and no-one disagreed.

They became Fort Lumber that day, shared the news at the next mealtime and communicated that back to HQ. No-one argued. It seemed so logical.

Steel was the next to go. He said, "Once we have a roof over our heads and a secure method of holding what we have. We need to make sure we have enough food. That is our next priority."

"It needs to be viable and we should not rely on dry provisions and canned food for ever. It is a finite resource anyway. There is simply not enough for more than a year."

So, Steel laid out his suggested plans for a sustainable future.

He sketched out the areas of the hillside that had been cut down and others that were next and said, "This will make suitable arable land, with some effort. The severed tree trunks and root balls will have to be lifted. Machinery would help."

Then Steel laid out a simple three field rotation plan.

Martinez interrupted and said, "When we cut the timber down, we will dig up the roots at the same time and create some efficient use of the machinery. The root balls can be dropped with the remaining off cuts into that chipping machine to make fuel for the iron stoves and heaters."

Steel nodded in agreement then explained how his three-field rotation would work. "One will be planted with wheat or rye next autumn, which gives us a year to locate appropriate seeds. That would be for bread."

"A second field will be used in the spring to raise peas, beans, and lentils for the camp and oats and barleys for the livestock. Which we do not have yet but we will need."

"The third will be left fallow for the livestock. The animals will help to fertilise the fallow field so it can be nutrient richer the following year and ready for planting again."

"We need to be able to feed horses, cattle, sheep and / or pigs. What I am proposing is to rotate the use among the three fields is a standard farming technique."

"in time, we will also need a paddock and stables for horses. The stable will also need to house the livestock in the dead of winter too. Building materials will be needed."

I know that we do not have any horses yet but they are going to be needed as a sustainable form of transport going forward. We cannot rely on the fuel we have in the tanks." Stated Steel.

"Vehicles will become something we use on special occasions only."

"The woods are well populated with deer and other wildlife, but we must not hunt them out. We send out longer range patrols whilst the weather is good, and I mean several miles away."

"Then when winter sets in and we need to supplement our diet, there may well be wildlife nearby we can hunt. Easier with less travel. Horses will help with those longer-range patrols and hunting parties."

The non-poachers in the group, which was pretty much everyone else nodded sympathetically at what he was proposing. They had not thought of that.

Steel went on to say "I want to commence the patrols tomorrow. Start as we mean to go on. Reconnoitre the immediate vicinity. The valleys either side and beyond. Map out what is there and systematically deploy the patrols to new areas."

Point stood up to provide a report on the transport fleet, which was now quite large. "We have accumulated a large transport fleet, with what we drove here with and the amount of well-maintained mobile machinery and plant already at Fort Lumber."

"Not including the workshops, sawmill, maintenance bays and storage sheds. I have made a full list of what we have." Then he allocated them across the plan with Martinez and Steel agreement, adding a note here and there before continuing with his briefing.

"The generator runs on fuel and I estimate that we have enough for at least this autumn, winter and spring but we need a smarter energy solution if we are to become sustainable." Then he sketched out a simple wind turbine and made a list of places where they could site solar panels.

Solar panels had not featured in their planning list when they left the steel stockade and therefore were the first thing on the shopping list, or shipping manifest as Martinez called it and there would need to be at least one return trip down to the stockade. Something else that was listed on the Last Planner.

"Furthermore, with some effort, we should be able to construct a waterwheel on the river below the hilltop, add a generator and create another, year-round sustainable source of energy."

The need for the mechanical equipment and electrical engineering went onto the burgeoning shopping list at the end of the planner.

Carla reported next. She said, "Bar a couple of gripes, everyone seems satisfied with the general sleeping arrangements. The bunkhouse is made up of a series of 4-bunk rooms, with one or two single and twin bed arrangements here and there. It is probably because of the construction of the building and best use of its space."

"Each floor has a bathroom at either end and have been dedicated as male at the east side and female at the other."

"Simple rosters have been written out and nailed to the bathroom doors, which essentially give a time of day for each bunk room to be in and then out of the way for the next group."

"The showers are rudimentary but do work." Much to the relief of the clan who had barely kept themselves clean on their quest. They could now look forward to the relative comfort of the facilities. Still, not everyone could shower, wash, or bath every day.

"Water has to be manually pumped up to the water tanks on the roof. It is a tough chore but one that every member of the camp will take part in." There were water tanks on the roofs of each wooden building across the facility. They formed the key response to any building fires, along with creating a water source in that building.

"Checking that the tanks remain full will be added to one of the daily inspection regimes."

"The bath in each set of bathrooms will be in full demand, I am sure. They do take up a lot of the hot water. Therefore, we need to keep a keen eye on those rosters."

"There are some electrically powered heaters, but they can only run when the generator is on and heat up the water in the copper cylinders."

We will have to take care on the generator fuel levels until we can connect it up to Point's future target of the site's hydro-electric capability. Once that is in place it will clearly lessen the demand." Point nodded in acknowledgement.

Carla concluded with a catering report. "Gastro, Bee, Med and one of the soldiers who used to be a chef before he joined up have galvanised themselves into a catering team."

"They plan to cook for the whole of the camp in one sitting for a breakfast, lunch and a late dinner, along with a supper. They have already started to create a list of menus."

"At other times, they will leave out cooked snacks and food on the go pouches for those on security or hunting patrols. To make sure that all of our people stay fed and healthy."

"There is a small hot water boiler. It will be left on around the clock, to provide hot drinks, morning, noon, or night." Then Carla sat down.

Radar "Harrumphed," as he complained, "My input is quite limited and I have to ask why I am even here?".

Raven put her hand on his arm and said, "Because you are a wise old fella who can see things we cannot," which got a few low laughs and "hear hears" from around the room and another "Harrumph" from Radar.

"Plus, you know I enjoy your company," she carried on.

Radar felt himself blushing, but no-one could see through his mangled face and the cosmetic bandage.

"I think we are good to go!" announced Raven, standing up. "Let's get on with it then" and the team meeting ended in a positive mood as everyone went off to get their own teams together and start with the tasks, they had taken responsibility for.

Raven said, "There was a hell of a lot to do" but said that in a low whisper that only Radar heard.

He in turn gripped her hand and whispered back "Yes but we now have some good people with us. We are going to make this work. We are survivors."

Then they headed off together to help with the tasks.

Chapter Twenty-Six

2031 – New World Homestead

In another planning meeting, almost two hundred miles away, on the other side of the mountain range a different leadership style was being demonstrated. One that was less collaborative and far more autocratic.

Chief was pacing up and down the campaign room, whilst his squad leaders in the tribe were giving him their weekly updates on productivity.

Warlord sat at one end of the long table with a clipboard making notes as each of the squad leaders gave their input. "Engineering?" was all the Chief said.

The diminutive pale skinned lady to the right of Warlord reported first, "Engineering are on top of the energy situation. The small waterwheel is now functioning as designed and is generating sufficient power to run the wheat mill and provide all the lighting needs of homestead."

"Production from the solar panels continues to provide the bulk of our energy demands and doe create a surplus. It remains a challenge that we do not have any other method of storing surplus energy at the moment. Other than the tank batteries."

"However, I am working on a plan for that. I just do not have any of the electromechanical raw materials to build a bigger battery just now."

She continued with her report. "I am in the process of constructing a wind turbine for additional energy which had the potential, along with the waterwheel, to provide year-round production, given the prevailing winds in the valley."

"No more power cuts would be a welcome change." Thought the Chief but he did not alter his up and down pacing. Instead, he gave a small and slightly theatrical round of light applause by tapping his hands lightly together as he looked at her.

She blushed and bent her head down. *"To receive such recognition from the great man was indeed a holy thing."* She thought.

Then he said "Mechanic!" and stared at the always messy looking wiry lady in crumpled and greasy overalls. Her black afro hair held up with a bright red headband highlighted a face that at times shone so beautiful, if it were not for her style of screwing it up in a grimace almost constantly. She generally snarled out her reports and he expected nothing different today.

"Mechanics worldwide seem to have a permanent grimace" thought Warlord. He did wonder if they looked in mirrors to practice them, but he did not say anything because she was his nightly squeeze.

Warlord felt he had drawn a lucky ticket when Chief allocated all the women to a man when they arrived in the New World Homestead. He had got the bundle of fun now known as Mechanic and the squad leader of the small vehicle maintenance team.

Her name was Amber, and she was a tough little thing that he absolutely adored. Something she was acutely aware of and knew she could have him do absolutely anything for her. They had a mutual agreement though, to never, ever, let their guard down in public. Hot and sultry in bed but ice cool in their daytime interactions.

Amber gave a sigh and a slightly grimaced look around the table before she growled out her report, "The transport fleet is all fully maintained and can be used at immediate notice. Fuel stocks remain at 55% of capacity."

She did not mention how much fuel had been used up on the costly chase of those nomadic folk a few months previously, or the "Gunboat Diplomacy" missions just recently. However, she knew from experience with Chief, to just stick with the facts. Let others procrastinate at their peril with this dangerous man.

Amber continued, "Work has progressed well on charging the tanks batteries and with my assistant, who has thankfully made a full recovery from her neck wound in that chase." She said that chase carefully of course.

"Together, we have been able to free up and fully lubricate the tank turret. It is now possible to rotate the turret around its 360-degree axis, using the normal controls."

A matter which caused Chief to stop and nod firmly at his Mechanic, she puffed out her cheeks proudly before concluding with her assessment of the heavy machine gun cupolas in use around the perimeter fence.

"Most of the machine gun cupolas are operating fine but a couple have seized up with lack of movement and some inclement weather. We have inflicted some heavy maintenance using lump hammers and brute force, but they are unlikely to recover from their demise and swivel again."

"The guns are fine. It is just the cupolas that have been slowly rusting into fixed positions." She gave a shake of her head in recognition that not everyone was following planned maintenance schedules she had created but it wasn't a point worth labouring on and so continued. "I have now altered the planned maintenance to make sure that the rest do not follow suit." They all knew that it was imperative that they retained the ability to swivel around and provide covering fire.

Chief acknowledged no further he just worked his attention to the next person round the table and stared at his agricultural and farming squad leader, causing her to blush before issuing the command "Farming?" without any pretence on politeness or familiarity.

Farmer Sue was an athletic looking redhead with whom the Chief quite often shared a bed. There were times though when he wanted solitude and she would be despatched back to the bunk room to sleep by herself. It was a fuck he wanted. Not a relationship.

Sue knew that. She despised the man but not as much as she feared him. His temper was uneven and difficult to identify how and why he would suddenly explode. She had been hit by him on several occasions but only around the body. Never the face. He seemed to need to preserve some sort of good guy persona, but everyone in the farmstead knew he was a complete arsehole and a madman.

Sue thought, *"It was only that stupid Engineer who held the Chief in some sort of awe. Saying things like he was the new messiah, sent from God himself. Deluded fool."*

Sue did not show any of those thoughts though and provided the report in a monotone voice.

"Farming is on target. Though we had lost some of the heifer calves to an attack by a pack of wolves that had got very brave. Security had mounted a hunt by horseback and claimed most of the animals." She exchanged nods of appreciation with Warlord.

"That has been our only loss. Other than that, the milk yields are good," and she nodded over to the Chef, who nodded back, "We have produced yoghurts and cheeses that will last into the winter."

"Eggs from the chickens and ducks are being laid on a regular basis and I have no concerns about them."

"There has been plenty of wheat grown to make bread throughout the winter and plenty of livestock to cull for our winter meat needs." Sue exchanged nods again with the Chef.

"Lumber cutting is now largely at an end for this season. We have plenty of trunks rough cut for building material in the spring, as well as fuel for the winter." As she nodded in conclusion.

It was a good report. Chief though did not acknowledge it and clearly dismissed her when he uttered the word "Cooking!" Then he continued to pace up and down their team briefing room.

The Chef, as he preferred to call himself rather than just Cooking Squad Leader, as it sounded much more professional. It was also in keeping with his previous roles in high class restaurants.

It was only that he was part of a group fleeing into the wilderness that was caught by the madman he now knew to be the Chief, that he was here. It would not be by choice that is for sure.

Chef Henri was classically trained back in France. He was trying to do his best with these country bumkin types and the horrible military people. He had been used to sophistication and smooth skinned young men under his tutelage. He avoided shivering and falling back into his falsetto voice to provide his report.

"We have a full set of menus in place until spring." He acknowledged the red-headed farmer with a nod as he continued to explain, "My menu and raw material needs have been shared with Farmer and I have no doubts that they would continue to be met." She nodded back but whether Chief saw that or not, was not obvious.

Henri could see the Engineer eyeing him slyly from across the table. The shrew was his allocated bunk partner, and he could find no words to describe how much he abhorred being with her.

Her scrawny but incredibly strong hands would work on him until she had him hard enough to ride. There was no finesse. No love. No attraction. She just liked forcing him to service her.

When he could not rise to the occasion, she would physically force him to go down on her. Twisting his ears and pulling his hair to get him in the right place, making his rather large French tongue lick her to satisfaction. Ugh. Most disgusting.

Henri's only release was to spend as much time in the kitchens as he could. There was a Hispanic boy in his late teens, Javier with the soft mouth. He seemed to welcome the occasional touch and stroke, which he responded to with excellent oral abilities, but those moments were all too rare. The Chefs eyes momentarily misted over.

"Security!" was all the Chief said. His way to shut the effeminate cook up. *"A rather odd man and probably hopeless in a fire fight but what a chef"* was all he thought as he prepared for the important report from his trusted number two.

Warlord commenced his security report. "Training all the security squad to ride horses has been a master stroke. It has extended the variety of task my people can achieve. Everyone is now proficient in their riding capabilities."

"Our long-range patrolling has run right up to the mountain range." He announced.

"Where the disastrous encounter had taken place with the nomadic group and their former archers." Thought Warlord but didn't say that part out loud.

Retreating from that incident had gone against the grain but those wilderness people were accomplished fighters out in the field. Warlord admired what they had achieved against his own better armed and arguably more professional soldiers. Inflicting more damage on their adversaries than they had taken themselves. It was impressive.

Chief had stopped pacing to look at his number two who had paused in his report. He was looking into space and clearly needed a prompt "Security?" questioned Chief, which snapped Warlord out of his rumination.

The big man continued with his report. "There is little of value out west, other than a couple of small herds of grazing deer. Worthy of a hunting party if we need to supplement our meat for the winter."

"As you now, we have achieved much higher rewards when our patrols have gone north, east, and south of New World Homestead."

They had found several different highly productive farms and ranches out on their travels. Some had been fortified by outsiders, others by the farmers themselves. It had been agreed that they would seek to extend their influence more by diplomacy than by domination.

Rocking up as a fully armed mobile armoured group had done the trick. The Chief called it "Gunboat Diplomacy." It was costly in fuel, but the demonstration of overwhelming power was what it was all about.

Assault gun toting, helmeted and armoured soldiers smoothly stepping out and forming a spearhead formation led by the APC's, had looked slick and impressive. It immediately drew the anticipated and immediate surrender by less well armed civilians, or small militia type outfits.

The "protection" arrangements were much easier to arrange with far superior armament and the farms all came under satellite control of New World Homestead. Paying homage in grain, cattle, and other tributes to ensure they remained at peace.

There was the added benefit of mutual protection as each farm and ranch pledged to support New World in their endeavours to create a much better society than had been in place previously.

Chief called it his Pledged Army and it consisted of over two hundred and fifty souls capable of handling a gun, a bow, or a crossbow.

Largely it meant little change to the farms and ranches. Rather than selling cattle and grain to pay taxes to the government. They sent produce to the New World Homestead in a different tax. They did so begrudgingly but recognised the protection that such a well-armed force could provide should it ever be needed.

It was the modus operandi of gangsters and bullies all over the world prior to the plague and came as no surprise to anyone.

Following another prompt from Chief with a cough, Warlord roused himself from his musing and continued with his report.

"The tributes have flowed well this week and in accordance with the pledges of each farm and ranch. It is my belief that we will be no need for any rationing at New World Homestead anymore." He said with some satisfaction.

On their more home-grown efforts to increase the size of the population, Warlord reported "Two of my Security squad and one of the farmers are pregnant. There will come a time when they need to be taken off their more arduous duties." To which the Chief raised his hand and curled into a fist, thumb up.

The final part of his report concerned the stockade.

"With all the recent occupants assimilated into the Tribe and carrying out useful functions."

"Or having been fed to the pigs if they didn't," Thought Chief.

"It has left the stockade empty and that has raised a question as to its future purpose. Given the protection arrangements now in place and new ones being negotiated with farms and ranches much further afield as new ones were discovered."

"Our patrols are no longer encountering any nomadic groups at all. None had been spotted at all in the last month. That is matched by reports from the Pledged, who arrest anyone they see on their land and hand them over to Security."

"With the bunkhouse now full, and the prospect of new babies, I wonder whether it is now time to convert one of the barns for additional accommodation and perhaps create the school that you had previously mentioned Chief?"

He snapped his clipboard shut with a "snap" as he ended his report with a question.

Not the way that Chief and Warlord normally dealt with things and it drew a curious look from Chief.

"I think that Warlord has raised a very good point" stated Chief looking around at his leadership team, "I want you all to go away and think over how we can make this happen? Come back to me next week with your plans."

"Removal of the stockade will send a strong message to all the Tribe that we have moved up into a new level. No longer do we need to incarcerate anyone. Those who are here and contribute to the whole, do so because they want to. Not because they have to."

If only he could read the minds of those faces around the table, he may have come to a slightly different conclusion.

Chief clapped his hands twice. Loudly. To indicate the briefing had ended, which was followed by the noise of everyone standing and leaving the campaign room.

"Not you Warlord." He said and waved his arm to indicate he should sit back down. "We need to discuss some things."

Chief waited until they all left, and the door had been closed. Then he smiled wanly and asked, "What is the matter my old friend?"

It was a long moment of silence before Warlord spoke. "I know that we still have a lot to complete before we can honestly say that we have a sustainable future, but I feel that we are missing out on something."

"I just don't know what it is. Something is not right here. There have been whispers...." As he tailed off and looked directly at his blood brother. "Things that I cannot put my finger on, but I don't want to carry out a witch hunt to find out. It would cause more harm than good." Then he sat in silence.

Chief just continued looking at Warlord. He knew what his number two was getting at. The Engineer was his best informant. She talked to people all over the farmstead, but she also listened when it looked like she wasn't. She too had brought him snippets of unrest.

Morale seemed to be lower for sure but what to do about it? Chiefs first thought was to rip out the heart of the discontent by a public shaming, a flogging or an execution to get people back in line. That would be his normal approach.

A short sharp lesson in what happens to people who try to rock the boat. However, he needed something else. Perhaps a distraction, something to take their minds off things but what would it be?

He ended the discussion by asking Warlord to leave whilst he gathered his thoughts. There was much to ponder. How best to move forward?

It was a new challenge for him for sure. He was so used to deploying military solutions. This god thing, this community leadership thing was so vastly different, and it was giving him a headache.

He needed time alone to think things through.

There was one thing that he did know. *"This was not a time to take down the stockade. We may have to put some resistors inside of it."*

Chapter Twenty-Seven

The Alliance final assault in the future – in the year 2531

The Alliance assault on Home Citadel was progressing well. Reports were arriving in through the personal communicator in Effendi's ear, from his Tribal Chiefs who were now laying siege to the final keep within the citadel. The bunker where the enemy's leaders were still directing their defence.

All the remaining defenders outside the bunker were either dead or now captured prisoners.

The Patronne who had survived the battles, had come out of their homes and workplaces to provide additional support to his army. Most did not have weapons and just threw themselves at the citadel defenders and many died in the attempt. It was a battle that was costing thousands of lives on both sides.

"Any defence now was futile!" He thought. *"It was only a matter of time before the pulse cannon broke through the final blast doors to complete their victory."*

"Time to gather at the control bunker for the final assault." He spoke to the other Alliance Leaders, Li Khan and the General. "We must join our troops and witness the fall of the bunker. Come, follow me."

Then without another word marched out of their temporary field HQ, located in a services control room on the citadels inner wall and ran straight into a cheering throng of his tribes. Together they marched forward, back slapping and fist bumping whilst singing old war chants.

It took all of Li's self-control not to turn his top lip in contempt at this pagan display, whilst General kept her aloof look on show as they made a much more dignified exit.

Li's enciphered personal communicator had been running non-stop, churning out update after update. The Eastern Commands parallel tunnelling had utilised the sounds of battle to complete their final push. The single tunnel had been shaped into four separate lines, each with its own tunnel boring machine. It remained a complete secret to the Alliance.

On Li's retina display, it looked the head of Hydra.

The aim was to disgorge thousands of Eastern assault troops simultaneously into the fight from four key locations and overwhelm everyone that was left from the final battle. This would complete an Eastern victory that he knew would shock his allies.

Unable to resist such a thought, his face creased slightly as a sly smile took over. Then he recovered his wits and Li Khan returned to his inscrutable self as the march continued towards a rhythmic thumping sound that was getting louder, the closer they got. The tell-tale sound of a pulse cannon working its way through steel and reinforced concrete.

"This was going to be an interesting finale." Thought Li Khan.

Chapter Twenty-Eight
2032 – Fort Lumber

Steel sat astride a horse and looked around him at his wings. Boy, Girl, Bullseye and Jose, also all mounted. He thought it was funny that Boy and Girl had never been appointed names, either their real ones or nicknames. He shook his head gently in wry amusement.

He was pleased with the progress made by Jose. Firstly, that he had survived the surgery and the fantastic prosthetic that Basher's team had made for him using a digital printer back at HQ. The wonder of such things escaped Steel completely. It was like magic to him.

Jose took to hunting and riding like he was born for it. Whilst sometimes his prosthetic hindered what he could do down on the ground. On horseback, he was something else. Steel likened him to a Mongol warrior, able to ride fast and shoot his recurve bow from the saddle without using reins. A fine compliment on his excellent capabilities.

Bullseye had worked with him for hours on end to perfect not just letting loose the arrows but to do so with unerring accuracy and from a variety of positions.

Jose had also developed the silent and covert hunting techniques that Steel had taught them all.

The teenagers were a close-knit group of their own. He wasn't quite sure who was shagging whom because they seemed to swap about quite a bit. Cuddling and kissing one and then the other, including between the boys and between the girls. He was cool about the whole thing and just pleased how well they all worked together. The four of them were inseparable these days.

Their little recon unit of five communicated only by sign language when they were out and about together. Short hunting signals, hands raised, use of fingers, waves and as a closed fist. It was their own language and developed around the one that Boy and Girl had brought into their camp. Neither of them had ever spoken a word.

They each hauled a travois on which there were two or three deer that had been hunted from a migrating herd in the next valley. A fine haul of a dozen carcasses that would give them a feast now and swell their pantry.

It was a good haul. Some would be prepared and eaten. Some of it would go into the chest freezers they had recovered from a looted diner out on one of the highways back near the garrison town. Some would no doubt be traded.

Steel mused on a very productive period at the Fort. One of their earliest patrols had encountered a large family run farm in the valley on the other side of the Fort, over to the west. Made up of three generations, plus in-laws and some employees and their families. It was quite a large group and completely self-sustaining.

The initial meeting was incredibly tense, and parley was conducted under a white flag of truce that thankfully both sides acknowledged.

Steel remembered that It had been a long walk up the track to the farm, which had guns bristling out of every door and window. It was not for the faint hearted for sure.

The farmers were acutely away of their countries demise but had not been touched by it. No plague here and their remote farmstead was too far from any of the Wars or factions trying to take control of the distant towns.

They had just got on with their seasonal activities but had not traded with anyone since seeing the night sky lit up by distant explosions and fires on the horizon where towns used to be.

The farm had always produced its own energy from a small wind turbine, solar panels on the roof and a generator run from a watermill at the side of the main farmhouse.

In the absence of money, which was of no use anymore. They commenced trade discussions quite easily in Steel's opinion. He guessed that they were creating surplus and with no town to head into, would want to exchange for goods they could use.

Steel had wooden planks from the sawmill he could offer. Good wood was hard to come by without putting the effort in. The farmers had resorted to splitting saplings to repair fences, barns, and the farmhouse itself. Plus, other construction challenges around the farmstead complex.

The farm did indeed have surplus seed and were prepared to sell some of their livestock. A dozen chickens, a rooster, some steers, and a few sheep but kept their dairy herd themselves. Though they were prepared to travel over to the fort to trade milk for planks and other things on a regular basis.

To be fair, they had the equipment to keep milk, yoghurt, and cheese production in a safe and as sterile a process as possible. Nothing like that was available at the Fort. Better to trade instead.

The jewel in the crown was a trade in horses, which Steel knew were going to be in great demand at Fort Lumber.

The farmstead fuel had run out and they enquired about any surplus fuel that the Fort may have but Steel said they only had a small amount and needed what they had. The farmers were not too fussed as they had already resorted to older farming techniques using horses. To pull ploughs, to haul wagons and to ride on for transport as well as rounding up the cattle and beef.

The farmstead had a growing population of around forty people, mixed ages from the direct descendants of the original owners, down to their youngest grandchildren. Growing because two of the women were pregnant.

The ranch was named after their forebearers and based on the surname of the pioneer twins who had made his way out here all those decades before. Jimmy and Frank Daniels who had titled it Double-D.

The farmers were relieved to find out the good intentions of the new folk up at the lumber mill, now a Fort. To be fair, Steel made no mention of the crazy man and his farm on the other side of the mountain range. That was still a thorn in the side of progress as far as he was concerned.

It was interesting that the farmers complained about the lack of education for the children, no access to medical facilities and other things that Steel thought were quite mundane but from their perspective of being untouched by the Plague, the Wars, or the Struggles, he supposed they were their priorities.

Knowing that one of the military bases out on the coast remained in good order and there was access to a doctor and nurses, also favoured the negotiations.

Steel made plans for the medical team to come out to the ranch. Doc had wanted to travel in a vehicle, but they were now held in reserve as their fuel stocks were limited. It was a funny sight watching them use a horse drawn wagon for the first time, but it got them out of the HQ and into the fresh air.

Steel gave himself a nod of satisfaction as he thought about the medical visits. They had become a monthly routine for both Fort Lumber and the Double-D ranch. To provide care, advice, and the occasional procedure to keep everyone in generally good health. The wagon also conveyed items in each direction. Fresh meat back to HQ, some specially engineered parts from the digital printer out to the Fort and to the Double-D ranch.

Efficient and effective use of their combined logistics was considered paramount by all the survivors in each of their three key locations.

It was a definite change in practices for Doc and her team, who had to come to manage things they had never thought they would when they volunteered for military service. They all knew it was a good thing though.

Cresting the rise, Steel brought his musing to a close. Fort Lumber came into full view on the horizon. A formidable looking set of wooden fortifications like a throwback to the late 1800s when such things were considered fundamental. It gave protection to the pioneers then, as it did today.

The fort may have looked a little old-fashioned, but it belied a wicked set of defences including heavy ordnance set for enfilade fire, supported by well-ranged mortars and handheld rocket propelled grenade launchers.

Around that were placed some minefields, with claymore mines and improvised explosive devices, along with snares and spike-filled pits.

Sergeant Martinez, Steel, Point and Gunner had collaborated very well, to create an extraordinarily strong defensive position.

There were a number of trails that led to the gated entrance to the fort. All of them knew which ones to use on any given week. There was a regular exercise of lifting and relaying some of the mines and snares, so it was less obvious which was a safe approach, and which one wasn't.

It required the utmost discipline from the Forts population to know which was which. So far, all had been well, and no accidents had occurred.

Their neighbours at Double-D had been warned to use only the main road approach when they were making deliveries for trade or anything else. They were to always approach under a white flag of truce. The track that was covered in extensive enfiladed cover from some distance out from the Fort. The trails were not used by visitors. Ever.

Steel led his hunting party in through this week's safe trail and knew that once the venison was spotted, that it would create a bit of furore in the fort as everyone knew it would lead to a series of BBQ events. The rest of the meat would be dried and hung in the big walk-in freezer that they had managed to patch up and make work.

As predicted, the travois were centre of attention from the moment they approached and were admitted through the gates into the fort. Lots of whooping and clapping from those not on duty.

They began to unload and haul them into the kitchen area and handover to Bee, Gastro, Med, and "Sue", as the soldier chef had been nicknamed. He was their Sous chef. Number two to the other three. *"A boy named Sue"* thought Steel. Remembering the old Johnny Cash song from the previous millennium.

Steel was awoken from his amused thoughts by a shout from Raven up on the new "Keep" that had been constructed in the middle of the Fort. It had no windows on the ground floor, only some firing slits. With a reinforced balustrade around the top floor, it afforded good views across the whole of the fort, with a short tower on top that contained their radio aerial, some solar panels, a small wind turbine and their wind-up warning siren.

The Keep was independently powered and situated over one of the three wells that had been sunk in the fort. Their last defensive position if the outer wall fell. The top floor was also their leadership teams operational planning room. The walls in between the firing slits were covered in simple maps and wipe boards.

An underground bunker network had also been dug out and reinforced with timber. It provided secure access into the Keep and was where their main armoury was located. Other tunnels led to remote points within the fort. Two others led to booby trapped exits outside of the walls. Escape routes.

Steel left the tendering of his horse to his wings and loped over to the Keep. When he got to the top floor, he was surprised to see Basher and Corporal Yoshida amongst the usual leadership team of Point, Radar, Carla, Sergeant Martinez and of course their leader Raven. This could only mean one thing, but pleasantries were expected first, and Steel shook the hand of everyone present. Then he took the opportunity to briefly hug and kiss his partner Martinez.

Basher asked, "Has the hunt been successful?" He knew it was, but it was just a prelude to asking Steel for one of the venison carcases to take back to HQ. Everyone knew that HQ would get one, but it needed to be handed over by the hunter. That was the right thing to do.

Steel duly obliged and said, "I would like to offer Basher the choice of whichever one he wants". Unsurprisingly, he pointed at the Stag. The biggest carcase. Everyone laughed. Then they got down to business.

It was a rare thing for Basher to visit. He only did so to convey world news or advise Fort Lumber on their festering sore. Avenging the deaths of the archers and their children.

All through the winter, the arguments had ranged from one thing to another.

It was clear in Point's mind that he would avenge the death of his wife, two children and his friends. Steel had originally pledged his full support but had mellowed somewhat through the cold dark winter months. However, he did not want to let his friend Point down. It was just an argument of how and when.

Steel was concerned about losing any of his friends in a firefight. An action that they would initiate and not be the defender. Different to almost anything they had done since coming together.

Carla was a little non-plussed. She wanted to help the people who had become her new family, who had saved her son Jose's life, who had given him purpose, training, and the chance of a future when everything seemed lost.

Martinez was keen to see proper action. Sat inside a steel fortress at the HQ had not been her choice then but in this new world, this new outlook on life. Surviving here with these good people and the wonderful little Steel in particular, had created a need to help. To deploy all her skills in making war. In dealing death to enemies. She could add a lot to the party and saw nothing wrong in taking the fight over the mountain.

Basher had left them his copy of The Art of War by Sun Tzu, the Chinese general, military strategist, writer, and philosopher from 500 BC. He suggested that it be essential reading for Raven and her leadership team through the winter. Point had commented that he had read it sometime before but would read it again to remain in solidarity with everyone.

The leadership team agreed not to include any of the thinking in their debates until everyone had read and digested the Chinese military strategists' quotes. Some clarification had been sought about what some of the excerpts really meant but it wasn't until they had all read it that they got their heads around planning on taking revenge.

The team had got used to throwing quotes at each other to substantiate their position. They had agreed on writing up what they considered to be their top ten most relevant, in no particular order.

1. *The greatest victory is that which requires no battle.*

2. *There is no instance of a nation benefiting from prolonged warfare.*
3. *It is more important to out-think your enemy, then to outfight him.*
4. *He will win who knows when to fight and when not to fight.*
5. *If the enemy know not where he will be attacked, he must prepare in every quarter, and to be everywhere weak.*
6. *Move not unless you see an advantage; use not your troops unless there is something to be gained; fight not unless the position is critical.*
7. *The supreme are of war is to subdue the enemy without fighting.*
8. *Let your plans be dark and as impenetrable as night, and when you move, fall like a thunderbolt.*
9. *Do not engage an enemy more powerful than you. And if it is unavoidable and you do have to engage, then make sure you engage it on your terms, not on your enemy's terms.*
10. *It is easy to love your friend, but sometimes the hardest lesson to learn is to love your enemy.*

It was Basher who started the discussion by pointing to the quote marked number ten.

"I would like to remind you that if we are all to survive, at some point in the future there would need to be some end to the fighting. To the war. A negotiated settling of the feud."

Point knew this was coming but did not rise to the bait. He knew what he was going to do. It just depended on how many others would be with him. He had no need to comment at this stage.

Basher continued by expanding into an update from HQ on communications with friends and former foes across this country and abroad.

"It is now clear that the cost to humanity has been enormous. Almost catastrophic. The plague, the wars and the struggles that ensued afterwards have been harmful to our very existence."

"Millions upon millions of people have died and with them have gone essential skills and capabilities. We may never be able to resume anywhere near what could have been considered normal just two or three years ago."

"Natural resources have remained but are largely untapped as there is a lack of fuel for heavy plant and machinery. Some carbon energy sources are being tapped into, such as coal but those opportunities few and far between. It is currently impossible for anyone to refine oil into fuel for vehicles, let alone aircraft."

"Most countries and regions are now using wind, solar and water to create energy. Travel has been limited to foraging only. Sail boats are in use at sea but primarily for fishing as communities are striving to be as self-sufficient as possible. Travel between continents is just not happening right now." He paused to look around the room to make sure that everyone knew the perilous situation that the worlds survivors had found themself in.

"Some good news to share. There has not been a single report of the plague, anywhere in the world now for over six months." Something which generated a muted cheer from around the table, some smiles and some nods. Not from Point though.

Basher continued. "There appear to be countless fiefdoms that have sprung up across the country and abroad. Our scientists at HQ have been able to connect up and use the new satellite tracking capability to start building up a picture of who was where."

"The imagery is clear that most surviving communities had adopted fortifications of a variety of types, as they clearly strive to hold onto what they have."

"We can report that some of the communities have commenced trading with each other but there are also some violent feuds, as some groups still seek to take over another group's resources. This must stop!"

"I therefore want to draw this leadership team's attention to the fact that lasting peace will only be achieved through negotiation and diplomacy. Continued violence will only reduce our ability to survive."

Raven interrupted his briefing with a question. "What if the violent feuds were the result of a tyrant, someone who used extreme measures? Surely, they cannot be ignored. They could grow and cause more damage and mayhem!"

She decided to continue with a lesson from history to illustrate her point.

"Think how the world reacted by appeasing Hitler in the 1930's in Europe. All it did was to leave him the time and space to grow his strength and begin his conquests. We must not allow something like that to fester here, not at such a difficult time for humanity. It must be stopped. Ended now before the cancer of it spread."

Everyone knew what she was leading to.

Raven looked around and saw the determined looks on the faces of her clan leaders, the new friends that had been made with the people of Carla and Martinez. They gave her the confidence to continue.

"We must deal with this now whilst we have the means to do so!"

Basher gave reluctant nod to acknowledge the argument but repeated his message, "Any military action will cost lives. It is my preference that we seek a diplomatic solution. I think my position is clear."

"Perhaps this was in keeping with his self-appointed leader of the western communities." Thought Raven

Basher continued. "There are others. Many others who claim to speak for many of the communities across the central part of the country, others in the south and one or two on the east side of the continent."

The old states, districts, towns, countries, county lines meant nothing anymore.

"What I do know is that there is a common thread to all the communications. We must work together, support each other, and ensure that we have as good a quality of life as we can make under these difficult circumstances."

Basher looked at his audience one by one as he concluded. "I expect there to be further discussions between the fledgling communities before we can even begin to become organised again. To begin to plan our future. A collaborative and supportive future. Not one of enmity and feuding!"

The room fell silent for a moment.

It was Martinez, who surprised them all with her thoughts.

She said, "I detest extremists with a passion. I have listened to all the words spoken today and I support Raven. This tyrant must be stopped now. I also understand vengeance, perhaps almost as much as those who have lost family." and looked directly at Point before continuing, "Revenge must be swift though and complete. Otherwise, a feud is created that could last a lifetime or longer."

She used several of the Sun Tzu quotes in her oration, although she used her own words to describe it.

"We take every single piece of armour we have. The convoy will need to maximise ordnance for an assault on what has been described as a formidable defensive position."

"We choose the battle we want to fight."

"Firstly, it will be a show of strength that may cause the defenders to rebel against their despotic leader. We offer them a way out. Give up the Chief and survive or face the consequences of what he has created."

"If that fails, our contingency plan will be an assault that is overwhelming and complete." She concluded by looking at Point again.

Point nodded but continued to remain silent.

Raven and Radar spoke as one these days. Their relationship could be awkward at times but everyone in the fort recognised them as a couple. Their wise words, their leadership and decision making were sought out by everyone at some point in time. So, they looked at their leader, Raven, to share with them once again what she thought.

However, it was Radar who spoke first. He spoke quietly and said "I agree with Martinez, but we must approach with several options in mind. Not just a full-frontal assault. I know from personal experience just how costly they can be in terms of casualties."

"I wanted to add that without Point and the archers, without Raven and this clan, we would not have completed my quest to find out what happened. Without Carla and her team and certainly without Martinez, we would not have created our own sanctuary here at Fort Lumber."

"I therefore want to support my friend Point and take the fight to this so-called New World Homestead. That is all I have to say."

Raven had put her hand on her partners arm at the mention of her name and once he had finished, added her own thoughts. Raven said "I remember the difficult journey we have all been on. I recognise that we are carving out a future here, but a promise is a promise. I cannot sit this out. We stop this madman once and for all before he gets too strong and before he decides to look West for us!"

They all looked at Steel, as the last of their Forts leaders to say his piece. He did not say much but it was all that was needed. "How could I not support my friends. We plan an attack together."

Yoshida then threw his cap into the ring. "We don't need many, if any, to defend HQ but we must also leave protection here at the Fort. However, I want to support the attack as well." He looked at Basher for agreement.

Pausing for a moment to look around the room, Basher said "We are no longer set up as a military or civilian government hierarchy. We have come this far together by providing mutual support and by sticking together."

"I have made my position clear that I believe we will only achieve a sustainable future without war and bloodshed. However, in saying that. If we are going to war. Let us do it properly."

"We need a plan!"

Chapter Twenty-Nine

The Alliance Victory in the future – in the year 2531

In the Home Citadel Control Room there was not much left for the defenders to do. Only wait for the inevitable breakthrough from the ever-present thumping of the pulse cannon outside.

The monitors showed all their surviving defenders and citizens being rounded up by the overwhelming and jubilant enemy. What was more galling to Leader, was the final act of the Patronne to join in with their attackers in pinning down Home Citadel forces. Many picking up arms against their former neighbours, killing and being killed.

"Perhaps all the reforms had been too late." mused Leader. "For that amount of hate to fester for all this time. Another great error that should have been foreseen and dealt with better before it became this. An act of treachery that had undone Home Citadel."

In the final scenes being depicted on the monitors, it was difficult to separate who were Patronne and who were the tribes from the Central Nations with their facial tattooing and the injuries from the fighting, they all looked alike.

Leader could see the enemy massing outside the control bunker. There were thousands there. Then she spotted the war leader of the alliance. The massive figure of the one they called Effendi. A giant of a man. urging his forces forward.

"This would be the right time to sue for peace." She thought. "To throw in the towel as the old pugilist afficionado's spouted."

"Well, that may be so if any communications links remained. There was no way now to indicate they were ready to capitulate, even if that were the case."

"For now, they would have to wait for the physical barrier to be felled and see if they survived any overzealous shooting from the first enemy to penetrate the bunker."

Leader tried her best to look as though she was still in control. Though she was not sure how that may look from her people around her. She put on a stoical look. Yes, that would be best. Proud but resigned to defeat.

Leader had lost communication with her lover, the chief tech scientist.

The science block was less well defended than the bunker. She hoped that she had survived. Been taken prisoner. There was always a need for good scientists, and she was the best. A brilliant mind and a thoughtful lover. If she could remain alive then at least she would have a future.

If she survived the final solution that is.

Leader spoke at last "Do not offer any resistance. It would be completely futile at this stage. We have lost the day." She saw her people sag. Shoulders slumped and their faces looked what they were. Vanquished.

She continued, "I will see if we can save what we have left and sue for peace if we get the chance. If not. Then I want to thank you all for your diligent work in this terrible war.

We have done our best, but it just wasn't good enough." She paused, then bowed her head slightly to those around her and said, "Thank you." Just as the blast doors fell inwards with a loud bang and a big cloud of dust entered the control room. Along with a shouting mob.

****

Effendi wanted to be on the front line, be the first into the control room. To demonstrate it was his victory. He wanted to see the face of the one that Home Citizens referred to as Leader. He wanted to see her face as he triumphed.

The pulse gun stopped as the blast doors to the control room collapsed inwards with a loud crash and a big cloud of smoke.

Effendi leapt forward with some of his key chieftains and entered the bunker. They were ready to fire but as the smoke started to clear he could see the few enemy remaining had all put their weapons down and raised their hands in the air as a signal of their defeat. To be sure he shouted out, "Put your weapons down and raise your hands in the air!" then he looked around for his adversary.

There she sat on a little raised plinth, surrounded by a small group of controllers still plugged into their equipment. *"So, it was true, they really were physically connected to their equipment."* Effendi had always assumed it was a falsehood wound up in a fantasy to propagate lies and subjugate their foes.

Effendi shook his head and repeated his order, "Everyone will lower their weapons!" and stared straight at the haughty looking woman facing him. He never could understand why any woman would be chosen as a leader, when all men were far better and stronger.

She replied, "I only have a data pad which I am using to keep in contact with my remaining team."

Effendi instructed her "Put it down!"

She tapped a key and placed the data pad face down on a little utility table that served just such a purpose.

He angrily shouted at her "Stand up!".

She smiled and said, "I am afraid that it is not possible," and pointed to the hover chair she was sat on.

It dawned him then, that it wasn't a control chair, on a plinth she was sat on and connected to, but a support for some kind of mobility impairment.

She saw the quizzical look on his face and smiled condescendingly and said "It was the result of an accident during tunnelling. My overalls had got caught in the whirling blades of a manual boring machine when we still have need of them. Only stopping when my leg jammed the semi-portable machine I was drilling with."

"Incredibly painful and I would have bled out were it not for my quick thinking to apply tourniquets."

"Accidents like that occurred only too often back when autoboots were in their infancy and we still operated manually controlled drilling equipment."

"It is a hover chair, with some essential life dependent equipment included, if I may demonstrate?" Asked Leader. Effendi waved his approval and so Leader picked up the data pad and with a deft movement of a finger on the screen, made the chair swivel around in a smooth circle.

If he was at all impressed, Effendi did not let his face demonstrate that, as he gruffly said, "I demand the unconditional and immediate surrender of Home Citadel to the Alliance and to me as their Chief!"

Leader nodded her head gravely and issued the command over her audio network. "Home Citadel has unconditionally surrendered to the Alliance. Lower your weapons and hand yourselves in to Alliance forces."

She knew that her message would be heard in every headset, of every armed defender, the control centre and displayed on any remaining monitor screens anywhere throughout Home Citadel.

Effendi signalled that his technical support was to assume control of all the systems still under control, whilst he continued with his need to dominate the one-to-one situation with the woman in the disability buggy.

She needed to know that he was victorious and soon would be the new world leader. A patriarchal society with no place for the delicate.

He called for the weaker elements of his alliance to join him in this moment of triumph. Only a minute or so behind, General and Li Khan arrived shortly afterwards. He wanted them to witness this, before he commenced the plan to displace them and take over their armies and homelands.

As he waited for them, a whispered verbal report was provided by his senior tech chief, and Effendi was a little dismayed to find out that so much of the Home Citadel infrastructure and systems had been destroyed in the battle.

This was not going to be the complete takeover that he had planned. It had been his ambition to take over the superior technology of Home Citadel so that he could eliminate his rivals but would now be faced with a massive rebuilding programme instead.

Needing to maintain his composure he thought he would take it out on the defenceless woman. "All of this is your fault!" he snarled. "I don't know what you did but you caused this. The death of my tribespeople, of my allies. You forced this to become a war of survival, and it is we who have survived to conquer you!" He spat out.

Leader continued to match his stare. She was not frightened by his demeanour. However, she did acknowledge with a slow nod of her head. General and Li Khan arrived just as she commenced her response.

"Yes, we have brought this upon ourselves. It was not of course, our intent for a war, nor for the war to end this way but it is, what it is." She sighed. Then she waved her hand over to the holography display beside her desk.

"We have created time travel using holography." Pointing down at the small figures travelling through a green and lush wilderness. The Alliance leaders gathered round to see. They had some hologram technology but not like this. This was something else. A product of the greater technical and scientific knowledge possessed by the West.

Leader continued, "We wanted to alter history and so went back in time. Five hundred years to be precise. Back to a time of world stability. When the known environmental challenges were being faced by a mature humankind. A world intent on maintaining peace without the devastating nuclear weapons of the day and taking a greater care of nature."

"We felt if we could descend underground with the same level of technology and skills worldwide. The East, Central, North and the West. Then it would not be so imbalanced to the point that hate would drive resentment. It would have minimised the losses of life and prevented this war."

"We went back then to try and help key bloodlines of all our ancestors. Yours as well!" she said waving her arm to include the three alliance leaders. "To make better use of knowledge. To create a better balance. For all our subterranean worlds to be successful!"

"Unfortunately, our time travel was not successful. Worse still we managed to export some form of bacterial infection to our past which spread like wildfire. Sadly, it killed off millions of people, which in turn has devastated the populations of our respective underground nations."

"Our ancestors then commenced a series of international wars, civil wars and degenerated into fighting to retain the limited resources that remained."

"We estimate as many as 97.5 percent of the world's population died. That obviously impacted on all of us, as people simply did not exist anymore. It was an error of magnificent proportions."

The Alliance leaders continued to stare at the slight figure of the seated woman, with a mixture of looks. Horror by the General. Anger from Effendi and the impenetrable mask of Li Khan, giving nothing away.

Leader continued with her briefing. "We have endured the demise of our ancestors and then the attacks of the Alliance. We never wanted this. We wanted to be more benevolent."

Her oration was interrupted by General who spat out "You could have been more benevolent anyway. You did not need to lord it over us. To take our best scientists, our skilled and capable engineers!" She shrilled.

"Or take the young people from the Central Nations and put them into slavery." Stated Effendi.

"Or watch us all die in the East.", stated Li Khan calmly.

They all stopped speaking for a moment, and they could all hear the keyboards being tapped in the background and the rustling sound as controllers were carefully unplugged from their workstations.

The uneasy silence was broken by Leader, who said, "There is a silver lining in this cloud."

The Alliance heads all looked at her like she was mad but none of them tried to interrupt her and so she continued.

"I have a report from my Chief Tech Scientist. A brilliant woman who has extrapolated the data we have been monitoring. Via the holography and by accessing our own systems data."

"The vast reduction of the world population five hundred years ago has had a dramatic and hugely positive effect on our planet."

"There are fewer people. A deliberate decision to minimise the use of carbon. A different kind of industrialisation utilising more natural and sustainable sources of energy. It has led to a hugely different world on the surface."

"The ozone layers have not broken down. There are no Tsunami's. No harsh weather conditions saturating the surface and making it untenable to live up there. Quite the opposite."

"The earth's surface is now a veritable oasis of calm. Nature has thrived. We can go up there now and flourish in a vastly different world. Of course, the people who have survived up there will have no idea of who we are but with diplomacy, we can make that right."

"We can leave this subterranean prison and breathe fresh air. See the sun. Swim in the sea. A million and one things we never thought possible."

Effendi was now stood with his mouth agape. General was thinking a thousand different thoughts and Li Khan's mask of inscrutability had dropped as his eye was twitching.

Something was wrong with his neural communication device. He could see the Eastern Command assault forces forming up on his iris display but was unable to communicate with his battle shoguns. This was not a time to attack.

The Eastern Command had factored in the potential for Li Khan to die in the final throes of battle and his lack of communication would not stop their assault. It was timed to coincide with the end of the fighting for Home Citadel. When it was least expected that a third force would enter the fray.

It was then that the control centre lighting started flashing red and an attack alarm sounded.

"What is this? shouted Effendi, looking around quickly. The monitors showed four tunnel mouths exploding out of solid rock in different parts of the citadel, followed by an outpouring of heavily armed and armoured Eastern Command Shock Troops firing weapons at anyone in front of them.

A very unsurprised Leader said. "It is probably the east forces that have arrived to win the day. Did you think we did not know about your plan Li Khan? You are not the only one with spies."

Effendi turned and fired a single shot from his gun that struck Li Khan in the face and caused his head to disappear as he shouted "Traitor!"

Leader could see the deteriorating situation and spoke quietly but enough to attract Effendi's attention "You know that it didn't have to come to this. It could have been so different," as she clicked a small icon on her data pad. Entitled *Final Solution*.

A series of seismic shocks began to rip apart Home Citadel and detonate explosive materials in the four tunnels full of Eastern Command assault troops. The monitors then all shut off and they were briefly cut off from all the data.

Unseen and unknown by those in the control centre. Similar explosions were taking place all over the world. In the northern, central, and eastern homelands.

The technology to provide magnetic levitation transport that Home had shared with the rest of the world, contained hidden and well-disguised self-destruct capabilities, linked to the matter and anti-matter mixes that propelled the system. All of which would devastate their own parts of the subterranean world.

Effendi screamed loudly and shot Leader in the face as the explosions rippled all around them, causing massive damage and serious loss of life. Then the control centre ceiling crashed down onto all of them.

Chapter Thirty

2032 – Battle for New World Homestead

Chief woke to the beautiful sound of a songbird outside his window. Its chirpy and cheerful sound drew a smile to his face as he lay there with the sun beaming in through the blinds warming up his room.

"All is good in the garden of Eden," he thought. *"However, there is still much to do."* He rose easily from his bunk where he had slept by himself. He had not required sex the night before and so stood alone with his own opinions as he opened the blinds and peered out into a lovely Spring morning.

All of that was shattered by a loud clanging sound from the alarm bell at the tank gateway along with shouts and cries from outside that immediately removed him from his musing. His instincts made him instantly aware of impending danger.

Gritting his teeth, Chief grabbed his handgun and an assault rifle, then he sprinted outside to see a picture of chaos with people running in different directions. Some dropping what chores they were doing to go and get armed, with others leaving the bunkhouse trying to pull on Kevlar armour and bumping into people trying to get in.

It was messy and lacked co-ordination.

Anger at what he saw brought a reddening of his cheeks and Chief knew that he would have to chew them all out afterwards. This was not supposed to happen this way. All their training and drilling meant that they should be always armed and ready. They were soldiers dammit.

Right now, though, he needed to understand what the threat was.

Warlord, his right hand, and blood brother was jogging towards him at a controlled pace to brief him.

"Sup?" was all Chief uttered.

"Riders are returning at a hell of a pace Chief. They will be here in a few moments. I don't yet know what they have seen but it must be a threat at the pace they are racing the horses."

Both Chief and Warlord jogged side by side over to the gate where the tank stood guard.

Chief looked around and saw that some semblance of order was now being put into place with weapons being checked, heavy machine guns on the cupolas cocked and the tank turret gave a short test swivel left and right. Indicating that someone had clearly got into the hull and was preparing it to fire.

Chief gave a nod of approval to his left and to his right. He could also hear check calls going on around him as their mesh net radio system came alive, as each operator was being verified. Who they were and where in the fortifications they were standing guard.

Warlord handed him a headset. There wasn't enough to go around for everyone. Each squad leader had one and they were allocated to key stations around the perimeter.

Chief knew that the headsets were normally not used and left on charge from the solar panels until really needed. Seemed this was just such an occasion to distribute them out.

Coming towards them was one of their long-range patrols, all carried out on horseback these days. Four riders pushing their horses hard, with a massive dust cloud trailing in their wake as they pounded along the dirt track sloping down toward the farmstead.

The gate and chicane were opened to let them ride straight through at pace and then immediately closed behind them. Everyone looked back out, trying to peer through the dust cloud with weapons pointed towards whatever was coming.

The horses were all pulled up and the patrol team leader dropped down to her feet and reported to Warlord. He was the Tribes Security squad leader, and it was right that he received the report. Chief would hear it at the same time anyway, but protocol was to report to her squad leader.

Chief thought she looked a bit scared. Not one of his original team of soldiers, she had been a recent recruit from his Pledged Force. A natural leader and terrific rider, her only weakness was a lack of real fighting experience.

Perhaps that was what was on show here. Something she may have thought about but had not expected to react in this way. "*Maybe she would get that action today. Let us see?*" He thought.

"Tanks!" she blurted out, which caused a few gasps from the security team around them at the gate.

Before she could continue Warlord put up his hand to stop her and said "Calm down. Take a deep breath. Compose your thoughts and give me your report soldier!"

She looked left and right. Nodded to herself. Took a deep breath and slowly exhaled it. Then she took a calmer intake of air and started with her report.

"Two lines of military vehicles are heading towards us. Mainly armoured cars and small tanks. Some trucks and Humvee's. Difficult to assess the size of the force. It may number hundreds if all the trucks and personnel carriers are full. We didn't hang about to check and thought it was best to return here immediately to inform you. Sir!"

A call came over the radio net from a spotter who had climbed up the wind turbine to get a better view. He had a monocular and calmly called out what he could see on the horizon facing them several miles away.

"No tanks, as such." began his much calmer report, "What I can see, is a mixture of Humvees, armoured personnel carriers, a half-track and some armoured cars. They have heavy calibre machine gun turrets that look a bit like tanks, but they certainly are not tanks. Not like our tank anyway."

"Several trucks and other bits of kit back beyond them. Lots of personnel on the ground. Looks like they are digging in and setting up mortar pits and it looks like heavy duty mortars. Probably 120mm judging by the size of the mortar barrels."

He paused to wave at a soldier looking back at him through a similar field lens waving back at him. Then carried on. "They look well-armed and very organised. I estimate more than 120 soldiers. Could be as many as a hundred and fifty. Hard to tell with all the activity underway."

"Shit!" was all Chief said in response as the spotter's report came to an end.

Those around him had heard the report. Everyone on the mesh net radio had heard. They would now be relaying that to those around them who did not have headsets. Pretty soon, everyone would know that Homestead was vastly outnumbered and facing an unknown enemy.

The Chief issued an order. "Send riders out for our Pledged Army allies. We are going to need every available gun carrying member of our society to help us here today!"

Warlord did not need telling twice. He called out on the radio for two riders to race out to the outlying farms and smallholdings. It would not be a quick reinforcement that was for sure but if they could gather all their guns, they would be a match for whoever this new enemy was.

He also instructed all the non-combatants to pick up arms and return to the bunkhouse and be prepared to defend it. One of the security squad ran across to the buildings and alerted everyone.

Chef Henri became a tad outraged when he was instructed to turn off his cooking ranges and grab a gun. His spluttering's were cut short by the stares of others around him, so he shut up and did what he was told.

Inside the bunkhouse he made sure he was stood with those he trusted. His friends Sue and Amber. They often spoke quietly with each other on occasions when they knew they were not being heard. The three of them felt like they were prisoners in this new world and went along with things only as far as they needed to. They too clutched weapons and the three of them took up a spot in a corner by one of the windows.

Henri noted that the shrew of an Engineer had a gleam on her face as she stood by the door of the bunkhouse looking out over the assault gun that looked enormous in her small but strong wiry hands.

Outside, Chief knew that he was out ranged by the mortars if they chose to fire. He shouted instructions for all personnel to seek cover. The tank could have lobbed stuff out with less accuracy close to but would not reach the siege line as the turret had elevation restrictions.

It would only work as a bombard if the tank could be moved back into a depression and thereby raise the angle. Then he shook his head and thought if the tank could move it would be sent forward to take out the flimsy armoured cars, not dig itself into a ditch. *"Fool!"* He told himself silently.

None of this was helping his anger right now. He was quietly seething.

****

Back on the rise looking down on the farmstead, Sergeant Martinez could see the frenzied activity going on in the ranch. She was looking through her field monocular and picked out a spotter up what looked like a wind turbine mast, so she waved at him. Just a single hand gesture to let him know she could see him.

She smiled as he acknowledged and waved back. Around her the activity that they had drilled and drilled over again was underway.

Everyone was dressed in military camouflaged fatigues, kitted out with all the Kevlar armour they could retrieve from the bunkers at the Steel Stockade and the Coastal HQ.

It would look impressive from a distance. She knew that. It had been her intention.

"It is more important to out-think your enemy, than to outfight him" she mused from the Sun Tzu quotes, then *"Move not unless you see an advantage; use not your troops unless there is something to be gained; fight not unless the position is critical."*

The turrets were all swivelling round as she had asked for. Crewed by mothers, children, and non-combatant males from Fort Lumber, Double-D ranch and some other communities that had become aligned. Groups of others moving with purpose around the makeshift camp. All dressed to look like a larger military force was besieging the ranch. *"Play with their minds."*, she thought.

All the trained military teams were setting up and ranging the mortars and laying out anti-personnel mines in front and at the sides of their position. Driving the armoured cars into depressions to minimise small arms fire damage to tyres and fuel tanks but retaining the full field of fire needed by the mounted guns.

Martinez continued musing as the plan unfolded around her. Dig in. Set up the enfiladed fire patterns for the mounted heavy machine guns. Lay out the mortar pits and prepare.

"The supreme act of war is to subdue the enemy without fighting but if you have to engage an enemy more powerful than you. And it is unavoidable, and you do have to engage, then make sure you engage it on your terms, not your enemy's terms." Which was exactly what she was doing.

The satellite photographs provided by Basher were invaluable to their entire plan.

The layout of the ranch below them. The roads in and out. This slight hillock provided excellent visibility, some natural defences and blocked the defenders only motorised exit. Martinez knew that their position could be outflanked by horse riders leaving by the high pastures and crossing the big hills and small mountains, but she knew that was less of a problem right now.

Martinez noted that the tanks turret was now in operation. Something they had discussed before the convoy departed on this mission. Its firepower was unmatched on this field. They needed to stay out of its range. It could take out their armoured vehicles with little effort, just accurate firing of its rounds, in anti-tank or against their people using high explosive rounds.

It took a while for the different aspects of preparation to come together but it was all carried out swiftly and diligently. It would look very impressive from the spotter's perspective down in the ranch. As it was supposed to do.

It was all part of the preparation and the illusion of a stronger, more able force than those of the defenders. The sad fact was the population of their combined communities was still quite small. Many of the farmers had joined them but the force was mainly made up of Coastal HQ, the Steel Stockade and Fort Lumber. They would not know that down there though.

As she mused, the non-combatants were slowly replaced by the seasoned and well-trained gunners in a smooth and well-rehearsed set of actions. The mums, dads and children safely moved back towards their fallback position.

The fallback area was where the tanker, tractor and baggage trucks were guarded by a small rear-guard force. Where all four armoured personnel carriers had formed a defensive wall with some natural rock features.

The non-combatants had been trained to load, aim, and fire assault guns and would have to do so if the fight were carried back there but Martinez knew that if it came to that, the day would probably have been lost by then.

Tents had been put up. Just behind the siege line and back at the rear guard. Cooking fires were lit. All to embellish the illusion that this was unlikely to be resolved quickly. That the enemy (us) were digging in for the duration.

She knew they needed to control the day. Continue with the charade of setting up but being prepared for any move from the fortified ranch down below.

If it were not to be resolved on this day, they would need to revert to a more defensive posture, as darkness would bring with it some challenges if the ranch defenders chose to mount a night attack.

For now, they waited and demonstrated that they were preparing for a siege.

"He will win who knows when to fight and when not to fight." Mused Martinez.

****

Back down in New World Homestead, Chief was discussing his options with Warlord. The delay of the enemy setting up on the only main track into the farmstead would stand Homestead in good favour if he could get the reinforcements in from the Pledged Army.

Each hour that went by would be better for the defenders than the attackers. Chief knew that a long siege favoured the defenders with their sustainable supply of food and water. The attackers would have to bring all that with them and have a finite limit on how long they could sustain a blockade.

However, all the indications from the spotter were that the enemy was digging in. Standard siege preparations.

Chief thought that if only they still possessed their night vision capability from when he saw active service. He could have waited out the light and then ordered a night raid to cause damage and fear. Hopefully capture one of their guards and through selective torture, work out who they are and at what strength. Then determine what action to take next.

No parley had been attempted, which slightly confused the Chief. This meant that the enemy had not outlined its intentions or its terms.

He grabbed his number two and marched over to the farmhouse so that he could discuss with Warlord what those terms could be and more crucially, what to do about it.

Their views were not aligned.

They heard the galloping of two hand-picked security team members on horseback, racing out of the farmstead and up into the higher pastures. The two riders would separate on the mountain trails and head south east and north west, to alert their neighbours and call in their pledges. It would only be a matter of time before reinforcements arrived. In the meantime, they needed a plan.

Warlord started first. "We have an enemy at the gate that clearly outnumber us in terms of personnel, if not in heavy ordnance. However, they do possess mortars that could possibly rain down on us. They have not asked for parley. So, should we find out what they want?"

Chief was clearly frustrated by the whole turn of events of the morning and vented his anger with an angry retort "For fuck's sake!" he shouted. "I can see all of that. Tell me something else I already know!"

Warlord had never seen him quite like this, so he took a few moments of silence before continuing.

"It could be that major force out west you were concerned about. The one that those nomads were from. It could be them. It could just as easily be another group who are completely different."

Chief looked perplexed and remained silent, so Warlord continued.

"We did get some rumours that passed through our pledged ranches and smallholdings that someone from the old government was trying to get organised."

"Some messages were transmitted on some of the old civil defence frequencies, but they were from way a way. Out on the coast, with some from the old central time zone communities and even out on the east coast. However, it has always been a conversation with someone who had a conversation with someone else. Hard to validate."

"It could be the government, whatever that consists of these days?"

"We do not have any aerials out here or equipment to receive so it has been hard to verify. Perhaps these are government forces. Here to bring us all back into line. Start paying taxes again and keeping politicians sweet."

Chief banged the table and stood up shouting "I won't have it. We are not going back to those ways. We are creating our own new world. A better society. We do not need anybody else. Weak and bent politicians with a government taxing us. No, they need to leave us alone." Then he sat back down glaring across the table at Warlord.

"Then we should parley." said Warlord quietly. "Let them know we mean no harm and just want to be left to our own devices. They should move on. Find others who want to fall in line again. Not us."

Chief waited a while and said "Okay. We will go and see if we can parley but at the same time, we bolster all our defences facing the siege line. Minimise those held back to monitor the fields and the bunkhouse."

"Make sure all the non-combatant squads are armed and holding the bunkhouse as our final fallback position if they assault. And hope we get our reinforcements soon!"

****

Up on the hill, one of the new recruits from the Steel Stockade. Hector. Strode up to the command post that Martinez had set up and reported that a small group of mounted defenders were preparing to come out of the ranch carrying several white flags held up on poles. Four horses in total.

Martinez nodded and thanked Hector for his calm report. This had been expected.

She nodded to those around her and signalled to the eight designated colleagues to crew two of the Humvees. They started up the engines and immediately rolled down the hillside on the track towards the horse riders.

The gambit was to meet them much nearer to the ranch than to the siege line. It was achieved without any obvious sense of urgency. Just motorised vehicles making better speed than trotting horses.

A white flag fluttered from each vehicle radio aerial. Indicating parley but of course, it did not guarantee anything and both sides carried cocked weapons. To be sure, to be sure.

Martinez wanted to show force and had selected the eight toughest looking troops she had. More though, she had selected the Humvee fitted with a public address system and would use it to control the exchange. She wanted as many defenders to hear as possible.

Chief, Warlord and two of their best soldiers from the old days walked their horses slowly out through the chicane, then the gate and started up in the direction of the siege line. As they set off and before they had even left the gates, two Humvees peeled away from the line of armoured vehicles and made their way steadily down the slight rise towards them.

The horses had not got more than a hundred yards when the Humvees stopped their downward journey a good two hundred yards away from them and a loudspeaker system kicked in with a slight whine. A voice stated "Stop there. That is far enough!"

"An instruction. The cheeky bastards!" Thought Chief, as he and his party reined in and stopped.

They looked over and saw two well-crewed reconnaissance vehicles. Each had an armour wearing gunner in the machine gun swivels and equally well armoured soldiers stepped out of each of the rear doors, using them as a barrier and aimed assault rifles at the four riders.

The voice continued. "We are here from the Governor of the West. To welcome you into our federated communities. You should return to your ranch and get all your defenders to lower their weapons and surrender them to us. Then we can explain the next steps."

Chief looked lazily at Warlord and gently shook his head before looking back at the Humvees in front of him and shouted back "What if we don't want to be part of the...err" he paused, shook his head quizzically, shrugged and then continued "err, Federated Communities" then spat in the dirt.

The loudspeaker responded with "The Governor of the West also requires you to hand over the two men known as Chief and Warlord into our custody. It is for the murder of innocent children and women under their duty of care. If you do not hand them over, we will attack."

"Enough!" shouted Chief as the ultimatum threatened to push him over the edge. He turned and whispered to Warlord and his two companions, "Follow my lead and return to Homestead." Then continued out aloud, "We will return and send you our message!" Before swivelling his horse around, followed immediately by the three others and trotted back to Homestead.

Chief could see the faces peering out at him as they got back to the defensive line. Some white-faced had clearly never seen any proper action. Others, more battle hardened, merely checked their weapons, and nodded back to Chief as he rode through the gate.

He realised then, that the vehicles had deliberately driven nearer to the Homestead so many more would hear what was being said over the loudspeakers. "*Clever bastards!*" he thought. "*Try to turn the heads of our society.*" He knew in that moment, that he needed to take the lead.

He shouted over to the tank, "Try and take out the fucking Humvees now!"

The tank turret swivelled slightly, and the barrel lifted upwards.

It had not been lost on the Humvee drivers that the parley was over and they had already put their vehicles into reverse and were headed back up the track as soon as the soldiers stepped back into the cabs.

One of the swivel gunners shouted an alarm when there was a bright flash from the tank gun muzzle, followed by a loud bang.

The explosion when it hit was phenomenal. Thankfully, it did not hit either of the Humvees directly but did hit the ground in front of the left retreating one that caused it to lift into the air and come crashing down onto its roof. Killing the gunner instantly and throwing one other out to the side. The wreck landed badly.

Martinez saw the whole thing almost in slow motion but was already issuing orders. She yelled "Smoke!" and then "Mortars! Now!"

The remaining Humvee commenced zig zagging in reverse at full speed, but it was an uncontrolled drive and crashed into the grassy bank next to the track and came to a halt. Severely damaged. "Bail out!" was the shout and all four soldiers threw themselves out of the vehicle seconds before a direct hit blew the Humvee into a thousand pieces.

Martinez had only half expected this response, she had thought the defenders may involve themselves in a more peaceful resolution. She grimaced at the risk of loss to her people when the first shot was fired but had reacted immediately.

A third shot struck the upturned Humvee and bits of body mixed with vehicle parts were thrown into the air.

Corporal Yoshida and a companion, after setting off early and wearing ghillie suits had leopard crawled very slowly for over an hour and a half before the parley commenced. They had done so to get into a position between the siege line and Homestead. Whilst all eyes were on the siege line.

They had already radioed co-ordinates to the heavy mortar crews who had their weapons set out in the half track and one of the trucks. 120mm mortars. Smaller ones had been set up in the pits. The heavy mortars were aimed at the gates, the lighter had smoke bombs ready to go to cover the retreat.

A series of "Whomp, whomp's" were heard as the different mortar crews launched their bombs."

Smoke bombs landed around the stricken and destroyed Humvees as the tank fired a fourth round of high explosive.

It was devastating. Crew members who were nearby were blown about like rag dolls.

"Medics!" went up the shout from the siege line and two combat medics did their best to run out to the ravaged scene. Two of the crew were alive and relatively okay other than cuts and bruises, three others were alive but only just. Limbs missing, gaping wounds but the other three lay dead.

The smoke was helping to hide the medics from the defensive positions down below.

The heavier mortar rounds then began landing at the homestead just short of the gates and to the left.

Yoshida calmly spoke into his microphone, "Add 100, right 100, call for fire. Two rounds."

Two more "Whomps" were heard.

Yoshida watched the explosions bracket the gate and cause some of it to collapse. Then he calmly said, "Fire for effect, twenty rounds" and the mortar bombs rained down on and around the gatehouse area.

Bits of defensive vehicle fortifications and some bodies were thrown into the air as the mortars caused havoc in Homestead.

Yoshida was reminded of the Sun Tzu quote, *"Let your plans be dark and as impenetrable as night, and when you move, fall like a thunderbolt."* Not quite thunderbolts but enough high explosive to kill, maim and cause damage.

The tank was useless now against the armoured vehicles, as the main siege line was out of range. However, it began firing indiscriminately into the bush and grass covered hillside between the siege line and the ranch, with high explosive rounds.

Clearly, the defenders assumed that a forward observation post had been set up and was calling in the mortars. They just could not work out where it was and were trying to hit any likely area.

This came as a relief to the combat medics who called back for stretchers to carry the three gravely wounded survivors back behind the siege line, where Doc and her small team had set up a casualty trauma tent in the rear-guard area.

Yoshida's companion kept an eye on the positioning of the tank barrel and for any other incursion towards them. He was also a sniper and was ready to use his weapon but not yet. The firing was indiscriminate and there was no risk or need to move just yet. To do so could expose their actual location.

The plan was to hold the siege line steady up on the hillside and mortar bomb the entire farmstead of key defensive positions.

Yoshida calmly called in new co-ordinates for the mortars. "Left one hundred, call for fire. Two rounds" and after seeing another heavy machine gun post bracketed calmly said "ten rounds, fire for effect."

Then he began working the fall of bombs along the ranch defensive line either side of the gatehouse, before directing fire towards the buildings.

They knew that families were in there, but this had to be a decisive action and maximise destruction to reduce the defender's willingness to fight. Just as Sun Tzu proclaimed. "*Fall like a thunderbolt*" thought Yoshida.

However, he held back on hitting the bunkhouse for now. There were many defensive positions to take out first. The bunkhouse would be the last main target.

****

Chief cheered the success of his tank gunner's accuracy, whilst Warlord screamed for everyone to take cover. He knew that there would be an immediate response. Sure enough. Mortar bombs rained down and started taking out their defensive positions. It was accurate fire and so he shouted over to Chief to get the tank gunner to use high explosive rounds on spots that looked capable of being used as a forward observation post.

"Get the FOP" screamed Chief over the cacophony of sound as the bombs were landing.

The tank turret swivelled around, and the aimer and gunner inside tried hard to find obvious spots on the hillside where a FOP would be located. However, the view was blocked by dust clouds from the explosions and the smoke bombs. Therefore, they just fired randomly in a left, right, up and down format until the small magazine in the tank ran out of HE shells.

The gunner screamed out for an ammo reload. The only rounds he had left were armour piercing. Fine for taking out the flimsy armoured vehicles the enemy had arrived with but next to useless against troops on the ground.

Chief recognised he was losing his defensive capabilities as each machine gun post was blown up. He shouted out for everyone to fall back to the bunkhouse but first they needed to re-arm the tank with HE.

The retreat was chaotic. Many of the defenders had already died in the mortar onslaught, some were relatively intact, and they helped the wounded who could be moved, back to the bunkhouse.

Two security squad members carrying wooden ammunition crates tried to get across the open ground to the tank but were struck by mortar bombs as the carpet of explosions moved from the gate line on towards the buildings. Neither survived. The high explosive rounds lay in the dirt of the exposed area between the buildings and the gate.

Chief cursed their luck and then heard slightly duller explosions from behind the farmhouse and a grimaced smile creased across his face. *"So, it was a two-pronged attack, as we had always feared."* He thought.

****

Back up in the high pastures on the trail the two riders reined their horses in and stopped when they heard the tank firing and then the mortars. They both looked at each other. They knew what that meant, and their faces showed how relieved they were to be out of that sort of fighting.

It was all the time needed by the archers.

Neither of the riders were wearing armour and neither knew what hit them.

They had decided to ride light. Stopping only to pick up some provisions from the kitchen, water bottles and their guns. Their mission was to ride at speed to mobilise the Pledged Army. Then together they could see off their attackers. Not anymore.

They were brought down silently. Each body had been pierced by two or more arrows.

Basher's satellite photos had enabled the clan to head out weeks before the armoured column. To work their way by horseback out and around some farms and ranches that were out East and South of Homestead.

Camping out like they used to when they were traversing the wilderness west. Then, once they were in position, lay in wait on the trails that led from the high pastures on the day that the main armoured force was due to arrive. Point had listed all the tracks and pathways.

Each trail was guarded by two or three members of the clan. One or two archers and the automatic weapon carrying Gunner, Gusto, Med, Raven, Carla, and Radar as back up.

It had raised a few eyebrows, of those that could of course, when Radar volunteered to be part of the early flanking attack force. He rightly explained that his visionary powers would be of good use and he was still capable of firing a gun. "Albeit perhaps not as accurately as I used to, but I am a soldier and you don't forget things like that", he had said.

It was hard to argue and for the first time in the short clan history Radar had selected and carried his own assault gun and ammunition. All of them were wearing ghillie suits, which made them indistinguishable amongst the bushes on the slopes. They moved off once they were on foot and the horses had been hobbled and hidden in the trees.

Radar had called out the movement of horses on the mesh net radio system that Basher's team had provided. It was just a matter of the time and the place. They needed to be taken down before the trail split across the ridge of the mountain slopes and they had done just that.

Two teams had already converged on the trail junction. Walking down each one to make sure they did not miss anything.

It was as they were lay in wait that they heard the explosions. Three loud cracks followed by the "Whomp" of the mortars and the continued if sporadic louder retorts from what could have only been the tank.

Raven recognised that the fighting had started earlier than they had expected but it was in their contingency plans. The loudspeaker broadcast had not achieved the desired effect. The hope was that some of the defenders would revolt and hand over their leaders to avoid a battle, but clearly that option had now gone.

The fallen enemy were checked that they were dead, then a quick scavenge took place. "*Old habits die hard*", thought Raven. The two horses were hobbled and left to collect later.

Job done. There would be no reinforcements.

Basher's satellite monitoring had shown regular patrols out to several outlying farms and ranches. It would be likely that they had formed a loose collaboration and may try and support the despot. However, if the ranches didn't know, then they couldn't help.

It was in the plan to visit all the known working farms and ranches, once the action was over. However, they needed to win the battle first.

The clan had agreed to rendezvous lower down the mountain slopes and commence their approach on the Homestead. It was hoped that their part of the attack would be the one that was least expected.

As they moved closer together Raven reminded herself of the Sun Tzu quote that amplified their position. "*If the enemy know not where he will be attacked, he must prepare in every quarter, and to be everywhere weak.*"

"*And we are here to exploit that.*" she thought.

The mortar barrage could not continue indefinitely. It was to serve two purposes.

Take out the forward defensive positions in preparation for a frontal assault but that would be extremely difficult given the presence of the tank. Its second purpose was to pin down the defenders and allow the clan to infiltrate the farmstead from the high pastures. It was the main reason they were all ghillie suited.

Once they had rendezvoused, there was a quick reminder of how their formation would work.

Steel, Point, Fletch and the teenagers minus Jose, would form a forward skirmish line. Moving forward through the pastures with Radar, Raven, Carla, Gunner and Med in a similar second line but all carrying automatic weapons as back up. They each carried backpacks with explosives and grenades.

Gastro and Jose took up a defensive position back where the trail split off. Their role was to stop any reinforcements from coming in from that direction. They could also be called forward to back up the clan if needed. They set up two concealed tripod heavy machine guns to create an enfilade, just as Yoshida had taught them.

****

Back at the siege line Martinez was receiving reports. The first came from the mortar crews that they had now used up over seventy-five percent of their ammunition.

The report went on to state that Yoshida was continuing to call in mortar drops onto each of the farmstead forward defensive positions. He was nearly ready to drop onto the main buildings at the centre.

Doc had sent word forward that one of the three Humvee survivors had died whilst wounds were being treated and she continued to try to save the lives of the other two. This triggered Martinez to carry out a mental count of what resources she still had.

It told her that she had Sixty-five troops at her disposal. Including the mortar crews, Yoshida, and herself. All trained to fight. Many of them regular military and some drawn from the former civilians from the Steel Stockade and the ranches close to Fort Lumber. It left a rear guard of about twenty-five active troops, plus medical and family members manning machine guns.

"Time to change the perspective." Thought Martinez.

She sent word back to the rear-guard that those families trained to prime and drop the mortar bombs into the tubes were to be brought forward. They would not be able to re-set the aiming of the tubes. It was just about continuing the volume of bombs at that point whilst it released the assault troops to enter the fray. She also brought forward fifteen of those regular troops.

The order was enacted, and a dozen people made their way forward to relieve the mortar crews.

Martinez told Yoshida to target the buildings now. That is where the remaining mortar bombs would land. Then she checked her own kit and equipment before striding forward to lead the assault.

Yoshida reported that the tank had stopped firing. Perhaps it had run out of HE rounds? He queried. Martinez could not rely on that as a fact, but it did not alter the plan in any case.

The mortar bombs were now aimed in a rolling carpet on to the farmhouse buildings. Then left in that position whilst the families dropped the remaining mixture of explosive and smoke bombs onto the buildings to try and confuse the defenders.

Martinez waved out her assault and the Eighty or so with her fanned out in a wide and well-separated loose attack formation to make their way down the hillside and into the farm for the final stage of the attack. She hoped that Raven and her clan were doing the business from the rear.

Unfortunately, there was no way of knowing as the mesh net radio only held good over a short distance. Each member of the troop extended its range only by moving forward and together. Once they got too far apart the communications link broke down.

A perfectly fine system for infantry unit's in a single action but additional radio systems would normally be used in a wide battlefield scenario like this one. They just did not have the kit available to them. Mesh net was all they had.

This would separate their communications. One net covered the siege line and rear-guard, it may stretch to the farmstead below. The second net supported the clan in their flanking move from the rear. The net would become one within the farmstead, then Martinez would know how the clan had fared.

For now, it was stick to the plan.

It would take about twenty minutes to walk down the hillside and be within reach of the defensive perimeter line. About the same amount of time, it would take for the mortar crews to run out of ammunition.

"This really was a one-time only attack. Better make it a good one." Thought Martinez.

****

Walking at a crouch and staying low, the still ghillie suited clan were making their way past grazing cattle and using as much cover as possible on their approach to the buildings.

It was as they clambered over a fence designed to keep the animals in the pastures that the wheels of their approach fell off.

Two loud explosions sounded that threw Boy and Girl into the air and thirty yards away, Point just seemed to disintegrate.

They all froze.

Steel scrambled over to the mute teenagers. Boy was clearly dead. Both legs blown off and horrible injuries to his abdomen and face. Most of his body was a grisly mess. Girl had fared little better. One leg and an arm were missing, and she was bleeding heavily.

Med had raced across the pasture to help. Everyone else went to ground as soon as the explosions happened. They blasts would draw attention and they were out in the open.

Raven shook her head at her, as she looked over the fence at the entrails and body parts spread around of the person she had once admired. Point was gone. Her guts wrenched.

Med switched her run over to where Steel was crouched. He told her to step over the fence carefully. The defenders had clearly mined the area on their side of the fence.

The rest of the clan used their ghillie suits to good effect and blended into the foliage.

Med did her best with Girl's wounds. Trying to stem them before she bled out. She quickly applied tourniquets to the stump of her arm and around the thigh, but it wasn't enough. The damage was immense, and the blood loss was too great.

An incredibly sad look came over Girls face as her life slipped away with a last gasp and her remaining good hand patting Med's forearm. Before it dropped back down. Med burst into tears and sobbed over her.

Steel pressed his hand over her mouth and slowly shook his head from side to side whilst big tears rolled down his own cheeks. "Now is not a time for mourning." He said, "We need to focus on our attack. Martinez is depending on us. Okay?"

Med nodded slowly and they both made efforts to hold their grief in.

Raven called on the mesh net. "As you can see, the bastards have mined the fence line. Girl, Boy and Point have all died." She paused for a moment, then continued.

"We have not got time to reconnoitre the field and make it safe. I cannot countenance a forward movement across the fields, we will have to follow the fence line and use one of their tracks."

"I realise that is where it will be guarded but we do not have time to hang about. We will just have to push on!"

There were no dissenting voices. It was Radar who made the call. He said, "There are no more guards outside as far as I can make out. They are all in the bunkhouse and the farmhouse now. The mortar fire must have made them retreat. I cannot see any more out here with us."

"Right." said Raven firmly. "That's made up our minds then." She took a quick look at the folded-up satellite photograph that had all the trails marked up. "*Shame it couldn't show mines*" she thought but it was too late for that now. They had to complete their manoeuvre and back Martinez up.

"We go left. That is the nearest gate, then it's about five hundred yards to the buildings. We need to be swift. Let's go!" With that they removed their ghillie suits as previously agreed. They would only slow them down at this stage.

The clan moved off down the fence line at a steady trot but spread out in a straggle line. If someone did have a machine gun trained on the tracks, being spread out would save some of them at least and they could continue to press home their part of the plan.

****

Inside the bunkhouse Chief was revising the Tribe's tactical position. They would be sitting ducks if they remained here. The bunkhouse and farmhouse were not fortified anywhere near enough to withstand an assault with automatic weapons, grenades or anything rocket propelled. This was rapidly turning into self-preservation and he intended to survive. With or without his tribe. His mind was made up.

He looked around at what was left of his tribe. A mixture of experienced soldiers, some conscripts, and the non-combatants. Some fatally wounded would not make it out. They all looked at him for direction.

"We cannot stay here!" he announced. "Our best means of survival is to become mobile again. Everyone who can, must make their way to the barn and get into the APCs. Now let's go!" he screamed.

There were some shrieks and moans from the non-combatants. Some said they didn't want to go. Others froze where they were. Unsure of what do to. Locked in shock at the chain of events. A couple screamed for assistance, but no-one stopped for them in the panic of everyone for themselves.

A mad scramble took place as people made their way through the bunkhouse and into the barn. Amber held back and pulled Sue and Henri with her to one side. "Let them go." She spoke quietly. "We will wait here and surrender. I think that is the only way we can survive this. It is madness to try and run away from the government forces. I am sure they will understand that we are not all part of this... this horrible new world."

Henri trembled and looked scared. He did not have the strength to move anyway and just plopped down on the floor behind the bunk he was cowering behind.

Sue was made of sterner stuff and pulled a couple of the bunks together to form a mini barricade inside the bunkhouse and pulled mattresses around them to help protect from any shrapnel or other stuff that may come their way. Amber helped and they created a small, padded area resembling a child's den.

Sue could see others trying to fend for themselves, to crawl and cower under bunks.

It was a wise move as the mortar bombs had now found the range of the buildings and the walls shook under the blasts.

Debris and shrapnel smashed all the windows of the bunkhouse in, which urged on the stragglers running out and into the barn. Some weren't quick enough and were cut down by the shrapnel and flying glass.

As Chief and Warlord got into the barn, they each took control of an APC and tried their best to divide what was left of their tribe equally into each of the vehicles. Chief placed soldiers at the wheel and to operate each of the pair of machine gun mounts up top to try and maximise the use of his most experienced squad members. The rest were quickly ushered inside.

Warlord noticed that Amber had not made it out of the bunkhouse and turned to go back for her, but he was pulled back by Chief. "We don't have time for stragglers. Our bed squeezes will not help us now. We need fighters to get us out of here alive. Leave it man!"

Chief then spoke over their closed radio net and asked that the tank crew remain in place to guard their exodus and be ready to evacuate the tank and transfer into the APC's. They could not exit to the rear as he knew that forces were approaching from there and in any case, the APC's would not be able to traverse the mountain trails.

It was going to be a rush out of the front door.

He needed to be sure he could get some movement up towards the siege line but then go around it. He just could not work out which way would be best just yet. That would come to him once they exited the fortifications and engaged with the enemy.

What he needed was some covering fire and all he had was the tank. Though he knew that he wouldn't be stopping for them. Unlucky. He needed the cover only they could provide.

The tank aimer reported that he could see ground troops making their way towards the farmstead and asked again for HE rounds. Chief said that was not going to be possible, but he wanted to know how many armour piercing rounds were left. Six was the reply.

Smoke bombs continued to pepper the area around the buildings, interspersed with high explosive rounds. The area was becoming increasingly dangerous for anyone to be outside.

Visibility was poor with all the smoke.

Chief called for the gunner to use the AP rounds on the ground troops. The impact may take some of the out. "*Better to use what he had than not.*" He thought and he needed the covering fire. Then he said, "Fire the six rounds then get out of the tank and we will pick you up."

Though he intended to be moving out through the gates long before completion of the six rounds. He needed them as cover only, "*Otherwise he would never get out of here alive. A necessary sacrifice to save the Messiah*" He thought.

****

Yoshida and his sniper compatriot held their position at the FOP and were awaiting the arrival of their comrades. The plan was that they would join in with the ground assault as it rolled forward.

In the meantime, he continued to monitor activity within the farmstead below and some unusual movement caught his eye. He pressed his microphone and said, "The barn doors are opening. They are going to use their vehicles!"

With that information. Martinez called a halt and ordered half a dozen of her team to return quickly and start up their 8-wheeled twin gunned armoured cars forward whilst she pressed on with their frontal approach.

Six soldiers jogged back at some pace to bring the armoured cars into play. There was some nervousness amongst all six because they knew the tank was still in action. They had to trust their comrades to do their thing.

It wasn't helped when the tank began firing. The first round didn't cause any concern, but the tank fired two more shots and it took out a pair of their ground troops setting up a tripod mounted machine gun. They, the gun and the tripod all blew up into the air with the impact of the round which did not detonate until it had penetrated some of the ground.

Yoshida kept the observation reports coming over their mesh net. "Two Armoured Personnel Carriers are leaving the barn. The tank remains a threat. It appears to be firing armour piercing rounds only. There are no soldiers on foot."

It was a simple message but held so much information of the present and clear danger around them at that time.

The battle plan had altered. It was standard military knowledge that no plan survives its first encounter with the enemy and why they had discussed several different contingencies. A swift exit in APC's had not been one of them. They expected the defenders to hold tight behind their fortifications.

Martinez and another comrade slid in next to them as another explosion struck the hillside. "It is using AP shells. Probably run out of HE." Said Yoshida. Still remarkably calm.

* * * * * * * * * *

The clan were on their approach to the buildings where Radar had seen everyone congregate. Then they heard motor engines fire up and two armoured vehicles shot out of the barn, drove across the open ground, around what looked like a cage and then headed for the battered gate area.

The explosions had stopped. "*That must be the end of the mortar rounds.*" Thought Raven. Then she called on the radio. "Armoured vehicles are leaving the compound!"

Martinez now she was nearer to the farmstead, noted with satisfaction that they were now all on the same net, picked up the call and acknowledged it with her own message.

"We know, our own armoured cars are joining us. Secure the buildings and prevent any retreat back to them."

"Roger" was all Raven said. It meant yes, I understand and will comply with that instruction.

All the clan heard it at the same time and moved towards the buildings. It was Radar who spoke next and said, "There are still half a dozen people in the bunkhouse. The barn and farmhouse all look clear."

The clan surrounded the bunkhouse and were preparing to enter it when multiple explosions and gunfire outside the gate caught their attention.

****

Chief's APC was the first to exit the barn, followed closely by the one with Warlord in. he told the driver to crash through the debris that the gate and former chicane entrance had now become following the mortar onslaught.

Through the smoke clouds wafting across the hillside, Chief could see a field full of troops and two armoured cars careering down the hillside towards them. It was then he heard the third retort from the tank and a loud explosion just missed everyone. Guns opened fire all around them, making it difficult to see everything that was going on.

A rocket propelled grenade shot towards Chief's APC and exploded with a loud crash on the front and bullet fire clattered off its sides. He assumed that Warlord was experiencing the same.

The tank fired a fourth time and missed again as rocket propelled grenades and bullet fire raked the two APC's and the tank alike. Both forces were now locked into a battle. The APC's were still on the move past and through the ground troops all taking cover in the limited bush and shrub covered hillside.

The four gunners swivelled and fired their high calibre machine guns. Two of them were hit by shots from the ground troops and a wheel was blown off Chiefs APC with a direct hit from a rocket propelled grenade. It caused the vehicle to career wildly before tipping over onto its side.

Martinez shouted for Raven to support by taking out the tank before it got their armoured cars, but it was too late. An armour piercing round was fifth time lucky for the tank and the direct hit caused one of her armoured cars to disintegrate in a massive ball of flames. The three occupants would have been killed instantly.

The clan converged on the tank and it was Gunner who unclipped a couple of grenades, pulled the pins. Then he lifted the tank cupola hatch, dropped the two grenades, and then threw himself to the ground in an ungainly dive from the tank housing.

Two muffled explosions rang out and the tank threat was neutralised. To be sure, Gunner popped back up, poked open the hatch and sprayed the inside with his machine gun.

"Good work" said Martinez from her advanced position near to Yoshida.

Her teams armoured car now closed with the one remaining APC which had moved past its stricken twin and was trying to escape. Both its gunners were sprawled dead in their swivel mounts, so it wasn't providing much in the way of threat, but it had to be eliminated.

Without anyone needing to say so, all fire concentrated on the only mobile APC. It only stopped moving when the big twin heavy calibre guns on their armoured car came into play and devastating fire raked the APC from front to back and then back again.

The APC crashed into the bank running alongside the track and came to a halt. Gunfire from the armoured car, another rocket propelled grenade and continuous small arms fire continued to rain down on it, killing everyone inside.

Martinez ordered that all fire now be concentrated on the inert APC but before anyone carried that out, a tatty piece of white material was waved from beside a body hanging out of one of the machine gun cupolas. A voice shouted out "We surrender!"

Martinez shouted "Check, check, check!" over the voice net. "Cease firing!"

One of her team leaders rose from the ground and shouted out "Everyone in the personnel carrier, drop your weapons and come out one a time with your hands in the air. Do it now or we will carry on firing!"

After a moment or two, the first person crawled out of a hatch. Then another, until about ten, mostly wounded figures in a hotchpotch of outfits. Some looked like soldiers. One had overalls on, another looked like he was a cook. All stood in a ragged line.

They were quickly overpowered, forced to kneel and the troops used cable ties to bind their wrists together.

"*It's over!*" thought Martinez.

****

Back at the ranch. The clan now paid their full attention to the bunkhouse. Steel shouted for everyone to drop their weapons and come out of the bunkhouse. If they did then no-one would be harmed.

It took a few moments for Amber, Sue, and Henri to extricate themselves from their timber and mattress cocoon and to exit the bomb-damaged building and they came out of the building unscathed and with their hands in the air.

Steel told them to kneel and applied cable ties to their wrists. Whilst doing so, a tall red-headed girl said that there were wounded people back inside the bunkhouse. So, after handing over to comrades to stand guard, Steel approached the door to go inside and investigate.

The remaining armoured car sped into the ranch compound, with Martinez hanging off the driver's door and dismounted with some aplomb like she had done it many times before.

It raised a small cheer from the clan stood over their prisoners as Martinez reported that the battle was over.

They looked out beyond the gate and could see a straggle of similarly bound figures making their way back to the ranch in a lot less order than they had left not long before.

Martinez looked around at the remaining clan members and asked "Casualties?"

"We lost Point, Boy and Girl." said a sad Raven. Then she looked up and asked "You?"

Martinez paused for a moment and said "Ten dead and fifteen wounded. Some very seriously." As she turned to glare at the tank and said, "Bastard tank!"

Some minutes later the prisoners limped and walked through the gate, accompanied at gunpoint by a few of Martinez's troops.

At that moment Fletch and Bullseye both spotted Chief and looked at each other. This was their moment. Without saying a word to anyone, they calmly lowered their guns and unhooked their bows. Each notched, aimed and loosed their arrows.

It came as a complete shock to Chief and everyone else present, as the two arrows struck him in the throat simultaneously and he fell over with a slightly shocked look on his face.

"Fuck sake!" shouted Martinez as Raven, Radar and Gunner all wrestled with Fletch and Bullseye to stop them firing any more arrows. In all the commotion. No-one was looking behind them at the bunkhouse when the tiny engineer had appeared in the doorway.

She had just seen her God felled by those horrible archer people and pulled the trigger on the machine gun she clutched. Her tiny hands belying the steely strength she possessed as she sprayed the gunfire indiscriminately across the group of people jostling in front of her.

Fletch, Bullseye, Radar and Gunner were all jerked about like puppets on strings, as the guns magazine was emptied into them.

It was Steel who responded the quickest. He had almost reached the door when she shot out of it. Already clutching his machete, he stepped forward and chopped down, severing both arms at the elbow and causing the gun to clatter to the floor. Then he swung it again to strike her throat and as her head detached in a spray of blood, she crumpled to the floor dead.

Then everyone's attention was drawn to the moaning coming from the wounded and dying lay on the ground. It was a scene of carnage, with blood pumping from wounds and desperate attempts by all present to save the lives of their friends.

Steel shouted into the bunkhouse that he would throw grenades in if there were any more trouble. A weak voice from inside shouted that he had thrown his gun down but couldn't move out.

Steel and Martinez, despite being wounded, then carefully entered the bunkhouse to find a scene of devastation. Four or five dead bodies, some of them almost whole and one arm waving from under a bunk was all that was left of the bunkhouse survivors.

****

The casualties were evacuated back to Doc's field trauma centre in a series of ambulatory moves using a mixture of the vehicles from the homestead and trucks sent down from the rear guard.

It wasn't long before she ran out of space to treat them all.

Following a discussion with Martinez and Raven, it was agreed to patch up the bunkhouse and use that as a hospital and the barn was set up next door as a makeshift mortuary, once the jeeps had been driven out.

Rows of dead people, from Fort Lumber and the Homestead were covered in tarpaulin and laid out on the ground inside the barn. The battle had been costly for everyone.

****

Over the next few days, several joint funerals took place. Some of them were accompanied by great tears and mourning, whilst others like the coward Chief had a somewhat ignominious end being thrown into a pit with Warlord and buried without a marker.

Fletch and Gunner were buried next to the remains of Point, Boy and Girl in a small cemetery that must have been created hundreds of years ago when the first settlers arrived.

The homesteaders buried their own in a separate side of the little graveyard, as did Martinez's troops. It more than doubled the size of the burial plots already there. It made a lot of sense to bury the dead of both sides in the same cemetery.

Raven, Martinez, Bullseye and Radar all spent some time in the care of the Doc and her team before they were allowed up and help prepare for the return home to Fort Lumber.

The homesteader survivors were offered a chance to make their peace with the western communities represented by Raven and Martinez. Sue wanted to stay. The ranch had originally belonged to her family when the army people arrived and took over. She wanted to carry on with the farming, as did some of the others, including Henri and what now seemed to be his boyfriend, Javier who had survived the mad dash out in the APC's. Amber was relieved now that they oppression had been lifted and was only too happy to remain there and make a go of the farm.

Some protocols were agreed on keeping in touch, with Fort Lumber and the surrounding farms and ranches, who were also thankful to end the "Protection" of Chief and Warlord. They also agreed to carry out mutual support and consider trading links with their new friends further west.

There would be a need for different commercial arrangements to be put into place. Money as such had no value to anyone right now, so they set out some schedules of how much a cow would be worth against a cord of planed wood, or a wagon load of potatoes versus a digitally printed piece of equipment to repair something.

None of that could be sorted in one go and so it was agreed to arrange a gathering of leaders sometime in the late summer, early autumn. People kept some opinions guarded and it would take effort to develop trust and respect. It was not going to happen just because the Chief and Warlord were no more.

Raven mused *"It is easy to love your friend, but sometimes the hardest lesson to learn is to love your enemy."* Because that is what was needed now. Repair the damage to hearts and minds as much as the physical damage to the buildings.

Thankfully, the home-made energy infrastructure had largely survived the battle and with some minor repairs and light maintenance led by Amber and supported by Fort Lumber people, the farmstead had every chance of surviving and thriving.

The bunkhouse and farmhouse were repaired but no-one could source any glass and so it was open windows and wooden shutters instead. All quite old school.

The barn was intact along with the tanker of fuel and the remaining vehicles.

Once all the wounded were declared fit to travel by the Doc. Raven and Martinez mobilised all their surviving forces and began the long trip back over the hills to Fort Lumber and those who wanted to, then on to Coast HQ.

As they travelled west again, Raven knew that whilst they had defeated the one person in the western regions who had the potential to have caused problems in the future. It had also completed the revenge that Point had called for and that had sadly cost him his life.

She felt that there was still much to do for their fledgling communities to survive but at least they could now do so without the threats and violence, that may have come to hurt them.

It was going to be a struggle, but Raven felt that they had the right people, in the right places. They just needed some luck and a long period of growth and development.

Chapter Thirty-One

2035 - The Way Forward

Raven reflected that it was now three years since that last battle in the west in 2032. The country had settled down considerably. Both her and Radar continued to be based at Fort Lumber. Raven sighed and thought that despite trying so ridiculously hard, they had not been successful in expanding their family beyond being a couple. Both of them had thrown themselves into work.

She looked around at the fort, which was now the heart of their commercial activity. Led by a Carla, who had a good head for business. Quality planed wood was in great demand as the regional communities began to rebuild homes and create places of work for commodities needed by others. Trade was good.

Raven waved to a couple with a toddler and smiled. She thought *"It was good that love had blossomed for Med and Gastro. More so when they were blessed with a pregnancy late in 2032."*

Steel gave a laconic wave, as led his now smaller team of wings out of the fort. They would be going out on a hunt. Raven noted with satisfaction that their patrols provided regular contact between a growing number of farms and ranches in their region.

There was now a need for vegetables, dairy products and meat. There were several markets that had sprouted up to supply the demand. They also provided opportunities for people to get together and celebrate as survivors.

Raven remembered those discussions that had been held that following summer in 2033. It had led to a more harmonious way forward. She smiled to herself as she watched Basher evolve from being a loud ex-military man into a great leader.

Basher was now the elected leader of the western regions. Together they had developed an agreed set of arrangements of community representation and oversaw any boundary or trading disputes.

Communication lines were initially set up on a version of the pony express. With riders carrying correspondence between communities to ensure that key people attended the regional gatherings to resolve disputes and ensure that trade continued.

The service also permitted the exchange of personal messages as people kept in touch with friends or family who had moved to different parts of the region. For work and to find love. It was led by the former military teams, Martinez based in the Fort Lumber, with Yoshida overseeing the horse stations and providing a security presence between the regions.

Plans were put into place to improve the generation of energy. Wind, wave, and the sun were harnessed to create a regional grid. Though wood and coal, when it could be dug up, continued to provide fuel for heating during cold spells and throughout the winter. It also permitted the creation of light industry to begin making things that the communities needed.

It was going to be a long haul, but Basher continually extolled the virtues of harmonising their existence with the natural resources available and to exploit them without creating any form of environmental disaster.

They needed to learn from their past if they were going to create a sustainable future for their children and their children's children.

New World Homestead had been renamed to Hope Farm. Led by Sue and Amber, the farmstead had gone from strength to strength, and they were soon trading surplus produce at the regional markets.

Similar arrangements were being put into place across the world, as those who could, remained in contact using the remaining satellite communications systems but who knew for how long those would last.

Raven thought *"The future looks positive, but a lot of hard work is going to be needed, if our lofty plans are to come into fruition."*

She smiled to herself and thought, *"We are after all, survivors."*

Chapter Thirty-Two

A new dawn in the future – in the year 2531

Emerging from the cave and seeing daylight for the first time ever, Effendi and the motley group around him, fell to their knees in sheer joy and exhaustion. Covering their eyes to the brightness. Some of those kneeling beside him were praising their religious deities and saying their prayers.

It had been an incredibly difficult escape from their subterranean tomb and only achieved by the combined efforts of people who had been at each other's throats at the time of the last great underground battle.

Effendi glanced around him and then back at the long queue of people emerging from the darkness to see a mixture of nations and cultures.

It had taken weeks. Many hundreds had died in the effort to get out, but they had made it. Leaning on a variety of different skill sets that each nation possessed.

Tech Mechs who knew some of the ducting routes for the air filtration and water pumps had led the way. Foraging for food amongst the rubble of the devastated Home Citadel. Eating what they could find.

However, it was the sheer brute force of warriors to drag themselves and each other over, through and under a massive number of hazards and obstacles.

Effendi thought back over the last few weeks. *"Thousands had died in the explosions set off by the crippled Leader as she brought about her final solution."*

"The Alliance had amassed almost all their human resources in the final assault. Including the treacherous EeGee's. It had been part of their initial plan to inhabit the greatest place on the planet, but that opportunity had been denied them by the battle and the so-called final solution."

"No contact could be made with their own home nation metropolises. It was assumed they had all died. There may be a few remaining that could try and make a way to the surface, if they even knew that it was an option. It was just not known. Their family and friends left behind would either exist or die in whatever was left of those places."

It made him incredibly angry.

Effendi remembered the words of the Leader and how she had said that all the fighting, all the tunnelling had all been in vain. History has been changed. There is no environmental disaster.

He knew then that the people of Home Citadel had indeed made a change for the good after all and here it was.

The sun shone in a blue, hardly cloudless sky. He stood up and felt the warmth of the sun on his skin. A new sensation. Then he stepped forward to see rolling green hills and animals roaming free. Beyond that there seemed to be a farm. He knew about those from the historical scriptures.

A veritable oasis and ripe for plunder.

Leveraging their superior knowledge of technology and battle-honed fighting skills, it was only a matter of time before they took over this soft world of surface dwellers.

He smiled to himself and thought, *"We are after all, survivors."*

Quest

My gratitude

Thank you to all my family for putting up with me taking the time out to write this book.

To my little brother Ged who provided me with many reviews and the need to tell the story properly.

For my niece Abigail who constructed my book cover, to make it a true family affair.

A special thanks to Lisa O'Boyle and my author friend Susie Kearley @KearleySusie for their intensive reviews, input, and guidance, along with the feedback from Paul Buckley.

Thank you for reading this book and if you would like to contact the Author or find out more:

https://www.amazon.co.uk/Maurice-Perkins/e/B08CM447T3

Twitter: @MozPerkins

Email: maurice.perkins@outlook.com

Printed in Great Britain
by Amazon

62171461R00129